HIGH HEELS AND HANDGUNS

A Kate Howard Novel, Book One

LISA HEARTMAN

Espresso Yourself Publishing, LLC

Cover design by Mariah Sinclair — The Cover Vault

High Heels and Handguns: A Kate Howard novel, Book One / Lisa Heartman

Dedication

This book is dedicated to all the women in my life.

You are strong, beautiful, and capable of anything you put your mind to.

—————————————

Chapter One

To most women, high heels and handguns didn't complement couture, but for Kate Howard, personal security expert, they went together like hummus and pita. In T-minus-thirty minutes, she could mark Senator Thomas's reelection campaign fundraiser a success punctuated by a hot bath and a cold beer. No seedy characters. No suspicious packages. No assassination attempts.

She studied the guests and waitstaff as the senator weaved her through a few tables and past the dance floor of the downtown Phoenix hotel. Keeping clients within constant arm's distance was an exhausting game. Too close, and your picture ended up in the paper. Too far, and your client ended up in the morgue.

Of all the private security events Kate had worked, this one took the booby prize. Literally. She checked to make sure her breasts were still securely smashed into the sequined evening gown the senator insisted she wear. The perfect red to match his tie for the evening but a bit too small. That would be the last time she'd accept a gift from a client.

Kate shifted her clutch under her arm. The weight of Ziggy, her Sig Sauer P938 pistol, was a comforting addition to her dare-it-all attire. Some girls didn't leave home without their lip gloss. Kate didn't leave home without Ziggy.

The senator stopped to shake hands with the one-hundredth benefactor of the evening, giving Kate a moment to scan the ballroom stage, bar, and buffet tables for unusual activity. The kind of trouble she was there to prevent. She caught a glimpse of the senator's six-year-old son, Robbie, and his nanny. *I thought they already left for the evening.*

Kate tuned back into the senator's conversation at the end of a joke. The same one she had already heard thirty times that evening.

She *client-smiled* at him, a smile she'd perfected over a decade of escorting the elite. Sincerity, with a touch of humor to make them think she liked them.

Senator Thomas placed his hand where the backless gown met the top of her ass to lead her away. As soon as they were out of earshot, Kate whispered, "If you'd like to keep that hand, you'd better move it."

"Kate." The way he said her name made her feel dirty, but she wasn't the pay-to-play kind of girl. "If people are going to believe we're together"—he slid his hand up her spine—"I need to show a little affection."

"Senator." She spoke soft and slow and sexy, caressing the side of his neck. "With the right amount of force on the vagus nerve"—she pressed her thumb into the soft flesh of the pressure point—"I can stop the blood flow to your brain. Killing you. Instantly." She gave him an I-dare-you smile. "Do we understand each other?"

The senator gulped and nodded.

"Good." She dropped her hand and pointed to the adorable carbon copy of the senator racing toward them. "Now kiss your son good-night, again."

Robert Thomas Junior ran straight for the senator, wrapping his arms around him.

"Hey, Champ. I thought you left." Senator Thomas ruffled the boy's sandy-colored hair.

The nanny held up a ragged, stuffed bunny of pale, quilted fabrics. "We forgot Patches."

"I want to stay." Robbie tugged his father's pant leg, looking up with a missing-tooth smile.

The senator ducked to hug his son. "You need to go home with Anna. But I'll make you pancakes in the morning. Deal?"

"Deal." Robbie high-fived him.

He stared up at her with his innocent green eyes. "Will you come over for pancakes too, Miss Kate?"

"Maybe another day, Robbie." Kate's tone was apologetic.

"Okay, little guy—let's go." Anna held out her hand for Robbie. "It's past our bedtime."

"We'll walk you out." The senator held out his arm for Kate to loop hers through. He maneuvered her gracefully past a few couples and around a server with champagne flutes. They crossed the hotel ballroom and headed for the winding staircase.

They descended the steps to a flurry of activity in the hotel lobby. Senator Thomas stopped at the bottom to shake a gentleman's hand. Robbie skipped ahead toward the revolving door, dragging Anna along.

"Sir, are you leaving?"

The senator turned back toward the voice. "Not—"

Boom.

An explosion rocked the lobby behind them.

The force of the shock wave knocked Kate and the senator to the ground.

She covered him with her body. Pushed his face to the side, protecting it with her hands.

Then a flash of light.

A ball of fire.

The screech of metal violently tearing.

Windows shattered.

The heat from the fire seared her skin, and bits of debris pierced her back and shoulder like shrapnel.

Kate clenched her teeth. She buried her face in the senator's jacket, her ears ringing amid the screams of panic and pain and muffled car alarms. In an instant, life was on a ten-second-delayed live broadcast. As if Father Time hit the slow-motion button, making seconds feel like minutes.

Fear like nitrous injected into her racing heart. It burned and blazed and bubbled up her throat. She held back a scream soaked in mistakes and memories. An image of the market bomb in Afghanistan flashed before her eyes, the weight of her captain on top of her. And as fast as it hit her, it was gone.

Kate gulped a breath of air thick with smoke, soot, and fragments of drywall dust. She coughed. Her shoulder throbbed. A piece of glass, embedded who-knows-how-deep, stuck out of the gash. It wasn't too bloody, so she left it, knowing she could cause more damage ripping it out.

Pushing past the pain in her left arm, Kate stood and helped Senator Thomas to his feet. She brushed bits of rubble from his suit. "Are you hurt?" She assessed him, checking for cuts.

He didn't even blink. "Senator?" Kate yanked out his pocket square, shook it, and gently placed it against his hair-line, where blood dribbled onto his forehead.

She checked the area for threats, looking for a safe way out. But nothing felt safe.

"We have to go," she said, giving the senator a little shake. Kate snatched her clutch from the step. She wasn't sure if she'd need Ziggy or her phone or both. The movement inten-sified the pain from her shoulder straight down her back and damn near knocked her over.

The senator mumbled something incoherent. It sounded like...*Bobbie?*

"Oh, God." *Robbie.* His name stuck in her throat, trapping air in her lungs.

Adrenaline gave Father Time the finger and kicked Kate in the ass.

Hard.

She braced her arm against her stomach.

Spinning on her heel, Kate looked to where she had last seen him.

She squinted. The revolving door. A mess of mangled metal and missing glass. She scrambled toward it, ahead of the senator, climbing over debris. Searching.

There were people on the ground. Bleeding. Crying. Begging for help. She stepped around and over them, promising she would get help. Finally, she found Anna. Her body was contorted. Blood, thick and dark, puddled on the carpet around her hair. Kate dropped her bag and felt for a pulse. Nothing.

Kate ran a trembling hand over Anna's face to close her eyelids. She hadn't known her well, but no one deserved an end like this.

"Robbie." Senator Thomas pushed past her. "Robbie!"

She grabbed his arm, pointing up to the still-teetering chandelier. "It's not safe. Come around this way."

He broke free, rushing toward a pile of rubble. Pieces of a window frame, furniture, a lamp. Then she saw him. The boy, eerily still. A glass shard stuck at least ten inches out of his chest, and no way to know how deep.

Like the little boy in the Afghan market bomb. A victim of chance. Wrong place. Wrong time. Her hands fell to her sides, arms and shoulders heavy with failure and sadness. Her wet, dull eyes searched his chest for movement. Was it one breath every three seconds or five seconds for children?

"Fuck."

Kate sat on an emergency room gurney at St. Joseph's Hospital, gripping the pillow in her lap. She squeezed it to her chest, slumped over, and buried her face in the sandpaper-like pillowcase, sucking air through her clenched teeth. The sound was more cat-hiss than human breath.

The ER doctor played a sadistic game of Operation on her back. Instead of a funny little buzzer sound, it was twinges of torment. And there were no winners.

"Are you sure you don't want something to dull the pain?" the doctor asked for the fifth time.

The sooner he cleaned her up, the sooner she could get upstairs and check on Robbie and the senator. They'd already been out of her sight for too long. Regardless of her current location in proximity to her client, Kate was still on the clock. That meant no pills, no booze, no kidding. She lifted her head. "Just get it over with."

"You don't have to be a hero." Another piece of glass clinked in the bowl.

I couldn't even keep my client safe at his own event. "There are no heroes here."

"The senator's son is in surgery because you kept him alive with those rescue breaths. I'd call that a hero."

Kate looked down at her watch. Two o'clock in the morning. Robbie had been in surgery for over three hours.

"That looks like the last of it." The doctor's tools clattered on the tray. "Seventeen pieces." He secured the last bandage.

Kate looked over at the bloody bits of glass he had dug out of her back. Not enough to fill a shot glass. Nothing like the one that sliced her left arm. And practically non-existent to the shard that had impaled Robbie.

"Because of the location on your shoulder, I'd like you to come back in fourteen days to have the sutures removed." The doctor tossed his gloves in the trash and pointed to the arm she cradled. "But I want you to take it easy for three-to-four weeks and wear a sling."

Was this guy crazy? There was a bomber on the loose, and he wanted her to take it easy. "Can I go now?"

She heard the curtain move behind her and expected it to be the detective she had spoken to earlier. Again. With more questions she couldn't answer. *Did you see the explosion? Did you see anything out of the ordinary?* Kate had decided to cut him off. "Did you forget to ask if I believe in Bigfoot and the Tooth Fairy?"

Her clutch thudded on the gurney next to her. She flinched, swearing under her breath at the jolt of pain up her back.

"Bigfoot, yes. Tooth Fairy, no." The voice was strong, direct, and painfully familiar. A voice she'd heard in her dreams. Memories. Nightmares.

It sent a ripple of awareness through her.

Paxton Banks.

Her former Army captain. Her current headache.

"I already know the answers to those questions." His footsteps got closer.

Kate's insides felt like a knotted ball of barbed wire. Cold and caustic, rusty and ragged, the metal reaching out like fingers stabbing, slashing, and scratching everything in their path. Every breath she took expanding their reach. Turning her vital organs to shreds.

She'd thought about this moment a few million times in the last ten years. Never once did she imagine it would happen here, like this. The mirror opposite of their last time together. She pushed out of her head the image of Paxton lying on the gurney, his skin pale, breathing labored, fatigues tattered and bloody, his leg littered with shrapnel.

He came around the side of the gurney, his steps controlled. Like a hunter approaching a skittish wild animal.

It had been a long night. Facing Paxton Banks right here, right now, was the last thing she needed. Kate was sore, tired, and scared. Scared her traitorous heart would split wide open. And this time, she wouldn't be able to hide her feelings.

Kate was relieved to not be wearing the hideous hospital gown the nurse had handed her earlier. She tossed the pillow aside and slid off the gurney onto wobbly legs.

"Easy, Katie." Paxton caught her around the waist. His strong arms wrapped around her, tempting and torturous. "I'm sure the adrenaline's worn off by now. You're going to hurt like hell."

The FBI logo on his windbreaker stared back at her. A generic black suit peeking out the bottom. She didn't need to look up to see his brown hair, soft lips, and blue-gray eyes. She could picture them perfectly in her mind. "I don't need your help." Kate pushed his hand away. "I told the detective everything I know. Go read the report."

"I did." Paxton stood in her way. His posture Army-approved. "I still have questions."

"Now's not the time." She grabbed her clutch, like having Ziggy close would give her strength.

"Katie—"

"Don't." Kate felt the weight of the day crushing her. The explosion. Robbie. Paxton. She stood tall. As tall as she could at a barefoot five-foot-eight. "Don't call me that."

"I have been calling you Katie since the day I met you."

"That was a long, *long* time ago." Kate hugged her arm to her chest. "That person doesn't exist anymore."

"You've had a rough night, so I'm going to let that one pass." He took a step back. "But I still have questions."

She slid past him and headed for the exit. "Sorry. I'm out of answers. I need to check on Senator Thomas and Robbie so I can get back to work."

"I just finished questioning Senator Thomas. He's in FBI protection, and Robbie's still in surgery."

Without a glance back she left Paxton, and hopefully her feelings, behind the curtain of the triage bay.

"Katherine Elizabeth Howard." Paxton came up behind her, placing his hand on her right arm. His touch was as warm as his tone. "You have no shoes, no car, fresh stitches in your shoulder, and from what I could find, only an ID, a key, and a gun in your purse. Where are you going?"

Anywhere you're not. Despite her reservations, Kate turned to look at him. Maybe to appease her curiosity. Maybe to say good-bye. Maybe her willpower was on the fritz. Regardless, she knew it was a mistake the moment their eyes met.

His brown hair was darker than she recalled. Longer on top, still high and tight. But his eyes. They were exactly the blue-gray she remembered. And those lips.

Her heart pounded in her chest like mortar fire. One devastating boom at a time.

So much for hoping he had become fat, bald, and ugly. The soldier she trained with, the one she fell in love with, the boy she couldn't be with over a decade ago, had turned into a man. A handsome man. And for the second time that night, Kate felt the world crumble around her.

"I need—"

"You need to rest, Sergeant Howard." A flicker of worry, relief, anger flashed across his face, and it was gone.

He was still angry. And she didn't blame him. Kate hated herself too. She'd relived the bombing in the Afghan market over and over in her nightmares. That shrapnel was meant for her. Now fate had settled the score.

Kate swallowed back the remorse, praying her voice would stay steady long enough to get out of there. "I need to get cleaned up and change my clothes and figure out what I missed. I can rest later."

"You are just as stubborn as the day I met you." He shot her a penetrating look.

Kate turned back toward the emergency entrance.

"Run away when things get tough. Is that what I taught you?"

"Go to hell, Paxton." Kate kept walking, the tile cold on her bare feet. Every step like a bolt of lightning across her back.

"Ms. Howard," a gentleman called to her. "Your prescription."

Kate didn't slow down to acknowledge him.

"I'll take it," she heard Paxton say, and his steps were behind her again.

Paxton placed his jacket over her shoulders. "At least let me drive you home." His tone more an order than an offer.

The scent of his cologne brought her back to a time when she would have done anything, including cleaning latrines, to spend a few more minutes with him. She'd fallen for the one person she wasn't permitted to, almost killed him, and ran like a guilty suspect to protect her heart instead of taking care of him. Kate didn't deserve him, not then and certainly not now.

She'd rather play hot potato with a live hand grenade than spend one more minute with Paxton Banks, but Kate was on the losing side of a never-ending day.

Chapter Two

The Saturday morning sun beat down on Kate's bandaged shoulder. Her loft was in a questionable part of town, but the views of downtown Phoenix were first-class. Penthouse-worthy. That view was the reason she had bought the dilapidated used-to-be drug den and remodeled it. Kate peeled her eyelids open one lash at a time. She hadn't been drinking at the campaign fundraiser last night, and she had refused pain medicine at the hospital. Why was her head heavy and hazy like a hangover?

What a soup sandwich the evening had turned out to be. The explosion. Robbie. And Paxton. Paxton being one of the investigators on the case was going to be a problem. And since when did he work in Phoenix? Had he been in the FBI building four months ago when she was there as a linguistics consultant and she didn't know it? Ugh. She had bigger things to worry about.

Kate needed to ruck up. She'd been through worse situations.

Assess the damage. Develop a plan. Implement.

By the amount of sun coming through the skylight, it must

be after nine o'clock. She had to call and check in on Robbie and the senator. Kate looked over at her docking station and focused her eyes on a pair of seen-better-days Chucks propped up on her nightstand instead. Beyond them, black skinny jeans and her laptop.

"Mornin' sleepyhead." A dark-haired kid peered over the screen at her. "You know, this thing is archaic. I'm surprised it hasn't given out on you yet." He tapped the side of her computer. "And how do you not have a television? All that gym equipment and no TV to watch."

Alarm bells clanged in Kate's head. Mayday. The distress message sent her muscles into a tense, ready-to-act state. She slid her hand under her pillow until her fingers wrapped around the cool comfort of metal. Taz, her Glock 17. She sat straight up, her stitches protesting under the movement. She fought against the exhaustion and pain.

Kate leveled the gun at the young, twenty-something hipster. Her heart thumped an SOS against her ribs. "Who are you?"

"Jeez, lady, chill." He put his arms up slowly, slinking behind the screen.

Taz was lighter than normal. And she immediately knew the gun was empty. Why, was beyond her. All that mattered was, he didn't know.

"Answer the question." Kate's voice was as serious as a hand grenade missing its pin.

"Kyle." He closed the laptop. Thank God her client files were password-protected. "I live downstairs."

Now that she could see his face, she recalled seeing him on the security cameras around the building. She loosened her grip on the gun. He was paler in real life. Not ghostly, but a little sun wouldn't hurt.

His place was like hers, only ground level with a smaller closet and bathroom—917 square feet of painted concrete, stainless appliances, and quartz accents. Of course, he probably had more furniture. Most people did.

"What are you doing here? How did you get in?" Kate wasn't exactly the borrow-a-cup-of-sugar kind of neighbor. In the year he'd lived downstairs, she'd made a point of keeping her distance.

"The guy—"

Her front door opened, and Paxton walked in carrying brown paper bags.

Kate pointed the gun in his direction, then back on the kid.

"That guy." Kyle pointed in Paxton's direction. "Uh, dude, a little help here."

"Didn't anyone ever tell you it's not polite to pull a gun on your guests?" Paxton pushed her front door closed with his foot. The metal clanged, sending her dull headache into a full throb.

Paxton slid the bags on the counter and turned toward her. He'd changed from the suit he was wearing at the hospital to a T-shirt and cargo pants. Just like she remembered him, only in black instead of desert-camo greens and browns. The look was far too casual and comfortable in her home. "Put the gun away, Katie. I asked the kid to watch you so I could run up to the office for a briefing."

And we're back to Katie. "How about I shoot both of you for breaking and entering?" Kate swung her legs over the edge of the twin-size bed and stood. Her body felt like a drill sergeant had cycled her through basic training again. Her muscles were sore and tight and stiff.

"A, I didn't break in. I used your key. And B"—Paxton picked up the handgun magazine from the island and waved it in the air—"it's a little hard to shoot me without bullets."

Bluff called. She swore under her breath, dropping her arm to her side.

Kyle put the laptop on the nightstand and stood. "She was nicer when she was sleeping."

"They all are." Paxton slapped him on the shoulder and walked him out. "Thanks for your help."

"Anytime, man."

Kate glared at Paxton, walked to the island, jammed the magazine into the chamber, and put Taz back under her pillow. "Why are you here? Why would you let a stranger into my home? I don't need a babysitter."

"He's the only neighbor you've got. You were a little out of it last night." He grinned like he had a funny little secret. The look softened his features and her stance. "One Percocet and you were talking about going dancing and freeing circus animals and how you think honey tastes like sunshine—"

"I didn't take any pain medicine."

Paxton pointed to the empty bottle of water next to her bed. "Yes, you did."

The memory of him taking the prescription from the orderly popped into her head. She thought hard about him getting her home. Coming upstairs. Bringing her a drink. Damn it, the water bottle. A trickle of disbelief quickly turned into a flood of embarrassment, the undertow threatening to pull her in. "You drugged me?"

"It's a painkiller. You winced at every bump in the road. Could barely walk up the stairs. There was no way you would sleep like that."

Kate pulled her injured arm into her stomach, realizing her attire, a baggy Army T-shirt barely long enough to cover teal panties. No bra. "What the hell am I wearing?"

"It was in my go-bag. I was afraid I'd hurt your shoulder shoving you in one of your little shirts, so I put one of mine on you."

"You dressed me?" Kate's voice eeked up ten decibels.

Paxton hung his jacket on the stool. His gun and badge on full display. "You weren't exactly in the position to do it on your own."

His tone aroused and agitated her. "Because you drugged me."

He pulled groceries from the bags and placed them in the fridge. "I didn't think you'd want to sleep on white sheets in a dress covered with blood. Nice hospital corners, by the way."

Before last night, the least she'd ever worn in front of him was a bathing suit. The idea of Paxton's hands on her, undressing her and dressing her. And without a bra under that dress. A delicious tingle started in her tummy. She shook her head. Nope. She wasn't going there. Kate let out a disgusted groan, walked into the bathroom, and shoved the door closed. She rested her shaky hands on the cool porcelain sink.

"Come on, Katie. We're all adults here." He hollered through the door.

"Go home, Paxton." Kate held her breath, manipulating the T-shirt over her head. She let the breath go slowly, gently working the stiffness in her shoulder. She turned to check her back in the mirror. Seventeen little flesh-tone bandages spread across her back. Not motorcycle-road-rash bad. Not lost-a-fight-with-a-cheese-grater bad. More like bag-of-angry-cats bad.

"The tattoo's a nice addition."

Kate placed her hand over the words scrawled down the side of her ribs. *Always in my heart.* Her mother's last words to her after an epic battle with cancer.

"Go. Home." She took a washcloth off the freestanding soaking tub behind her and made quick work of erasing the remnants of yesterday's makeup. Too bad she couldn't wipe away the memory of Robbie's pale face. The shard of glass impaled in his chest. The senator's cry for help while she stabilized him. Then, a flash of the little boy in the Afghan market. A little boy too far gone for her to help.

She ducked her head under the faucet, working up a

lather on her hair with her good arm, and rinsed until the sink was free of suds.

Kate pulled on a pair of sweatpants and matching full-zip hoodie and zipped it to her chin. She flung the bathroom door open. The smell of bacon and eggs smacked her in the face. Ugh. It would take a week to get the smell of meat out of her loft. "Here." She tossed the T-shirt at Paxton. "Thanks for the shirt. Have a nice life."

"Come eat something. You'll feel better."

Even one of Paxton's world-famous cheese omelets couldn't make her feel better about being drugged and topless. Especially topless in front of Paxton. She felt the heat of embarrassment settle on her cheeks. "I have work to do." She walked to the front door, opened it.

"FBI has a team on Senator Thomas."

"I still have work to do."

Paxton didn't move from the stove. "Not. Until. You. Eat."

Kate slammed the door hard enough to loosen a filling. She pulled an apple off the counter and took a giant bite. "Now go," she said with a full mouth.

"That's not food. It's the food you feed food."

She gulped down her bite of the apple and looked in the pan at the sizzling bacon. "I don't eat meat."

"I remember." He pushed a yogurt and spoon in front of her. Blueberry. Her favorite. And she was hungry.

Paxton turned to the island behind him, slid his breakfast on a plate, and sat on her favorite stool. No words. He just ate.

Fine. Kate pulled out the other stool, yanking the top from the container. The silence between them was thicker than her yogurt. Uncomfortable.

"What were you doing at the fundraiser?" Paxton kept his eyes on his plate.

Her client confidentiality excluded law enforcement. "Protection detail for the senator."

"I reread the file this morning. There was no record of security for Senator Thomas." Paxton's face was relaxed, but his tone was rigid. "What were you really doing there?"

"That's why I was there." Kate stood and collected a pile of papers from the window ledge. "He received a threat. They wanted to keep it quiet, and I was security that could blend in."

"Blend in. In that dress?"

"Less conspicuous." As if having boobs makes you less threatening. She knew twenty-five ways to kill a man with her bare hands. "And the dress wasn't my choice."

"As his date." The last word carried a healthy dose of disapproval. In her. In her life. In her choice of careers.

"As his aide." Kate pushed the papers at him. "I've been working in his office for weeks. Background-checking his staff, looking into his past, rereading his speeches, examining phone records, watching interviews—"

"He's a state senator. Why wasn't the FBI notified of the threats?"

"Threat. Singular." Kate pulled an email out of the pile. *"You will pay for the pain you have caused.* Phoenix Police Department would never have considered that a credible threat. He's a state senator, so he can hire anyone he wants for protection. And it was weeks ago."

"Who else knew about this?"

"Only his campaign manager." Kate gently sat on the stool so she didn't hurt her back.

"How did you get involved?"

"Why does it matter? And what are you even doing here?"

His fork clattered on the plate. "Indulge me."

Kate played with the string on her hoodie, wrapping it around her finger and letting it unwind. "A guy I know recommended me."

"A guy." The muscle in Paxton's jaw twitched. Anger. His

tell. The one thing he couldn't hide. Not from Kate. "Does this *guy* have a name?"

"None of your business." Her matter-of-fact tone set off a chain reaction in Paxton. The relaxed look he was trying hard to keep in place disintegrated. He straightened, shoulders back, head high, but his eyes. His blue eyes turned stormy gray. Interrogation face. She'd seen it before, but she'd never been on this side of the look.

"Katie, this isn't a game." Paxton's tone was harder, troubled, more unsettled than before. "This psycho blew up the senator's limo. Killed four people in the blast. Hurt twelve more. The senator's son is in critical condition. That could have been you."

"That's my job."

"You need a new job."

"Who the hell do you think you are?" Yes, Kate knew she was fanning the fire. And yes, she knew she might regret it. But no, she wasn't going to put up with his judgment. "You're not my captain anymore, Paxton. You don't get to come into my home and boss me around."

"Like you'd listen." He stood, gaining the vertical advantage on her. "You're out there alone. No team. No backup. No plan B. But that's the Kate Howard way. Isn't it?"

His words hit her like a tank. An overwhelming blow to the gut, splitting her wide open. Her guilt and scars and faults all on display. Past and present collided. He might have been there now because of the fundraiser bombing, but this fight…this fight was ten years overdue. And she deserved whatever hell-fury he could rain down on her.

"It's time for you to leave."

"I'm not leaving until I get a name." Paxton crossed his arms over his chest.

"Brazio." The name shot out of her. Vicious. Violent. "Now get out."

His brows drew together at the mention of their communications sergeant. "Brazio? You kept in touch with Billy Brazio?" His question, rhetorical. His tone, piss-fucking-poor.

"This has nothing to do with Brazio." Kate stood like someone had stuck a pin in her. The stool slid back with a screech. "Or the explosion last night. Or my job. Or anything else you want to blame. You're mad that I disobeyed an order. Your order. You're mad at me. I'm the one who went into the market. I'm the one who let my guard down."

"That shrapnel you took"—Kate pointed at his leg—"it was meant for me. You saved my life. And how did I repay you? I left."

Kate waited. Waited for Paxton to react.

Scream, shout, something.

Nothing.

Screw the proverbial elephant in the room; this was a herd. And she was bracing herself for a stampede. The air between them changed, and his silence was worse than any war or gunshot wound or explosion.

A muscle in his arm flexed, and she thought for a moment he might punch her. A small piece of her wished he would, to get the hate for her out of his bones.

"I'm an awful, horrible, wretched person. The lowest of the low." Kate pushed Paxton toward the door.

He stumbled back a step.

"It's nothing I haven't told myself since I left you at that base hospital." Kate pursued him, invading his personal space, pushing him again.

He took another step back.

"I never wanted to hurt you, Pax. When I saw you lying there?" She breathed deep, like it might be her last. "I just couldn't. When Major Hernández said he was disbanding our unit, I took a change of duty station. I welcomed the transfer. I hopped on a transport plane and disappeared like a coward. Is that what you want to hear?"

"No." Paxton made a fist and Kate braced for impact, her

muscles tight and tense. He leaned in, cupping his hands around her face, and pulled her in to kiss him.

The ambush startled Kate. It took her a moment to register the kiss. His lips, warm and lustful, overwhelmed her senses. Kate reacted instinctively.

She pulled back and punched him in the face.

Chapter Three

That did not just happen. Kate hesitated, torn by happiness and hysteria. All she'd wanted for years was Paxton. And there he was. In her loft. Kissing her. And this was how she reacts? By punching him in the face?

Paxton groaned and folded forward. Hand over his nose. Blood in his palm. "I forgot you had a wicked right cross."

Her fight-or-flight response needed serious recalibration.

"I'm sorry. Shit." Her chest constricted like a too-tight sports bra, making it hard to take a full breath. Kate grabbed a towel off the sink and handed it to him. "I thought you were going to punch me."

He walked back to the island, sat on the stool, and propped his arm on the counter, holding the towel to his face. "Why would I do that?" His voice was muffled.

"Lean forward. Pinch your nose." She grabbed a baggie from the drawer and filled it with ice from the fridge dispenser. "Because you hate me."

"I don't hate you." Paxton glanced at her, and she saw the apprehension settle around his eyes. Tiny little worry lines reaching out to a few gray hairs at his temple. She hadn't noticed them earlier.

Kate gave him the makeshift ice pack for his already-swelling eye. "You told Major Hernández you didn't want me in your unit. Special Forces was no place for a woman. I was a burden. You didn't care how good I was; you wanted me gone."

"That's what this is about? An overheard conversation a dozen years ago?" His volume dropped, as did his gaze. "Katie, I was afraid you'd get hurt."

"Because I'm a woman?" Kate's tone was ten pounds of sass in a five-pound bag. "I can take care of myself." She'd proven herself a thousand times in the military. Gone through the same training and requirements as the men in her unit.

Paxton pointed to his face. "I know you can. But it didn't make me feel less responsible for you. I couldn't afford to be overprotective of the girl on my team. Not thinking straight. Showing favoritism. Looking soft. I was the captain."

No matter how hard she worked, all they saw was a woman, not a soldier. Someone needing protection, not someone who could give it. To them, she was a liability. "I joined like you. I knew the risks. I was prepared to die for my country."

"I wasn't okay with that." He pulled the ice pack and towel away from his face.

"Is that why you tackled me when the market bomb exploded? You felt responsible for me?"

"No."

"Then why?"

Paxton squeezed the towel so tight his knuckles went white. He shifted, turning away from her.

Kate slapped her hand against the island, getting his attention. "Why?"

"Because I couldn't let the last image I saw before I closed my eyes at night be your dead body."

Kate swallowed hard. She couldn't fault his reasoning.

The last image she often wrestled with at night was Paxton, the pain and fear on his face, his leg torn apart by shrapnel.

His eyebrows drew together, and an agonized expression took his focus far away. "I didn't even know you were gone until I was out of surgery. All Hernández would say was 'special assignment.' It was like you disappeared…"

Kate opened her mouth to speak and closed it. She wound her fingers into the hem of her sweatshirt to keep from touching his hand.

"Then ten years later, I'm called out to a car bomb. My big chance to prove myself at a new field office. Police, fire, ambulance everywhere, and one of my guys hands me a purse with your ID he found next to a dead woman."

Nausea and guilt whipped up a wicked little remorse cocktail.

"I was worried out of my mind all over again. I thought you were dead. This time for sure." Paxton brought his attention back to Kate. "When I heard the reports of what happened, I rushed to the hospital. I had to see you. Make sure you were okay. When I walked in and saw your back and shoulder"—he shook his head like he was Etch-A-Sketching the image out of his mind—"I wanted to protect you all over again."

After a long pause, Kate placed her hand on the island to give her strength. "Why did you kiss me?" Her voice was steadier than she expected.

"I've wanted to do that since I met you." Paxton tossed the towel on the counter. "I wasn't allowed to do it back then, and I sure as hell wasn't going to miss the opportunity to do it now."

Since I met you? Kate's stomach sank like the marbles in a game of KerPlunk.

"I'd do it again if I thought you'd let me get away with it." He pointed to his face. "The shiner might be worth it."

Again? Her mouth went dry. Paxton ripped the pseudo-bandage off her heart, keeping her feelings—her unrequited, unwanted, unhealthy feelings—tucked away. He was her captain. Fraternization was strictly prohibited. She would never have acted on the feelings.

But now?

Kate's throat tightened, and she pressed her lips together. Her emotions, a land mine just under the surface, were ready to blow. She brought her fist up to cover her mouth. Falling apart in front of Paxton was not an option. She had to get out of here.

Her gaze ping-ponged around the loft, landing on everything and nothing. "I have to go." She scooped up the sequined red dress from the floor, jammed her feet into her sneakers, grabbed her purse off the arm of the treadmill, and slammed the door behind her.

I've wanted to do that since I met you. I'd do it again. His words ricocheted in her brain.

Kate got to the bottom of the stairs, pushed the building door open, and took a deep, cleansing breath. The cool fall air filled her lungs.

The empty field across the street, bare and bleak with its sunburnt grass and bundles of trash, stared back at her through a chain-link fence. Her SUV should have been right there where the oil stain darkened the pavement. She rummaged through her purse and pulled out the key fob. Pressed the lock button twice and listened. No *beep, beep*.

The door opened behind her, and Paxton stepped onto the sidewalk. "That went about as bad as I expected."

Kate ignored him and pressed the button again.

"At least you let me say everything I needed to this time before you ran."

Kate didn't have time to decipher his response. It was better she didn't think about it, think about him. Think about that kiss. No. She had more important things to do. Like, find her car.

"Where are we headed?"

"Not we. Me." Kate looked up the street, then down. No silver SUV. "I'm going back to the hotel to see what I missed." The hotel. Ugh. She had left her car at the hotel the night of the fundraiser.

"It's a crime scene."

Kate stared at him. He'd cleaned off the blood on his nose. A little swelling showed under his eye, but not bad. He's lucky her back hurt, or she would have hit him harder. "So?"

"The FBI isn't going to let you walk into an active crime scene."

Stiffness settled in her neck and jaw. She hated that he was right. Kate would rather eat MREs for a week than ask him for help, but she was short on time and federal agents. The sun glared off Paxton's badge, and the muddy waters of dread flooded her conscience. His blue-gray eyes told her he already knew what she was going to ask.

She conjured up her client-smile and softened her tone. "Would you be so kind as to give me a ride to my car?"

"Katie, you just punched me in the face and stormed out." His tone was more mock-mad than actual mad. Paxton tucked his hand in his windbreaker pocket. "And now you're asking me for a favor?"

Katie. The way he said her name ignited hot little trickles in her belly, but she ignored them and widened her smile. "Yes."

Paxton leaned into her, and she took a step back. "That smile doesn't work on me."

Kate pointed to her lips. "This smile works on everyone. It's a verified crowd-pleaser."

"It might work on your clients. But I know you." Paxton pulled keys out of his pocket and opened the passenger door of his black, government-issued SUV. "And I know your real smile."

The twenty-minute ride to the hotel was riddled with potholes. Every bump thrust her bandaged back into the seat. For all Kate knew, Paxton could have taken the roughest roads on purpose. A little payback for the sucker-punch. She clenched her jaw to hide the discomfort. When he finally put the vehicle in park, she was relieved.

Kate stared up at the mangled front entry of the hotel. She heard Paxton's door close behind her, but she couldn't take her eyes off the building. Windows and doors and walls had been propelled into the lobby by the force of the blast. Charred, black smoke lines licked up the front of the building from the fire.

The closer she got to the building, the heavier her legs felt. Her brain knew going in there was a bad idea, but Kate pushed past the stiffness threatening to lock up her knees in the middle of the street. In the daylight, it looked more like a toothless mongrel than a five-star hotel. The building gave her the willies, but Kate wasn't going to let it scare her away.

Instead of walking to the parking deck, Kate walked toward the crime-scene tape, which kept the media and lookie-loos from the metal debris littering the two-lane street. She lifted the obnoxious yellow tape and started to walk under.

"Sorry, ma'am." A police officer blocked her. "Only official personnel allowed beyond this point. You need to stay on the other side where it's safe."

"Safe?" Kate laughed. "I was in there when the explosion happened."

"I'm sorry to hear that." He dipped his chin. "But unless you have a badge, you need to stay on that side of the tape."

Kate spun on her heel to talk to Paxton, but he wasn't behind her. She popped up on her tippy-toes to look for him. His high-and-tight brown hair was nowhere to be seen. She pulled the zipper of her hoodie down to show some cleavage and turned back toward the police officer. "I really need to get in there." She gave him a wide smile. "I'm part of the investigation. A witness."

Robocop didn't even venture a peek at her chest. "Unless you have a badge or are with somebody who has one, I can't let you beyond this line."

Kate caught a glimpse of Paxton at the lobby entrance, speaking with a group of guys in matching FBI windbreakers. She pointed at him. "I'm with that guy."

The officer didn't even turn to look. A corner of his mouth twitched up in a *yeah-right* smirk. The cop was doing his job, but cut a girl some slack.

"Paxton," Kate yelled, waving in his direction. "Paxton." He didn't move from his spot or his discussion. She cupped her hands around her mouth, took a deep breath, and hollered at the top of her lungs. "Paxton. Elmer. Banks."

His head whipped around, shaking it disapprovingly. The guys he was speaking with broke out into laughter. He stomped over, stiff with indignation. His gaze dropped to her open hoodie. When his eyes met hers again, the lines of his lips had softened. She was inappropriately flattered by his interest, and her pulse kicked up a step.

"I thought you were getting your car." His tone was deceivingly dry.

"Officer"—Kate leaned in to read his name tag—"Shelton here will not allow me in."

"Good job." Paxton patted the officer on the shoulder and turned to walk away from them.

"Wait." She hated asking for help. Especially from Paxton. Especially twice in the same day. He made her feel so inadequate, but she needed him. Kate swallowed a big ol' helping of humble pie. The bitter taste left something to be desired. "Please."

Paxton turned, glaring at her, and crossed his arms over

his chest. She admired the way his jacket snugged his shoulders, stretching the fabric and showing off his muscular arms. Her pulse kicked up another step. Kate realized she was staring and averted her eyes. "I...I need your help."

The officer looked over his shoulder at Paxton. "Sir?" Receiving a nod of approval, the officer lifted the yellow tape high enough for Kate to enter the crime scene.

"Thank you, officer." Kate smiled at him.

She and Paxton walked in silence past the battered-and-barbecued limo, missing windows, a door, and part of the roof. The remaining metal fanned out like a ragged banana peel. The only time she'd ever seen anything like it was in war-torn countries. Kate's stomach sank faster than a Humvee in quicksand at the thought of someone doing this, so monstrous and malicious. What could Senator Thomas have done to make someone so enraged they would attempt to blow him up? How had she not found any evidence to suggest someone would?

Following Paxton, Kate took careful steps through the rubble of what had been the hotel entrance. She scanned the area, taking in the damage.

Paxton turned to her. "Where were you when the explosion happened?"

A pain in her throat made it difficult to swallow, let alone speak. Kate pointed to the base of the stairs, where the carpet was void of glass and debris. The perfect outline of where she threw herself over the senator, taking cover. Kate was suddenly aware of the cuts and scrapes on her back, like she could feel every. Single. One. She wondered for a moment if Paxton had felt the same thing about the shrapnel in his leg.

Kate stopped short, grabbed Paxton's forearm, then pulled her hand away. She squinted at the bloodstained carpet where Robbie's frail body had lain among the destruction. A casualty of conflict far beyond his childhood comprehension, like the little boy in the market she couldn't save. Nausea steamrolled through her, and Kate's yogurt threatened to make a second appearance.

"Are you okay?" Paxton's voice sounded distant. "You look a little pale."

The sting of tears burned her eyes like pepper spray. She blinked them back. She was too afraid to look at Paxton. To let him see her this raw. Kate was a soldier. She'd seen worse.

"This was a bad idea." Paxton took her by the elbow. "We should go."

Kate took a few steps toward the spot where she'd assessed and stabilized Robbie, praying for the ambulance to arrive in time. Senator Thomas had cried, begging her to keep him alive.

"Maybe you should sit."

The heaviness in her legs multiplied, weighing her down. She fell to her knees and wrapped her arms around her stomach. Kate had to pull herself together.

She heard Paxton speaking, but couldn't make out the words. She turned in the direction of his voice, and something pastel in a pile of debris caught her attention. Kate forced herself to stand. "Help me." She pointed at the garbage.

Paxton put his hand out to block her. "You're not supposed to be lifting." He moved a crumpled chair and piece of wood.

She crouched down and picked up the threadbare toy. Patches, Robbie's bunny, unblemished by the surrounding destruction. Kate's head spun. She stumbled, grabbing Paxton's arm to steady herself. The dizziness pushed the volcano in her stomach to the verge of eruption. She took a few breaths—in through her nose, out through her mouth—to soothe the nausea. If they hadn't come back for the stupid rabbit, Robbie would have been in the limo when it exploded. Kate squeezed her eyes closed, then blinked to clear her blurry vision.

"What is it?"

"This is the reason he's alive. I need to get to the hospital." Kate pulled her hand back.

"What are you talking about?"

She ran her finger over its floppy ear. "It's Robbie's bunny." Kate's voice was as shaky as her hand.

"Katie." Paxton's voice was soft. He lifted her chin, studying her. "You're not making any sense."

"It doesn't have to make sense. I have to go." Her voice cracked, and a tear slid down her face.

"Okay." Paxton wiped her cheek. "I'll drive."

Chapter Four

Kate stood at the hospital information desk, waiting for the overly bubbly, barely legal girl behind it to get off the phone. She'd called Senator Thomas's cell phone three times on the way there and all three went straight to voice mail. Paxton paced on the sidewalk, cell phone plastered to the side of his face, his expression not giving away the subject of the call. Good or bad. A moment to herself, without his eyes on her, was a relief. *When did he join the FBI? How long had he been in Phoenix? How the hell was she supposed to feel about this?*

In his cargo pants and matching black T-shirt, he looked more like the old Paxton than he did in the boxy suit he had worn the night before. And she wasn't hating the way his pants hugged his ass when he walked. She watched him take long strides with a slight limp in his right step. Kate hadn't noticed it earlier. No doubt a legacy from the market bomb. Her chest tightened.

"May I help you?" The young lady at the desk smiled up at Kate from behind her computer.

She turned back to the girl, clearing her throat. "Hi. I need to know what room Robert Thomas Junior is in."

"I'm sorry, ma'am." Her sugary-sweet smile made Kate sick. "That information is classified."

Classified. Was this girl serious? Kate had been on missions that didn't exist, in countries people rarely heard of, and a candy striper with a boy-band haircut had better clearance?

Her body temperature ticked up a degree. "Okay. Would you please ring the room and let Senator Thomas know Kate Howard is here? It's very important."

"I'm sorry, ma'am, but we've been asked not to disturb the patient or his family."

It was against her client confidentiality agreement to share that she was the senator's bodyguard. She jammed her fist into her thigh, the movement softened by something stuffed. She looked down at the ragged bunny in her hand, then held it up for inspection.

"This is Patches." Kate put the stuffed animal on top of the desk. "Robbie doesn't go anywhere without him. I'd hate for him to be in this place, scared and hurt, without his bunny to make him feel safe."

"Yes, ma'am. I'd be happy to have an orderly take it to him." She moved to take the toy, but Kate pulled it out of her reach.

"I'd really rather do it myself." Kate tried to keep the annoyance out of her voice, but she was reaching code yellow, a step above her typical, guarded blue.

"I'm very sorry, ma'am, but I can't let you do that."

"Yes. You can." Kate's voice teetered on surly. "I know you're doing your job, but I'm also trying to do mine. Just tell me what room he's in. I'll be in and out in no time."

"Ma—"

"Don't you dare call me *ma'am* again."

The girl picked up the phone receiver, holding it midway to her ear. "If you can't compose yourself, I'll have to call security. Ma'am." Her tone seeped sarcasm.

Kate's temper bypassed code orange, racing straight to

red. If Kate didn't hate her so much right now, she'd probably like this girl. Clenching her fist so tightly Patches probably popped a stitch, she took a step toward the open side of the desk. "Look—"

"What's going on here?" Paxton placed his hand on Kate's arm to pull her back.

"Little Miss Pixie Cut won't let me see Robbie." She yanked her arm free, and a twinge of pain darted down her back.

Paxton grinned at Kate, a cross between playful and patronizing. To say it wasn't sexy would be an understatement, but that didn't mean it wasn't shitty. He pulled the badge off his belt. "Special Agent Banks. We're here to speak with Senator and Mrs. Thomas."

"Yes, sir." She stood and pointed to the elevators. "Fifth floor. Room five-twenty-three."

Ugh. Kate glared at him, then turned the look on the girl. Kate did an about-face, stalked down the hall, and jammed her finger into the up button.

She deepened her voice, whipping up her best guy impersonation. "Look at me. I'm Paxton Banks. I have a badge."

"Is that jealousy I hear?"

Kate pushed a piece of hair out of her face. She stared straight ahead at the little gleaming light, acknowledging her desire to get on the elevator. "Of her? Please." Kate jabbed her thumb into the up arrow a few more times. "She wouldn't last three seconds in the ring with me."

Paxton let out a low, throaty chuckle. A dangerous concoction of goading, flirtation, and cockiness. The kind of laugh that made hearts skip beats and panties hit the floor.

She whipped her head around. "What's so funny?"

"I was talking about being jealous of the badge." Paxton leaned in toward Kate, his whisper silky and sexy. "Jealous of the girl is even better."

A delicious ripple of heat spread through her to places

only her massaging shower head had recently satisfied. She hated that he had that kind of power over her. This virile appeal that grew stronger the closer he got made her heart vulnerable and volatile. A powder keg.

The elevator doors opened, and Kate stepped in. "Don't flatter yourself."

Paxton penetrated her personal space, reached around her, and pressed five without a word, his grin still firmly in place. She willed herself not to fidget, but being that close was making her everything tingle. She focused on breathing and blinking until the door binged.

The doors opened, and Kate walked out of the elevator, head down so Paxton wouldn't see how he unnerved her. She heard a soft whistle behind her and stopped to look.

"This way, Katie." He pointed down the opposite side of the hall, where two agents sat.

She shoved the bunny in her purse, hiked it up on her good shoulder, and headed in their direction. One agent was skinny with a mustache that would make Tom Selleck jealous, the other agent bald and stocky. As she got closer, the Kojak lookalike stood to greet them.

Paxton flashed his credentials; Kate peered through the window into the patient room, expecting Robbie to be wearing the ashen, pained look she remembered from the hotel. Instead, he lay in the hospital bed, eyes closed and peaceful. A breathless relief washed over her.

A brunette sat facing Robbie, her hand on his. Myra Thomas, his mother. Kate had never met her but recognized her from her research and recon.

Something touched Kate's arm, making her jump.

"Katie." Paxton looked at her like she might crumble to pieces. The pity in his gaze was nauseating, but the slight swelling still showing under his eye proved she was not the fragile flower he thought she was. "He needs to check your purse."

She tipped it in his direction, her fingers covering the butt of Ziggy.

Cue Ball took the purse and pulled Ziggy from his custom, built-in holster.

"I have a concealed-carry weapon permit for him." Kate realized she was a little loud and turned the volume down.

"Procedure." He checked Ziggy's safety, then placed him in a lockbox the Magnum, P.I. wannabe held out. "Only law enforcement with weapons in the room."

Kate took the purse back. Lighter without her trusty friend.

The door swung wide, and Mrs. Thomas appeared in front of her, eyes bloodshot and ringed with dark circles deeper than her own eye color. Her clothes were rumpled and slept-in, for what little sleep she must have gotten, and her hair, normally straight and silky, put messy-buns to shame. The poor woman looked like she'd taken the express train to hell and back.

Mr. Mustache stood, and both agents placed their hands on their weapons like a synchronized freak-show of has-been TV investigators. Ugh. This was not going to end well with jumpy G-men and a mother skirting sanity.

Mrs. Thomas stepped into the hallway, closing the door behind her. "You have a lot of nerve showing up here."

Kate looked around. "Me?" She couldn't disguise the confusion in her tone.

"Our divorce isn't final. My son is in critical condition." She zeroed in on Kate, pointing a shaky finger, the nail bitten down to the flesh. "My husband's whore isn't welcome here."

Paxton moved to pull Kate back, but she didn't budge. It wasn't the first time she'd been called out by a jilted lover, angry business partner, or crazy ex-wife in her line of work. She was a personal security expert. Part of the job meant blending in, looking like she was with whomever she was protecting. She took her job seriously, always conducted her threat assessments, and she was damn good at what she did. She could thank Paxton for those skills, but she wouldn't.

Kate straightened her shoulders. There was nothing she could do to make the situation better but absorb whatever pain and fear Mrs. Thomas felt for her son. Words, sneers, and glares were the least of Kate's problems.

"I told you we didn't want to be disturbed." Mrs. Thomas addressed the FBI agents, whose hands remained on their weapons.

"She didn't come here to upset you." Paxton's negotiator tone kicked in.

Mrs. Thomas crossed her arms over her chest. "I want her out of here. Immediately."

"What is going on here?" Senator Thomas walked up from the left side of the hall carrying two cups of coffee, another FBI agent a few steps behind him.

"Senator." Kate nodded. His campaign manager, Christopher, must have brought him a change of clothes, taking in his media-ready freshly pressed suit and shined shoes. He looked like his normal, polished self, but his eyes matched his wife's, telling a different story. A father full of anguish, exhaustion, and agony.

"Kate?" He stopped at her side, and the young, blond, MacGyver-looking agent with him assumed the position of the other two agents.

Kate felt very naked without Ziggy at her side. She turned her attention back to his wife, whose face was getting more and more red.

"Myra, why are you causing a scene in the hall?" He placed the coffee cups on the chair where baldy had been sitting.

"Perfect." She threw her hands in the air. "Stick up for the homewrecker."

Senator Thomas stepped between Kate and his wife. A braver man than she would have given him credit for. "Why don't we step into the room to talk like adults." His voice was low and calm, very elected official-sounding. "We don't need the whole hospital knowing our business."

"Fine." She stepped aside to allow him to open the door. "But if you think your whore is coming in here, you're as dumb as she is."

Kate clenched her fist and released it. She'd been called all kinds of names. None of them true, but it didn't mean she liked it.

"Myra." Senator Thomas placed his hands on her shoulders, but she shrugged them off. "If you can't discuss this rationally you're welcome to leave."

"I'm not leaving my son."

"Then do this for Robbie." The senator escorted his wife into the room.

Kate followed them but moved to the opposite side of Robbie's bed. Better safe than arrested for murder.

"I didn't come here to cause trouble." Kate pulled the stuffed bunny out of her purse, tucking it under Robbie's arm. "I just wanted to see how he's doing, and bring Patches."

"He's in a medically induced coma." Myra choked back a sob.

The senator closed the door and stood at the foot of the bed. "The piece of glass pierced the pericardium and left ventricle. He had a lot of blood around his heart, but they were able to repair all the damage. Thanks to you, he should make it through this."

Paxton glanced at Kate and back to the senator. "That's great news, sir."

Robbie was going to be fine. The knot of tension that had appeared in her shoulders the night before started to unwind. "Yes, great news."

Mrs. Thomas scoffed.

The senator turned to his wife. "You can be angry with me to eternity, but Kate is the reason Robbie's alive."

"I suppose now you're going to tell me she's a doctor?"

"No. A bodyguard." Senator Thomas smiled down at his son, then up at Kate. "She saved us both."

"Just doing my job, sir." Kate felt the heat of tears forming. She looked up at the lights to ward them off. This whole damn ordeal had turned her into an emotional weapon of mass destruction.

"This." Mrs. Thomas pointed to Paxton in his black-on-black gear, arms easily twice the size of Kate's. "This is a bodyguard. Not that." She glared in Kate's direction.

"No, ma'am." Paxton stepped forward. "Sergeant Howard was top of her class and the best in our unit. She saved my life more than once. From what I read in the reports, she threw herself into harm's way to protect your husband and stabilized Robbie until the paramedics arrived."

All true statements, but taking a compliment when she clearly missed a bomber made Kate's insides harden.

Mrs. Thomas sagged into the seat. She slipped her hand over Robbie's and closed her eyes.

The senator pointed to Kate's shoulder. "And how are you feeling?"

"I've had worse." And she had, but not on American soil.

Senator Thomas rubbed his temple. "Who did this? Why?"

"We don't know yet, sir." Paxton tucked his thumbs into his belt loops. "But my team is working on it."

"I want Ms. Howard kept in the loop of this investigation. She already has top-secret clearance, and she has my full backing. I want to know who did this to my son."

Kate watched the muscle in Paxton's jaw harden. "I'll see what we can do."

Kate looked down at Robbie and back to the senator, shaking her head. She had to have missed something in her research. "I swear I'll get to the bottom of this, and the person responsible will pay."

Paxton's phone buzzed. He checked the screen. "Excuse me," he said and ducked into the hallway.

"Since when do you hire bodyguards, Robert?" Mrs. Thomas narrowed her eyes at him.

"About two months ago I received an email." He looked at Kate, and she gave him an encouraging nod. "I didn't think it was a big deal. People send elected officials nasty letters all the time, but Christopher insisted I look into security with the election coming up."

Kate glanced over at Paxton, wearing out the soles of his shoes in the hallway, pacing this way and that.

Mrs. Thomas stood, still holding Robbie's hand. Something changed in her eyes. The pain and fear for her son turned firm and flinty toward her husband. "Someone threatened you?" Her voice was deeper.

"Yes."

She dropped her son's hand, stepping toward her husband. The tightness in Mrs. Thomas's face was like a mama bear, fierce and protective. It made the hairs on the back of Kate's neck stand at attention, wishing she had riot gear.

"And you thought it was a good idea to have our son, my son, at your reelection campaign fundraiser?" Her voice hardened with every step toward her husband.

Kate walked closer to the senator. The family was under FBI protection, but Kate was still technically his bodyguard. It would look bad if she let him get murdered by his wife in the middle of a hospital.

"You knowingly put Robbie in danger." The threat in her tone imminent.

Kate stepped between the senator and his wife. "Mrs. Thomas—"

Paxton yanked the door open, turning all their focus on

him. The worry lines in his forehead hooded his eyes, but the twitch in his jaw was what turned Kate's hands clammy. A cold shiver of dread darted down her spine, announcing this was not good news. "We need to go." His tone confirmed her feelings.

"Where?" Kate whispered when she got to the door.

"Senator Gail's been in an accident."

Chapter Five

____

Kate closed the SUV door, staring up at the Phoenix Children's Hospital. The midday sky was quickly turning gray, casting an ominous shadow. A dark and heavy sensation of dread developed deep in her gut. A sign this day was about to get a whole lot worse. Kate tugged the zipper up on her sweatshirt, blocking out the wind.

"The police and EMT reports are starting to come in." Paxton took long strides toward the hospital. His phone hadn't stopped dinging since they'd hit the road ten minutes earlier.

Kate double-timed to keep up with him. She took in the surrounding lobby. It looked like they had stepped onto the Candy Land game board, bright and cheerful. The colorful decor a world apart from the other hospital they had just left with its white everything. But it still smelled like a hospital.

Next to the visitor desk, Paxton showed his badge to the tall, skinny agent.

The guy put out his hand to stop Kate. "Badge, ma'am?"

Again with the badge. This shit was getting old. She hugged her injured arm to her waist. "We're together."

The agent, with his fresh-out-of-the-academy haircut and

by-the-book look on his face, shook his head. She imagined for a moment that this had been what Paxton looked like when he started. All young and ambitious and infuriating.

"Paxton?" Kate's focus flitted from the agents standing guard down the hall to Paxton.

He turned toward Kate. "You should stay in the waiting area."

"The hell I will." Kate stepped around him, blocking his way down the hall. Of course, he could easily move her, but not without another bloody nose. She glared, daring him to try. "You heard Senator Thomas. I'm going with you." Her tone was point-blank.

"Kate, I don't have time to argue with you."

"Then don't." She forced herself to keep her head high. "I've been working on this for weeks longer than you. All the research I've done, the background checks. Maybe I could connect something Senator Gail saw or heard to the bombing."

Paxton looked over his shoulder and back to Kate. "Keep your voice down." His eyebrows squeezed together like he was debating and disputing her comment. "It's a car accident. I am here as a professional courtesy to the senator. For all we know, these two incidents have nothing to do with one another."

"Two state senators in two days?" Kate shook her head. "My gut says they're connected."

He took a step toward her, forcing Kate to lean back to keep her eye contact. "That's the difference between you and me. I act on facts and evidence." The lack of space between them was unsettling. The air palpable. His chest almost touching hers, radiating heat, ignited a spark in her core. "You just react."

"Come on, Paxton, you know this feels fishy." Her gaze slipped to his lips and back up to meet his eyes. The puffiness from her punch earlier practically gone, like it never happened.

Paxton smirked, the look sending heat north, south, and everywhere in between.

"I'm coming with you."

"This is a coincidence until I have proof otherwise." Paxton's tone was surprisingly serious in comparison to his look. "You're wallpaper in there. Got it?"

Kate nodded, straightened her shoulders, and stepped out of his way.

After she checked Ziggy with the next agent, Kate followed Paxton into the private room. Senator Barbra Gail sat on the bed next to one of her daughters. For twins, the tween girls looked nothing alike. The daughter with fiery red hair, knotted in a bun high on her head, jumped up, grasping her mother's arm. The little blonde, a carbon copy of her mother but sporting a fresh cast, looked up at them, her eyes still red-rimmed from crying.

A pang of sadness tightened its grip around Kate's gut.

"Senator Gail." Paxton reached his hand out to her. "I'm Special Agent Paxton Banks. I need to ask you a few questions."

The senator whispered something to her red-haired daughter, kissed her cheek, and stood. She lived up to the "Senator Barbie" nickname the social media haters had donned her. Blond hair, big blue eyes, and a figure disproportionate with reality. She shook Paxton's hand and turned to Kate. "And you are?"

"Kate Howard." She reached out her hand to the senator. "I wish we were meeting under better circumstances."

The senator glanced back at her girls, then motioned to the door. "Why don't we step into the hall."

Paxton held the door for the ladies, closing it behind him. "I've heard pieces of the story, but I'd like to hear it in your words. What happened today?"

Senator Gail tugged at the sleeve of her green silk blouse. She was still very well put together, but the look of anger and fear in her eyes left Kate sick to her stomach.

"We were taking Desiree and Danica to dance class."

"We?" Paxton pulled a small notebook and pen from his cargo pants.

"Patrick was driving."

"And what's his relation to you?" He jotted a note.

"Patrick's my personal assistant, driver, sometimes babysitter. He was supposed to be off today, but the girls wanted him to see their dance rehearsal." The senator studied her shoe. "He was rushed to surgery. The injuries to his left side were severe."

"I'm sorry to hear that." Paxton's eyebrows raised a fraction. "What's Patrick's last name?"

"Minard." The senator let out a deep breath. "I should have made him stay home." Her voice wavered.

"This is not your fault." Paxton's voice was soft and calming. "There is no way you could have known this would happen."

The senator nodded, but her eyes disagreed. Guilt was there, bubbling under the surface. A feeling Kate knew all too well. "We were headed to the dance studio, and out of nowhere this car slammed into the driver side. We thought it was an accident and started to pull over when the car rammed us again. It forced us onto the median." The senator wiped away a tear and sniffled.

"You're doing great." Paxton's tone was encouraging. He pulled a tissue from his pocket and handed it to her like a Boy Scout, prepared for everything. "Take your time."

"The girls were crying. Patrick was in a lot of pain." Senator Gail blotted her eyes. "Luckily, he was able to get us off the road and into the gas station parking lot a little ways down. The clerk called nine-one-one."

What kind of a nutball would go after a senator whose

kids were in the car? Kate wiped her sweaty palms on her pants.

"Did you see the other vehicle? Can you recall the color, make, or model?"

She shook her head. "The whole thing happened so fast." She paused to blow her nose. "I think it was light-colored. Silver, maybe, but it could have been white. I—I was more worried about Danica, Desiree, and Patrick than looking back at the car."

Kate followed the senator's line of sight to her daughters. The red-haired twin had taken her mother's spot on the bed next to her sister.

"But you're sure it was a car?"

"I don't think it was tall enough to be a truck or van."

"Did Patrick cut someone off or—"

"This wasn't some case of road rage." Senator Gail's tone turned as sharp as a Ka-Bar knife. "We were under attack, Agent Banks. They could have hurt my girls far worse than a fractured arm and some nightmares. What happened to Patrick was meant for me."

The senator wasn't wrong. If this was an attack, that driver-side impact was intended for her.

Paxton nodded, but Kate wasn't sure if it was in agreement or appeasement. "Do you know why someone would want to hurt you?"

The senator scoffed. "I'm almost three years into my term. We've voted on a lot of controversial legislation. Immigration laws, tax increases, health insurance, legalizing marijuana, teacher salaries, gun reform, veterans' affairs. If it pisses someone off, we've voted on it."

Kate's protective instinct, her core empathetic nature, the essence that kept her in the security business, ignited like a flamethrower. Sitting on the sidelines was not an option. She cleared her throat. "Have you received any threats?"

Paxton shot her a wallpaper-doesn't-talk look.

The senator scoffed again. "I've received dozens of threats over the years. My office manager keeps them on file."

Paxton dug in his pocket and pulled out a business card. "I'd like to look at them."

"Absolutely." Senator Gail's tone scaled back to normal, and she took the card. "I can have him send them over."

"Thank you."

"Anything particularly disturbing lately?" Kate focused on Senator Gail to avoid Paxton's no-doubt disapproving scrutiny. "Death threats? Bombings?"

Senator Gail's hand silenced a gasp. "Do you think this is related to the bombing yesterday?" Her voice got quiet. She checked the hallway around them. "Is that why you're here? Is someone targeting senators?"

"We don't know that these cases are related." The agitation in Paxton's tone was clearly toward Kate for suggesting they were. "It could be a coincidence, but the Bureau wants to be diligent in its investigation to rule it out."

Kate took a step forward. "Senator Gail, can you remember anything recently that stood out?"

The senator crossed her arms over her chest, her thoughts taking her away. "They're mostly *you're destroying our state, how do you sleep at night* type of things." She brought her attention back to Kate. "But you know, a few weeks ago I received an odd email."

"Odd?" Kate and Paxton said in unison.

"Perverted." Her voice was quiet.

Kate's gut constricted. "Do you remember what it said?"

Senator Gail leaned in. "'Your double Ds will look great in a casket,'" she whispered.

A sicko and a psycho on the loose. Perfect.

"The FBI will have a team assigned to you while we investigate." Paxton put the notepad back in his pocket. "We take death threats seriously. I think it would be wise if you wore a ballistic vest as well."

"What?" The senator's voice was a notch below panic. "Are you out of your mind? I'm not wearing a bulletproof vest. What would that say to my girls, to my constituents?"

Paxton ran his hand through his hair. "It would say you care about your girls and want to stay alive to see them grow up."

"No. Absolutely not." Senator Gail tossed her hair off her shoulder and planted her fists onto her hips as if she were a superhero. "It would say that I'm a coward. That I can be bullied. I didn't take this job to make the easy decisions, Special Agent Banks. I took this job to make a difference."

"Respectfully, ma'am"—Paxton's tone was disapproving—"I think you should reconsider. This person got to you once. What's to stop them from trying again?"

"I'll go along with this FBI security detail, but the vest? No."

Kate watched the muscle in Paxton's jaw tighten. As much as she respected the senator's passion and steadfastness, her vanity and pride could easily get her killed.

"What if there were a less-conspicuous option?" Kate put her hand on the senator's shoulder. "Something less obvious. Fashionable, even. No one would question it for protection. Would you at least consider it?"

The senator looked thoughtfully at Kate. "No one would know?"

"It would be just between us." Kate looked at Paxton and back to the senator.

Senator Gail shrugged. "I might consider it."

"Okay." Kate smiled. "Then that's exactly what I'm going to get you."

Kate's phone chirped for the ninth time since they left the hospital. She'd ignored it while they interviewed Senator

Gail, but could no longer. Maggie, her best friend, had seen the news about the bombing, and in true Maggie form, she had imagined the worst. Paxton was supposed to drop Kate off at the hotel to pick up her car, again, but based on the rapid-fire rate of Maggie's texts, Kate knew she needed to make a stop before her face ended up on a milk carton.

"Could we take a quick detour?" Kate tossed her phone on the console between them.

Paxton checked his watch. "I need to get back to the Bureau for a briefing."

"I'll make it quick; I promise." Kate's stomach growled, reminding her they had missed lunch. "Hang a left up here, and a right at the light."

They pulled into a parking lot, and Kate had her seatbelt off before he put the SUV in park.

"Mr. Chen's Dry Cleaners?" Paxton looked up at the building through the windshield. "Now we're running errands?"

"I'm working." Kate pulled last night's dress off the seat and draped it over her arm. "You can go. I can find a ride home from here."

"I'm not leaving you stranded." His tone was reluctant.

"Suit yourself. But you probably want to leave the FBI jacket here. Mrs. Chen's not a fan of law enforcement."

"You're kidding, right?"

"Nope." Kate knew firsthand being escorted through those doors by a guy with a badge and a gun was never a good thing. What she neglected to tell Paxton was that she was also on Mrs. Chen's least-favorite-people list. She didn't like Kate as a fifteen-year-old runaway living in her basement, and she didn't like her now as a thirty-four-year-old bodyguard.

The door chimed as he opened it for Kate. The smell of soap, starch, and chemical cleaners hung in the air. To most people, the smell was noxious. To Kate, the smell was home.

Mrs. Chen shuffled to the counter in a dress much too boxy for her small frame. Her face was set in the rarely-happy-to-see-you scowl Kate had grown to expect. At least she was consistent. She pulled her glasses up from the string around her neck, placed a wrinkly hand on the counter, and leaned in to examine them. "He look like police."

The woman had to be part bloodhound. She couldn't see worth a shit anymore, but she could sniff out law enforcement and chocolate cherry cordials from two towns over.

"He's not a cop." Kate stood in front of Paxton, strategically blocking his badge and gun from her view.

"What you want?" Her gray hair flopped into her face.

Kate client-smiled and held up the dress. "Is Maggie here?"

"Margaret not here. You go." Mrs. Chen shooed them away from the counter. "No trouble here. You go."

Maggie was there. She lives upstairs, works downstairs, and owns the building. She was always there. Kate looked up at the security camera and waved, hoping Maggie would see her.

Mrs. Chen said something in Mandarin, then swatted at Kate's hand.

"Mama C, please."

"What did she say?" Paxton leaned into Kate, his breath warm on her cheek.

"I don't know. Maybe she was complimenting my sweats." Kate pulled her phone out of her purse and texted Maggie. *The dragon is guarding the castle.*

"What do you mean you don't know? You speak Chinese."

"Mandarin. Yes, I do." She had learned the language in this very building. Mr. Chen would teach her while she cleaned lint traps, hung garments, and pressed slacks for hours after school. "But I'd rather imagine she's saying nice things about me."

Kate's phone chirped. *I'll rescue you.*

"She's not in the Kate Howard fan club?" Paxton's voice dropped in volume.

"Not even close," she whispered over her shoulder.

Mrs. Chen shook her finger at Kate, muttering about growing up and settling down.

"Mama, be nice." Maggie, a blur of pastel pink, came out of the side door, around her mother, and hugged Kate before she could move.

She gasped when Maggie put her arms around her. "Don't squeeze." Kate pushed out through gritted teeth, cursing the twinge of day-old pain in her back.

"You're hurt." Maggie pulled the black, cat-eye glasses off her head, sending her long, black hair flowing this way and that. She looked Kate up and down. "I knew it. I told you." She glanced at her mother.

Mrs. Chen took a step forward, softening her posture. "What's wrong?"

"I'll be fine. It's just some cuts. I've had worse."

Maggie shot her an I've-heard-that-before look before her eyes flitted up past Kate, and she knew she'd lost her attention. And why wouldn't she lose to Paxton? In the black T-shirt and cargo pants, he looked like a G.I. Joe action figure come to life. Chiseled jaw, strong arms, great ass.

"Well, hello." She put her hand out. "Maggie Chen, at your service."

"Special Agent Paxton Banks."

Mrs. Chen rattled on behind them about always being in trouble. She should kick Paxton for getting her started.

"Wait." Maggie eyed Kate suspiciously, tugging on her lace blouse. "Paxton Banks. *The* Paxton Banks?" Her tone was sing-songy.

For Kate, it was a little too suggestive, implying they'd gossiped about him like schoolgirls. She cleared her throat.

"Maggie this is Paxton, my former Army captain. Paxton, this is my best friend, Maggie."

"Pleasure to meet you." Paxton grinned. "Katie told me all about you when we were serving together."

Maggie laughed and bumped Kate with her hip. "*Katie* has apparently neglected to tell me all sorts of delicious things about you."

Kate tapped Maggie's shoulder. "Now that everyone's acquainted, can we talk in your office?"

"Absolutely." Maggie scooched her mother out of the way.

Mrs. Chen called after them to leave the door open and no funny business.

"What did she say?" Paxton followed Kate down the stairs.

Kate waited until they were out of Mrs. Chen's earshot, through the twelve-inch-thick steel door which held Maggie's studio. "She likes your boots."

Maggie and Kate laughed, but Paxton didn't play into their joke. He was too busy taking in his surroundings.

The basement, filled with racks of fabric, tables with sewing machines, and a full-length, three-way adjustable mirror, had been Kate's home for almost three years. Her rollaway cot was barely visible in the corner.

"This is for you." Kate handed Maggie the dress. She was almost two inches shorter than Kate, so the hem would hit her at what Mrs. Chen would consider a reasonable length. And she was a full cup size smaller, so Maggie wouldn't have the cleavage challenges.

"Red sequins? Va Va Voom." Maggie waggled her eyebrows. "How very Jessica Rabbit of you."

"It was a gift from Senator Thomas."

"The man has good taste." Maggie held up the dress, an over-exaggerated pout on her face. "Is this blood?" Her tone full of disappointment.

"Yes." Kate leaned against the cutting table. "But it's mostly not mine."

Kate put her purse next to the sewing machine, opened the bottom drawer of the file cabinet, and pulled two Mr. Muscle protein bars out of the box. She tossed one to Paxton and tore the other open. She savored the smooth, peanut buttery goodness.

Maggie grimaced. "What do you want me to do with it?"

"Mama C can probably get the blood out." Kate recalled how proud she once was for getting coffee out of a white cashmere sweater. Of course, Kate was the reason the sweater needed to be cleaned in the first place, but that was another point entirely. "If not, you could use it for target practice." Kate pointed to the other side of the room, where a mannequin, riddled with bullet holes, had seen happier days.

Paxton rested his hand on the top of his gun. "What exactly is this place?" His tone was curiously cautious.

Maggie tossed the dress on the cutting table. "It's an old bomb shelter. I've made it into my sewing studio."

Kate smiled proudly. "Maggie's a seamstress. The best in the business."

"And you shoot at the clothes you hate?" Paxton's tone was a forced joke.

"Oh, don't be silly." Maggie grinned, placing her glasses on her head. "I shoot the ones I like."

Paxton gave Kate a critical squint before turning his attention back to Maggie.

"Aside from the occasional pants to hem and skirt to take in, I dabble in social subterfuge." Maggie pulled a gray suit jacket off a rack and held it up to Paxton's chest. "Fashionable and functional clothing for high-profile individuals." Her voice was infomercial-worthy.

Paxton picked up the price tag and choked on his protein bar. "Four thousand dollars?"

"For you, thirty-eight hundred. We'll call it the 'friend of Kate' special."

"Are you kidding me? Who can afford that?"

"Executives. Politicians. Celebrities. Anyone who needs an insurance policy against bullets and knives." Maggie pulled the jacket off the hanger. "Try it on."

He looked from Maggie to Kate and back. "This is going to stop a bullet? It's a blazer."

"Not just any blazer." Maggie flipped open the lapel to show him the inside. "I use Kevlar for my anti-ballistic wear, and for some of my more flexible clothing I use Dyneema composite fabric."

"That's what she uses for most of my wardrobe." Kate pulled the remainder of the protein bar out of the wrapper. "It's the strongest, lightest, most versatile fiber in the world."

"Kate thinks she's bulletproof." Maggie's tone was full-on braggy-pants. "I'm the reason she is."

"This is Dyneema?" Paxton pointed to Kate's sweats.

Kate tossed the wrapper in the trash. "No. This is Old Navy."

Maggie held out the jacket for Paxton. "Come on, try it on."

"I'm a black suit guy."

Maggie laughed. "Don't be silly. A little gray in your life wouldn't kill you."

He slipped his arms in, and she pulled the mirror toward him.

"This one has Kevlar." Maggie let out a whistle. "Look at that. Perfect fit. Have I got a good eye or what?"

"It's light." He turned toward Maggie.

"And it will stop up to a 9mm bullet or standard blade. Now, it will leave a nasty bruise or a broken rib, but you'd be alive." Maggie straightened the jacket, lingering over his arms.

A niggle of jealousy reared its ugly head, but Kate shoved

it down with the last bite of Mr. Muscle peanut butter madness. "I'm happy to test it out if you like."

Paxton buttoned the jacket and turned back to the mirror, completely ignoring her offer to shoot him. "Wow."

Wow was right. Kate's heart was going to need ballistic wear of its own if she weren't careful. They say the suit makes the man, and they weren't kidding. The gunmetal gray made his blue eyes sparkle even in the dim fluorescent basement light. He was mesmerizing.

"The slacks need to be finished." Maggie held them out. "Here. Take your pants off."

"What?" Kate's voice cracked. She pushed off the table and turned away from them.

"Since when are you a prude?" Maggie threw them, hitting Kate in the back of the head.

"I'm not." Kate put the pants on the table but kept her face averted. She prayed the heat seeping into her skin would dissipate. This was not how she wanted to get Paxton's pants off. Not that she had thought about how she would get them off. Ugh. She needed to think about something other than Paxton's pants. "We need to talk about an actual client, and we don't have time for a fashion show today."

"Katie's right." Paxton's voice got closer to her.

Kate turned back toward them. "Senator Gail. Have you heard of her?"

Maggie laughed. "Sure. She's the one they call Senator Barbie with the blond hair and big boobs."

"The one and only." Kate slung her purse over her shoulder. "She needs a new wardrobe. I'm thinking a black blazer. Something cute, but versatile that she can dress up or down. And it's kind of a rush. Think you're up to it?"

Maggie beamed. "Girl, I've got this."

Chapter Six

"Damn it." Kate pounded the keys on her laptop as if typing harder would make it cooperate. It had been four hours since Paxton had dropped her off at her car and she'd driven home. Since beginning her research, the computer had frozen up on her twice already. Scooting the stool back, she paced a few steps in front of her kitchen island command-center. On a normal night, she could hit the weight bench or practice some drills on the punching bag to blow off some steam, but her back and shoulder were in no shape for that.

When the teakettle whistled, Kate turned her back on the infuriating machine, filled the *Better Late Than Ugly* mug Maggie had given her for Christmas, and dropped a tea bag into the steaming water. She leaned against the fridge, glaring at the business card Paxton had given her until her focus went fuzzy.

Regardless of the technical issues, her investigation into the senators was worthless. An unproductive, unusable, unbelievable waste of Saturday night. Except for their current job titles, that they had children, and were human, Senator Gail and Senator Thomas had zero in common. Sure, they had cast some similar votes over the years, but so did a dozen other state senators. Kate could not find one outward force indicating why they would both have been attacked. She took a step forward, placed her tea on the island, and flipped through the documents spread out on the quartz top. "Maybe Paxton was right about them being a coincidence."

But her gut said otherwise. She picked up the business card and her thumb aimlessly circled the embossed FBI logo. Kate needed more information and better resources. Paxton surely wasn't going to tell her anything. She blew out a breath.

She tossed down the card, picked up her phone, and scrolled through her contacts. Her finger hovered over Special Agent in Charge Gerald Dupree of the Phoenix FBI Field Office. Kate knew it was a bad idea to go over Paxton's head, but she owed it to her client to stay involved in the case. Not that she cared what Paxton thought of her. Or if he thought of her. She brushed her knuckles across her mouth, remembering the warmth of Paxton's lips on hers, and pushed the memory away. No, she was better off forgetting it ever happened. If calling in favors was what it took, she'd happily piss off Paxton to fulfill her contract with Senator Thomas.

Was this really how she wanted to use her one and only get-out-of-jail-free card she had earned, coincidentally, for spending a night in jail after punching a *Wild Girls of Spring Break* cameraman in the face?

"Oh, fuck it." She took a deep breath, pressing the call button. It rang once, twice, three times, and just before voice mail answered she heard a gentleman clear his throat.

"What?" Dupree's gruff voice sounded like she woke him up, but in the few cases she'd worked with him as a linguistics consultant, that seemed to be his norm.

"SAC Dupree?"

"Speaking."

She straightened her shoulders, strolling around the kitchen. "Good evening, sir. It's Kate Howard."

"Ms. Howard." His tone revealed his recollection of her.

"Sir, I'm sorry to call late on a Saturday, but I'd like to cash in the favor you owe me, and it's rather time-sensitive."

"I'm listening."

"You've been informed of the car bombing at Senator Thomas's reelection campaign fundraiser?"

"I have."

"I've been on the senator's security detail for a few weeks now. The fact that this incident happened on my watch infuriates me. And as you know, from when I was guarding Patricia, I take my client's protection very seriously." Kate hoped bringing up his daughter would remind him of her experience and reputation. The very reasons he cited for hiring her to protect his daughter on spring break a few months back. "Sir, I know it's unorthodox, but I'd like to stay informed of the investigation. Details I've seen or heard or come across in my research may prove a valuable asset in the investigation of this case. Plus, I witnessed the explosion."

The line was silent for what felt like a minute before she checked to make sure the call was still connected.

"In what capacity?"

"Frankly, sir, in any capacity that would allow me to help catch the person responsible." Kate swallowed back against the guilt squeezing her throat. "Senator Thomas requested I stay informed, and I owe that to him and Mrs. Thomas." *And Robbie.*

"Understood." His tone didn't give her a clue of which way he was leaning. "I'll see what we can do." And he disconnected.

"Okay. Good. Okay." Kate walked around the island, placing her phone next to the laptop. Still frozen. She pounded on the keyboard again, the screen flashed, and it tossed her an electronic-middle-finger—the blue screen of death. "Oh, you've got to be kidding me."

Kate's stomach sank faster than a Humvee in a lake. Her

research, client files, security system, Netflix—everything was on that laptop. Kate's stomach rolled, sending a chill all the way out to her fingertips. She pulled a blue flannel shirt off the back of the stool to cover her black tank top and running shorts. She racked her brain to recall the last time the computer had automatically backed up.

Midnight and Noon, right? Kate looked up at the clock over her sink. Quarter to nine. "Shit." What little info she had found tonight was lost.

She scrubbed her hands over her face in disgust. Kate recalled her neighbor, Kyle, saying something about computers that morning. Shoving the laptop under her right arm, she rushed out of her loft and bounded down the stairs like a tactical team storming a target. "Hey." Kate banged on his door hard enough to make her shoulder hurt. "Kyle. Open up," she shouted.

Kyle swung the door open, eyes wide, hair wild, Cheetos stains on his fingertips. "Is the building on fire?" His voice was panic-laced.

"What did you do to my computer?" Kate held the laptop out between them. "It was working fine until you touched it this morning."

"Me?" Kyle grabbed the laptop, turning it over to look at the manufacturer's tag. "This thing was old six years ago. I can't believe it's not in a museum somewhere." He handed it back to Kate and slammed the door in her face.

"Seriously?" Kate's body tensed up, making her injured shoulder throb. She kicked the door with the side of her heel. The pain of hitting her ankle against the metal door made Kate realize she hadn't put shoes on.

Kyle opened the door again. "Look. I'm in the middle of a warlock battle."

"I don't care if you're turning *into* a warlock." Her tone was ten shades of don't-mess-with-me. Kate shoved the computer back at him. "This is life or death."

He groaned as if this were the millionth time she'd asked him for a favor, when in reality it was only the second time they stood face to face. At least this time she hadn't pulled a gun on him.

Kate yanked on the sleeve of her shirt. "It was working and now it's dead."

Kyle laughed. "And that's my problem because?"

"Because you were the last one to touch it. And you said you were a computer guy."

He flipped up the screen. "This thing is toast."

"No." Her voice was whiny even to her. "It was just working. Can't you do something to untoast it?"

"Untoa—" Kyle ran his fingers through his hair, making it stand up even more. "You can't untoast a fatal system error. At best, you could try to recover some documents in safe mode, but the chances are slim. All this thing is good for now is a doorstop."

Kate tipped Kyle's watch toward her. Almost nine. A stiffness settled into her shoulders and back. "So, I'm screwed until the stores open up tomorrow? That's great."

The desperation in her voice must have been just enough to seduce Kyle's sympathy. He rolled his eyes. "Is it really life or death? Not Solitaire or Farmville or some shit like that?"

"Life or death." Kate made a cross over her heart.

When he stood up straight, he was an inch or two taller than her. "Fine." He stepped back with a dramatic sigh and motioned her in.

"Thank you." She padded barefoot into the apartment. It had been years since she was in there, not since she bought the building and had it completely renovated. The place looked like an IKEA catalog threw up, but what Kyle saved on building his own furniture he must have spent tenfold on computer equipment.

There were six screens all mounted on the wall and a sleek reclining chair with an attached keyboard. It even had a cupholder. Now, *this* was a command center. She'd never seen anything like it. "This is impressive." Kate ran her finger down a rack of flashy gadgets.

"Don't touch." He pointed to the equipment.

She put her arms at her sides. "What is it you do?" Her tone was more suspicious than she intended.

Kyle slid her laptop into the trash with a clatter, and she cringed. "I work with computers."

"You obviously don't fix them." Not hiding the sarcasm in her voice, she walked over and pulled the decrepit device out of the trash. "Do you program or do web design?"

He shrugged, leaning against the fancy chair. "I can do all that."

Something about his vague response made the hairs on the back of Kate's neck stand up. There was more, way more, he wasn't saying. "What does your business card say?"

"That's the beauty of being your own boss. No one to tell me what I can and can't do. And what about you?" He cut her off from asking more questions. "What do you do that requires you to sleep with a gun under your pillow and have life or death computer emergencies on a Saturday night?" He matched her suspicious tone.

He was deflecting. Something was definitely off. Kate spit out the standard response she gave to every non-client. "I work for a temp agency. And you can never be too careful."

"That's all right." Kyle pushed off the chair and rummaged through the rack of supplies. "You don't have to tell me."

"I just did." She flicked at a button on her flannel shirt. "I'm a temp."

"Riiiiight." He dusted off a sleek, black laptop and placed it on the desk. "And I was born yesterday."

Kate wrapped her arms around her middle. "What's that supposed to mean?" Her tone was a tad indignant.

He plugged in the laptop, flipped up the screen, and

pushed the power button. "You work out all the time and get dressed up a lot and get home late."

Creeper much? "I like to stay in shape, look good, and have fun. There's no crime in that."

Kyle put his hands up. "Look. I'm not judging you. I'm sure you make good money as…"

"What exactly do you think I do?" She took a step toward him.

Kyle put his head down focusing on the computer. "Escort," he mumbled.

"Escort?" Kate choked on the word. "No." She shook her head. "No. I'm a temp. Right now I'm working at Senator Thomas's office."

"Sure." Kyle's fingers raced across the keys. "Whatever. Like I said, no judgment."

Kate would have been more embarrassed, but sadly this was not the first or the tenth time someone thought she was an escort. She owed no one an explanation. As Kyle said, that was the beauty of being your own boss.

She pushed his comment aside. "Is this you helping?" She pointed to the laptop.

He tapped a few more keys and blew out a breath. "You can borrow this for the night. Should be good to go after it reboots."

"Thank yo—" Kate hesitated at the sound of knocking and looked around. "What is that?"

He paused and looked up. "A late-night visitor at your door."

"My door?" Kate wasn't expecting anyone. She glanced down at the dead computer in her arms. Guess she wouldn't be checking the security cameras. And in her haste, Kate had left her phone and Ziggy in the loft. She suddenly felt very naked. No cameras. No phone. No gun.

"Are you good here?" She looked over at Kyle.

"Yeah. Go. I'll bring it up in a few minutes."

"Thanks." She opened his front door wide enough to stick her head out, peeking up at her landing. Paxton knocked on her door again, a white plastic bag in his hand. He was still wearing the black cargo pants and T-shirt from earlier in the day. The seductive smell of Chinese takeout filled the small entry, making her salivate. Although she wasn't entirely sure if it was because of the food or the man.

"Come on, Katie. I know you're here." Paxton knocked again. "Your car's outside."

Kate stepped into the hall and closed Kyle's door behind her. "I'm not home."

Paxton spun on his heel and peered over the railing at her. "Hi," he said with a significant lift in his brows. "I, um, brought Chinese."

"I see." Kate rested the laptop on her hip. "What are you doing here?"

"I was hungry, and I thought you might be hungry too, so…" He pointed to the bag.

Kate gave him a who-are-you-kidding glare as she climbed the metal steps, stopping short of the landing. "Really." She stretched her neck to see the logo. Happy Panda. As she suspected. "I'm supposed to believe you just happened to stop by my favorite Chinese restaurant, picked up a smattering of vegetarian options, and drove over here at nine o'clock because you were hungry? With no agenda?"

"Yes. And Mongolian Beef for me."

Although she wanted to take him at his word, there was an eagerness in his eyes she couldn't explain. "Nope." Kate shook her head and rested against the metal rail. "Not buying it."

He took a step toward her door. "Our Chinese is getting cold."

She didn't take her eyes off his. The color of a perfect spring sky blue, flickering with excitement and interest and intrigue. "What if I had people over or was out?"

"I took a chance."

Her stomach quivered and not for the food. It was for the tempting man standing in front of her, making her hyper-aware of every tingle and throb in her body.

He flashed her an impatient smile.

"You found something, didn't you?" Kate's excited tone made his smile widen. A smile almost as delicious as getting lost in his eyes. She took the last step up to meet him.

"I'd rather not talk about it here."

Kate blocked their way into the loft. She gave him a let's-have-it eyebrow raise.

When she didn't move he added. "Please."

She turned toward the door, gave the knob a twist, and pushed. Kate put the dead computer on the island and slid the paperwork over so there was room to sit. She opened her mouth to ask what they found, but her cell phone rang.

Paxton's jaw slacked when he looked at the screen. "Why is SAC Dupree calling you?" His tone was angry and confused.

Nosy fucker. Kate grabbed the phone from the counter and pressed the green button. "Hello? This is Kate."

"Ms. Howard." Dupree's voice was as gravely as before. "It's done."

"Why is Dupree in your contacts?" Paxton whispered. He put the bag on the counter, making too much noise.

She took a few steps away toward the windows. "Sir, what does that mean?"

"You are a temporary and unpaid civilian consultant for this case, and this case only. You are to observe and report any pertinent information to the agent to which you have been assigned. You are to assume anything you learn about this investigation is confidential and to be kept in the highest surety as all top secret information."

"Absolutely." Kate wiped a sweaty palm on her flannel. "Thank you, sir."

"And, Ms. Howard." He cleared his throat. "You will follow our rules or you will find yourself in cuffs for impeding an investigation. I gave your lax interpretation of the law a pass last time because you were protecting my daughter. It won't happen again. Am I clear?"

"Yes." Kate placed her palm flat on her stomach to calm the nerves running amuck. "Thank you, sir."

"The agent on the case will reach out to you." And the line disconnected.

"Wait. Hello? Hello?"

"What the hell was that about?" Paxton's tone was flat-tire-in-the-desert serious. His voice directly behind her.

His phone rang, making Kate jump. *Nonono.* She didn't need to look at the phone to know who it was.

Chapter Seven

____

Kate knew SAC Dupree was on the line before Paxton fished the phone out of his pocket. She clasped her sweaty palms, lacing her fingers together. The most important thing was for her to keep calm and rational. This was what she wanted. Right? To have access to the details of the case. This is what Senator Thomas asked of her.

He pulled the phone out and grumbled at the screen. "Special Agent Banks," he said, placing the phone to his ear.

Maybe Paxton would take the news of her being on the case well.

"Yes, sir." He gave Kate a disapproving stare.

Or not.

"I understand, sir," he said through clenched teeth. "Not at all, sir." The muscles in his neck and jaw tightened. "Absolutely, sir. Thank yo—" He placed his free hand flat on the counter, slowly lowering his phone and his head.

He let out three breaths before looking over at her. "Katie, what did you do?" His voice was restrained, but she knew by the look in his eyes and the tightness in his jaw he was raging inside.

Calm and rational. She pushed her shoulders back and

cleared her throat. "I called Dupree and asked that I be kept informed about my client's case."

"How do you even know Dupree?" Paxton took a stiff step toward her. The tension rolling off him made her muscles tighten, tugging at the stitches in her shoulder. "Are you blackmailing him?"

"What?" The words hit her like buckshot, peppering her confidence with negativity. She wrapped her arms around her stomach. The burst of disappointment took her by surprise. How could he think she was capable of such brazen behavior? She should tell him that she'd worked with Dupree as a linguistics consultant or that she'd conducted protective detail for his daughter, but he didn't deserve that disclosure. "How could you even ask me that?"

"I don't know why he would agree to this otherwise. Temporary consultant?" He took another step toward her. "It's ridiculous. You're not law enforcement. You're not a profiler. You're not even a private investigator."

The heat in the room ticked up as Paxton ticked her off. Kate shoved her sleeves up to her elbows. "You're right. I'm none of those things. But I'm quick on my feet and I trust my instincts." She fired back at him. "It makes me a damn good bodyguard."

"For deadbeat douchebags and crooked CEOs." His voice was louder, angrier. Paxton slid the cell phone into his pocket and crossed his arms over his chest. "This is the FBI, Katie."

"You left me no choice."

"No choice? What are you talking about?"

"You were being all uptight about me being around the victims and evidence." She focused her attention on keeping her voice steady. "Now you don't have to. I already had the clearance. Now I have the approval."

The muscles in his jaw and neck went rigid and released. "Katie, I have rules and regulations I have to follow."

"I have rules too, you know."

"*Your* rules."

Kate made a dismissive hand gesture. "Rules are rules."

"You can make it up on the go if you need to, but I can't afford to skip a step. Not if it means a murderer or terrorist could go free."

Terrorist? The hairs on her arms lifted. The thought hit her like a bucket of ice water. Shocking. Sobering. Stoical enough to snuff out the shit between them. She took a step toward him, close enough to touch his arm. "What did you find in Senator Gail's car?"

He scratched the back of his neck, roughing up his short hair.

"Paxton, you can talk to me. We're on the same team." Kate rested her hip against the sink, trying to look casual despite the stiffness in her muscles. "I'm a consultant. Let me consult."

"Temporary consultant." His voice was quieter. "Under my direction, my orders. This"—he motioned between them —"This is not a democracy. Understood?"

Kate hid a gulp with a nod.

"I transferred to Phoenix for advancement opportunities, and this case could be the key to a promotion. I will not let you screw that up for me." He paced a few steps, stopping in front of her. "Are you in or out?"

Paxton and his verbal confirmations. Even on missions, which were direct orders that we had no option to decline, he always wanted a verbal agreement to the operation. Kate took a deep breath, bluffing away her nerves of working for Paxton. "I'm in. Under one condition."

He took a step closer to her. His eyes locked on hers, increasing the temperature between them. "You are in no position to make stipulations."

Maybe, but she'd do it anyway. She needed ground rules. From this moment on, Paxton was a business associate. And she didn't get involved with people she worked with, so pleasure was off-limits. She stood up straight, clearing her throat. Paxton was close enough if she turned her face up to his, leaning in slightly, she could touch his lips. She held his gaze, testing her own willpower. Heat started in her chest and crept up her neck to her cheeks. "That kiss never happened."

He stared at her, no change of expression to give away his thoughts.

Kate slumped against the counter. The effort to put distance between them was harder than she expected. "And you won't do it again."

Paxton took a step back. The muscle in his jaw tensed. When it released, his stance softened with it. "One hundred percent focus on this case."

Kate nodded, briefly closing her eyes. Her chest constricted, relieved and disappointed by how quickly he had conceded. "Tell me about Senator Gail. What did you find?"

He leaned against the island opposite her. "An explosive device."

"I was right. The cases are related." The words rushed out of her. Kate's excitement was quickly replaced by the somberness of the attacks, and that ugly, sinking feeling was back, weighing down her heart. The thought of Senator Gail and her girls in the car. No. She couldn't think about that. "Why didn't it go off?"

"The techs are looking into it. Right now the theory is the electronic blasting cap was damaged somehow. We think that's why they rammed the car. Trying to cause a spark to ignite it."

"Isn't C4 pretty stable?"

"Yes. But dynamite isn't."

"Dynamite?" Kate's voice eeked up. Her heart slammed into her chest like a flash-bang. "Who are we chasing—Wile E Coyote?"

"All I know so far is it didn't go off, so we might luck out and get some fingerprints off it."

She removed her flannel shirt and wrapped it around her middle. "Was it the same bomb as the one at the fundraiser?"

"Not sure yet." He turned and pulled containers out of the bag he had brought in. "But from what I've seen, there's a good chance they are the same. We'll know more soon." Paxton opened a few of the little white containers, letting the steam billow out.

Kate opened the cupboard, grabbed two plates, and put them at their seats. "That makes this I'm-sorry-for-doubting-you Chinese food."

"This is not an apology." His tone was stern. Paxton took a seat and pulled the other stool out for her.

She ripped open a soy sauce packet with her teeth and dumped it over the steamed vegetable dumplings. "I told you the cases were connected. My instincts were right. You should have believed me."

"It's not that I *didn't* believe you."

Sitting, Kate scooped some Kung Pao Tofu on her plate and popped a chunk of broccoli in her mouth. "But you didn't."

He shifted on the stool to face her. "I live in a black and white world. Everything I do has to be properly documented for arrest purposes. I need hard evidence or probable cause for a warrant. *Kate's gut said so* isn't going to hold up in front of a judge."

His knees brushed her thigh, sending her pulse all catawampus. Kate put her hand on his leg to push it away, lingering a moment too long before she pulled her hand back. Working under Paxton without getting under Paxton was going to be hard. Harder than the muscles she'd groped. She gulped down the broccoli so she wouldn't choke.

Kate slid off the stool, walked around the island, and pulled out two beers. She put one in front of Paxton, the other she twisted the top off and took a swig. "I understand. But sometimes you just have to trust your gut." Unless it's telling you to jump a business associate.

"If this *is* domestic terrorism"—Paxton dished himself some rice—"there is no margin for error. It's my job to identify, locate, and neutralize the threat."

The front door opened, making Kate jump. "Laptop delivery." Kyle strolled in like Maggie would have. Only she was welcome to do so.

"Don't you knock?" Kate shot him a surly stare.

"Why?" He put the computer next to the sink. "The door was unlocked."

Paxton stood to shake his hand. He looked from Kyle to Kate and back. "You two are friends now?"

"He's lending me a computer for the night. Mine crashed."

Kyle leaned over the containers, picked up a spring roll, and bit into it, letting pieces of the crispy crust fall all over her research.

"Seriously?" She scooped up the documents, brushing off the crumbs. Kate pulled a plate out of the cupboard and shoved it at him. "Were you raised by wolves?"

"No. My brother," he said with a mouthful. Kyle placed the spring roll on the plate and hopped up on the counter to sit.

She wanted to holler at him to get down, but there were only two stools at the island and she didn't want him anywhere near her bed, leather club chair, or weight bench with greasy fingers. She really should invest in some furniture, but why when she was the only one living here?

"What's all this?" Kyle motioned toward the pile of papers Kate was still straightening.

"Research." Her tone was very none-of-your-business.

"On what? Or who?" Kyle's eyes got wide. He jumped down, looking over at Paxton. "Are you working on a case? Is it top secret? Can I help?"

Paxton took a long sip of his beer. Kate wasn't sure if he was formulating a response or hoping the subject would change before he came up for air.

"You're FBI too?" Kyle pointed at Kate.

"Eeeh." Kate made a wishy-washy gesture with her hand. "More like FBI adjacent."

"I knew you weren't a temp. Or an escort."

Paxton choked on his beer, trying to cover it up with a cough.

Kyle clapped his hands like an excited toddler, bouncing from foot to foot. "How can I help? I'm really good at finding dirt on people."

Paxton sat straight up on the stool. "No."

"Let the kid talk." Kate cut Paxton off. "What kind of dirt?"

"I don't know." Kyle shrugged and shoved the last bite of spring roll in his mouth. "I used to know this PI. Sometimes I'd help him find out if someone was cheating on their spouse or their taxes and stuff."

Kate matched his enthusiasm. "Could you tell me if two people have anything in common? Enemies?"

"Sure." Kyle wiped his hands on his jeans. "That'll be fun."

Kate glanced over at Paxton. His face had *no* written all over it from the pinched expression around his lips to the furrow in his brow.

"My case. My rules."

She turned back to Kyle. "Is it legal?"

Kyle nodded. "Mostly. You just have to know where to look."

"No." Paxton's tone was authoritative-sounding. "The FBI will take it from here."

Buzzkill. Party of one.

Kate groaned at the sound of knocking, yanking the covers over her head to block out the morning sun.

"Katie?" Paxton's voice seeped through the frame of her thick metal door. "Katie, wake up."

She pushed the blanket off one eye and blinked over at her clock. Seven a.m. She'd spent most of the night researching the senators and hadn't even gotten three hours of sleep. Kate squeezed her dry eyes shut. "Go away." She hollered in the general direction of the door.

"Katie, you have five seconds to open this door or I'll tell Dupree you changed your mind about working this case."

She kicked furiously at the covers and scrambled across the cold floor, ignoring the bite of back pain from the cuts. Turning the dead bolt, Kate swung the door open. "What happened?"

Paxton stared. His eyes roamed from her hair to yesterday's clothes to her bare feet and back up to meet her eyes. She froze under his scrutiny. A deja vu reveille and muster of their time serving together.

"You look like hell." Paxton's tone was flat, but she caught a slight smirk as he headed for the loaner laptop still on the kitchen island from last night's research. He placed a white paper bag and two cups of coffee next to it.

"Well, good morning to you too. Please, do come in." She turned up the sass in her tone to ten. Kate closed the door, taking a few steps toward him. He was back to the boxy black suits that did nothing for him, but his masculine showered-and-shaved scent was waking her up in all the wrong places. "To what do I owe the pleasure of this early morning invasion of privacy?"

Paxton hit a few keys and swiveled the laptop, set to the local news station's website, in her direction.

Kate leaned in to read the caption, "Phoenix Fire Department called out to early morning garage fire. So?" She opened the bag and her stomach growled at the sight of powdered donuts. They were never one of her favorite treats until Paxton's mom and sister sent them in care packages. He would always share them with the team. From that point on they represented freedom, family, and friendship.

"Focus, Katie. Don't you recognize the house?"

She let go of the bag and squinted at the picture of a home in the early dawn light. Fire crews all around. A hint of red and blue shadows from the emergency vehicles nearby. "No. Should I?"

"It's on campaign posters all over town." Paxton opened a new browser and popped up Senator Diaz's website. "That picture there."

Kate examined it. The stucco structure with terracotta roof tile behind the senator was no different than half the Spanish-style architecture homes in the valley. "Maybe? I don't know."

"It's Senator Diaz's home."

Kate pulled napkins off the counter next to the sink and handed one to him. "What does a garage fire have to do with Senator Thomas's case?" She pulled out a donut and pushed the bag toward him.

Paxton clicked back on the news station's page and scrolled down the article. "It says here a neighbor reported hearing a *blast* before seeing smoke and flames coming from the garage."

Kate took a bite letting the powder sugar fall all over her napkin. "A blast." His words soaked into her tired brain. She straightened, looking up at Paxton. "Like an explosion?" Her words were donut-muffled.

The corner of Paxton's mouth lifted into a smoldering smile. The look was pure hunger, and her heart hummed in response. He brushed his thumb along her lower lip, sending a tingle down to all her naughty parts begging to be touched.

Kate gulped down her bite and put the rest of it on the counter, wiping the back of her hand across her mouth. There will be no touching. This is business. Not pleasure. She couldn't be distracted by his sexy actions. "Are you saying what I think you're saying?" She took a few steps toward the windows and pivoted back toward him. "Three senators in three days. Would someone be so bold?"

Paxton took a seat at the island and put his attention on the laptop. "I think we should take a drive and check it out for ourselves to be sure."

"Can we do that?"

"We can, but I'm waiting on dispatch to confirm the location." When he looked back up at her the smolder was stifled. She wasn't sure if she should be grateful or disappointed. "Sunday morning is only necessary personnel at the fire department."

She walked over to the nightstand and picked up her phone. "It was Phoenix fire, right?"

"Yes."

Without hesitation, Kate opened her contacts and hit number four on her favorites. A picture of Cody Stanton, her bartender and late-night get-me-some, popped up on the screen. A battalion of regret tromped through her gut, and she debated hanging up as soon as it rang.

"Kate?" A groggy, deep voice made her remember the time. Far too early for a guy who didn't lock up until nearly three o'clock. "Are you okay?"

She could hear rustling on the other end and imagined him naked in bed, sending heat into her cheeks. Kate turned away from Paxton, not wanting him to read her face.

"Kate?"

"Yeah, hey, sorry to wake you." Kate lowered her voice. "You're a volunteer firefighter with Phoenix right?"

"I'm a volunteer with PFD, but not a fireman."

"Oh." The fact that she knew that much was remarkable since most of their conversations were bar orders or bawdy bedroom talk.

"I'm part of their Community Emergency Response Team. It's more disaster-related than fire."

"Got it." Kate bit her lip. "Never mind. Sorry to disturb you."

"Kate, what's going on?" Cody sounded more awake now. More himself. "It's not like you to call before midnight. And never to *talk*."

He was right. She let out a breath. "There's a pretty big garage fire in north Phoenix. I read that PFD was on-site."

"And you were worried about me?" Cody's tone was teasing.

"No." Kate was a little louder than she expected. She glanced over her shoulder at Paxton feigning interest in something on his phone, but she knew he was listening to every word. "No. Not no, I wasn't. More like no, I hadn't considered that. I—I just thought maybe you could confirm the address."

"You think it's a client?"

Despite not knowing her, he knew enough. "You know I can't tell you that." She absentmindedly straightened the items on her nightstand. "Is there any way you can get me the location?"

"Since when do you ask for favors outside of the bedroom?"

She couldn't help the smile that splayed across her face. "Since now." Kate forced her shoulders back and cringed at the pain. "Please. It might be important."

There was an uncomfortable silence creeping through the line. All the times she'd shut him down at the slightest suggestion of something more than a sweaty-good time, this would be his chance to give it back to her.

"I can call one of the guys."

"Really?" She let out a breath she hadn't realized she was holding. "I owe you one."

"I like the sound of that." Cody's voice was suggestive.

On any normal day, it would have sent her driving toward his place. Today, with Paxton standing feet away, it would send her straight for a cold sponge bath.

"Text me the address as soon as you can. Thanks. Bye." The words rushed out of her, hanging up before he could describe his payment. Kate cleared her throat, tossed the phone on her bed, and turned toward Paxton. "We'll have it in a few minutes."

He looked up at her from the stool at the island. "Who was that?" His tone not giving any indication of his thoughts.

She walked past Paxton and rested against the sink. "Not important." She tried for a casual tone.

"If it impacts the case. It's important."

"Then it's a good thing it has nothing to do with the case." She grabbed her donut and a coffee. "I'm going to change. We can leave as soon as we have the location."

"How will I know who to thank?"

He was baiting her. Seriously? He was the one who taught *her* that trick. "Not to worry. I'll thank him for both of us." Kate headed for the bathroom with a little extra sway in her step.

Her phone chirped before she got to the door. She pulled it off the bed and smiled back at the picture of Cody.

Don't go.

Crime scene.

Body in the rubble.

Chapter Eight

"This is as close as we're going to get." Paxton put the SUV in park at the end of Senator Diaz's street. He reached into the back seat and handed her his FBI jacket. "Throw this on."

Kate took it but continued to stare out the window at the emergency vehicles blocking the road. The only things she could see beyond them were palm trees glistening in the morning sun.

"Are you okay?" He angled toward her. "You haven't said much since we left your place."

Kate nodded, afraid her voice would out her for being an economy-sized bag of chickenshit. Bodies on the battlefield were one thing, but walking into a situation where you know one is waiting for you? That's an entirely different thing. This wasn't war. It was plain old suburbia. Her stomach rolled at the thought.

"Katie?"

She took a deep breath and let it go slowly, grateful for the last half-second to compose herself before looking at Paxton. The sky-blue serenity of his eyes, the soft set of his lips, the way he held himself. *How did he do this every day?* If he were dreading this even half as much as she was, it didn't show.

"You don't have to go in there." His voice was softer, reading whatever he was into the quiet.

Admitting to Paxton she didn't want to be around a dead body was not happening. He'd use it to have her pulled off the case. Kate scoffed at his pity. It was just the fuel she needed to catapult her ass into motion. "Don't be ridiculous." She unbuckled her seatbelt and reached for the door. "Of course I'm going. I'm part of this investigation."

In an effort to be hands-free, Kate had opted for cash in her pocket and a holster on her hip. She wasn't used to carrying Ziggy in the open, but the concealed carry holster against her back was not comfortable in her current condition.

Kate rounded the first fire truck before she realized Paxton was alongside her. He held the back of his windbreaker, helping her to get her injured arm in it. It was far too big for her, covering up her T-shirt and dark, low-rise jeans almost to her knees. She probably looked ridiculous, but it smelled spicy like Paxton's cologne, sending a flood of warmth through her.

They weaved through uniformed response personnel until they reached the caution tape. Flashing his badge at a police officer, Paxton placed his other hand at the small of her back, encouraging her to keep moving.

The smell of smoke was strong in the air, but it really hit her when the detached garage came in view. An entire structure stripped down to rubble and charred studs. Luckily, the garage had stood twenty-five or thirty feet from the home. Pieces of wood and metal scattered between it and the house, untouched with the exception of a few blown-out windows.

Kate shoved the jacket sleeves up to her elbows so she could clutch her hands together, keeping them from shaking. Was this really what her life had become? One crime scene after another. *Soldier up, Kate. This is what you asked for.* She tipped her chin up and shoulders back, despite the pinch of pain, and followed Paxton toward the house.

"Whoa, whoa, whoa." A man in Phoenix Fire Department turn-outs put his hands up.

"Special Agent Paxton Banks." He flashed his credentials.

"This area hasn't been cleared by the inspector."

Kate blocked the sun from her eyes. "The house doesn't even look damaged."

"Until we get the all-clear, no one goes through those doors." He pointed to the front of the house. "It's for your safety."

"What about the senator and Mrs. Diaz?" Paxton looped his thumb into his pocket, looking around. "Were they home? Are they on-site?"

The man pointed down the street, opposite of the direction they parked. "Unfortunately, yes. EMTs are loading them now."

A glimmer of hope loosened the stranglehold on her. Maybe Cody was mistaken. Maybe there was no body.

"Were they injured?" Paxton looked over his shoulder to where he pointed.

The firefighter leaned in. "I don't believe so, but Mrs. Diaz didn't take the news about their son well. Not that I blame her. They'd have to sedate me too."

Fuck.

Cody was not mistaken.

An ache in the back of her throat made it difficult to swallow back the bitterness of a life lost. Of a grieving mother. Of a fucked-up situation Kate had no clue how to fix.

"Thank you." Paxton nodded, heading in the direction the fireman indicated.

"Now we're ambulance chasers?" Kate stayed close by his side.

"If we lose that truck it'll take us days to get answers."

Kate picked up the pace. "There." She pointed to a dark-haired man speaking with an emergency responder. He was taller in person than she expected. Almost as tall as Paxton. But his frame was far narrower.

"Senator Diaz." The urgency in Paxton's voice was obvious to anyone in earshot. He pulled his credentials off his belt.

Kate peeked in the vehicle to see the senator's wife being attended to by EMTs. Mrs. Diaz was slumped on the gurney, an oxygen mask across her face, clutching a picture frame to her chest. She was unnaturally still. Her unfocused stare falling to a spot on the floor. The look of shock clung to every crease around her puffy eyes. Kate's chest ached remembering the day her mother passed. The hurt and angst and loneliness she felt even in a room full of people.

"I'm Special Agent Banks. Ms. Howard and I have a few questions before you go."

The EMT stepped forward. "Senator and Mrs. Diaz have been through a traumatic experience. Can this wait?"

Kate focused on the picture Mrs. Diaz embraced, her fingernails forcing their way into the wood frame. A boy, late teens, in a green soccer uniform. An obvious resemblance to her husband.

Kate pulled her arms in, wrapping the jacket tight around her waist. She brought her attention back to Paxton and the senator.

"It's all right." The senator nodded.

Paxton handed him a business card. "We're very sorry for your loss."

The senator glanced back at his wife. A flicker of pain and worry flashed across his face. He took a few steps away from the vehicle. "Why is the FBI here?" His voice was hushed.

"Professional courtesy, sir." Paxton's tone was friendly. He pulled the notebook and pen from his pocket. "Can you tell me what happened this morning?"

The senator's mouth fell open, but no words reached his

lips. He stood quiet a few seconds until he cleared his throat. "Cora was in the kitchen eating breakfast. I kissed her good-bye and headed out to the garage." His voice wavered, and he took a moment to collect himself. "I'd just reached the front door when I heard the explosion." His posture slacked and he closed his eyes, the moisture evident around his lashes when he opened them.

Paxton jotted a note. "Where were you headed early on Sunday morning?"

"I belong to the Brews and Cruise Classic Car Club. We meet for breakfast every Sunday at Morning Rush Coffee Shop. Jessie and I—" The senator wiped at a tear with the back of his hand.

Kate squeezed her middle tight. "Jessie is your son?" She forced the words past the lump in her throat.

The senator sobbed quietly, taking another step away from the vehicle. He covered his face with his hand, nodding.

This poor man was trying to keep it all together for his wife, and she had to open her big fat mouth. Kate's chest tightened. The senator sighed heavy, wiping his eyes and nose on his shirt.

"What was he doing in the garage?" Paxton's tone turned from friendly to sympathetic.

"We converted the attic space into a studio apartment for him last year." Senator Diaz's shoulders shuddered with a deep breath. His chin trembled. "He wanted to live on campus, but we weren't ready to let him go."

"And your vehicle was parked below the studio?" Paxton asked.

Senator Diaz nodded.

The engine turned over, and activity in the back of the ambulance picked up as one of the guys put compartments on lock-down. They were getting ready to leave. Kate stepped forward. "Did he have any problems in school?"

"No." Senator Diaz's voice turned confused. "He was on the dean's list."

"What about work or friends? Any problems there?" The words rushed out of Kate.

Paxton flashed Kate a you're-pushing-it look.

"Jessie was a good kid. An upstanding young man. He got good grades. He was loved by everyone." The senator's face reddened. He lowered his head. "He was even supposed to be getting a humanitarian award for his work at a homeless shelter teaching kids to read. He and a few others." Senator Diaz scrubbed his hands over his face. "What does this have to do with a gas explosion?"

"Has the fire investigator already concluded the investigation?" Paxton's tone turned curious.

Senator Diaz raised his head; face red, nostrils flaring, breathing heavy. "What else could it have been?"

Paxton shoved the notepad in his pocket. "Senator, we don't mean to upset you. These are standard questions we ask in an investigation."

Kate checked up the street and down. She didn't recall passing a gas company truck, but maybe she had missed it. If this was a gas explosion someone from the company would be on-site, right?

"Senator"—the EMT tapped him on the shoulder—"if you are going with us, it's time."

"Yes. Of course." Senator Diaz took an uneven step toward the ambulance.

"One more minute, please." Kate smiled at the driver.

"It's okay." Paxton gave her a back-off look, turning to help the senator into the vehicle. "We appreciate your time."

But it wasn't okay. Paxton said it himself. If they waited, it would take days to get their answers. And if this was related in any way to Senator Thomas's fundraiser bomb or Senator Gail's car accident, they were on borrowed time.

"Please, senator." Her voice louder than expected, Kate grabbed the door before it closed.

"Katie." Paxton put his hand on her shoulder. She shrugged him off, hurting her injured shoulder in the process.

"Have you received any threats?" The words escaped in a rush. Not waiting for a response. "Do you know of anyone who wants to harm you?"

The senator turned, his face hard, flinty. He shifted his gaze to Paxton behind her. "You'll be smart to control your partner or I'll inform the FBI director of your conduct."

"Yes, sir." Paxton pulled her hand from the door and pushed her out of the way. "It won't happen again."

The driver closed the doors and disappeared around the side of the truck.

Kate balled her hands into fists, watching the ambulance take off. They had left them with fume-filled air and nothing to go on. "Shit. Now what?" She turned to face Paxton. His posture was stiff as a saber.

"Do you even hear me when I talk or is it all just white noise to you?" His curt voice sliced at her.

"That was—"

"Insulting? Insensitive? Uncalled-for?"

Kate glared back at him. "He was about to leave. I had to do something."

"Jesus, Katie. They lost a child."

The reminder of their situation made her head heavy.

"You don't drill grieving parents with questions like that. He's not a suspect. We're not trying to break a terrorist." Paxton dragged his fingers through his hair. He took a few breaths. "If he files a complaint with the Bureau—"

"He won't."

"My neck is on the line." Paxton folded his arms over his chest. "I'm in charge or did you forget?"

"I'm sorry. Okay? I know I screwed up. I'm not used to dealing with politics and emotions." Kate pulled the sleeves of the jacket over her hands and rolled her fingers in them. "If Senator Diaz calls I'll tell SAC Dupree this was all my fault."

There was a quiet minute between them. The silence amid the busy scene was grating. She didn't dare speak until the throbbing muscle in his jaw slowed. "What do we do now?"

"We use what we have to keep investigating."

"How? We just lost our witness."

"We lost *a* witness. And he told us plenty to get started." Paxton surveyed the surroundings. "We still have the neighbors and the police and firefighters first on the scene. See if there are any security cameras in the area that picked up the incident or anything leading up to it. There is plenty here to help us."

Kate stared at him in awe. Paxton was always good at organizing their missions, going over all the details, finding all the angles, making sure objectives were met. Seeing him now took her back to that feeling of a military operation debrief. Knowing Paxton was in charge always made her feel safe, even in the worst situations.

"First we have to speak with the fire inspector." He started walking back toward the house. "We need to get our hands on the inspection report."

"Doesn't that take, like, days?"

"It could take weeks, months even." He showed his badge to the cop, and they slipped under the caution tape. "But maybe the captain can confirm if this was an accident or intentional based on what they know already."

A breeze picked up the sides of the jacket, and Kate pulled it close around her. They backtracked their path to the garage. "What if it was a gas explosion?"

"We're lucky."

Her stomach hardened. That didn't seem lucky, but in the grand scheme of things, it would have been a better circumstance than her gut told her it was. That chickenshit feeling from earlier settled in. "And if it wasn't?"

His silence solidified her own fears. It was a tragedy either way. One the Diaz family would take years to recover from, though the loss would forever be a part of them. Paxton kept walking, not looking over at her. "Then we've got a much *bigger* problem on our hands."

Chapter Nine

Kate and Paxton made their way over to the garage. The scene was a mess of fire crew and police. The smell stronger the closer they got. "How are we going to find the captain in this mess?"

"We're looking for a red helmet."

"Red?" Kate looked around. "They're all yellow."

"Yellow are the firefighters, red are captains, and white helmets are typically worn by fire chiefs."

"How do you know that?"

"You learn a few things after ten years on the job. And it's not my first fire." Paxton pointed to the far side of what used to be the garage to a woman holding a clipboard, wearing a red helmet. "See."

"FBI?" The fire captain addressed them as they walked over. "I didn't call for FBI assistance on my investigation."

Kate focused her attention on the captain. She didn't want to accidentally set eyes on Jessie's body. Or parts of him. She swallowed back the bitterness in her throat.

Paxton handed the captain his business card. "We heard about the incident and needed to check it out."

"You're not here to piss on PFD territory are you"—she

looked down at the business card in her hand—"Special Agent Banks?"

"No, ma'am." Paxton shook his head. "I'm working a case this might be related to. I wanted to see for myself."

Her brows raised up under the helmet. "FBI investigates fires now?" Her tone was sarcastic.

"Not exactly." Paxton pulled his notebook and pen out. "Do you have any idea how the fire started?"

The captain's facial expression changed in an instant. Like it was wiped clean of emotion. "The Origin and Cause Report won't be complete for forty-eight to seventy-two hours. You can read it then."

Kate reached over, took the notebook and pen, and shoved it in her pocket. "We're on a time-sensitive case. If this *is* related, waiting could delay catching a killer. I know it's not protocol, but can you tell us anything?"

The captain's posture relaxed, and her features softened. "Completely off the record?"

"Yes." Kate pushed a strand of hair away from her face. "Off the record."

"No." The captain shook her head. "We haven't completed interviews with the first responders, witnesses, and home-owners. Photos and evidence retrieval are still underway. Until I know the whole story, I'm not going to make any assumptions."

"We understand." Paxton nodded.

Kate lowered her voice. "Could it have been a gas leak?"

She scratched under her helmet. "My crystal ball's broken."

"I only ask because I didn't see a gas company truck anywhere on the street, but the senator suggested it was a gas explosion." Kate took a step closer. "Your professional opin-ion. Could this have been an unfortunate accident?"

The captain blew out a breath. She looked from Kate to Paxton.

"We just need to know if this was accidental or not." Paxton motioned toward her clipboard. "It could be related to another time-sensitive case."

"The radius of the debris and location the fire *appears* to have started is too far from the wall where the gas water heater was housed, but that does not confirm or deny an accident."

A troop of soldiers skittered up her spine, spreading suspicion along the way.

"Thank you." Paxton nodded.

The fire captain rested the clipboard on her hip. "But your lack of surprise tells me you knew that already."

"It was a consideration." Paxton pointed to her hand. "You've got my card. I'd like copies of the report when it's ready."

"Should I be looking for something in particular, Special Agent Banks?"

"I'll take anything you've got."

"Putting out the fire likely destroyed any evidence the fire itself didn't. There won't be much for you to go on, but we'll give you everything we can."

"Thank you." Paxton and Kate said in unison.

"Where to next?" Kate handed back his notebook and pen.

"Kate?" A voice emerged through the mess of emergency workers behind them.

She swung around toward the voice, but she already knew who it was. Cody. *What is he doing here?* She put her hand on Paxton's arm, stopping him from turning the rest of the way. When their eyes met, she pulled her hand away. "Why don't we start with the neighbors?"

She stiffened and noticed Paxton did the same. Kate swore under her breath. "Be nice." She wasn't sure if the comment was for her or Paxton.

Paxton eyed Cody, his expression not giving away his thoughts. He would make an excellent poker player. Cody, on the other hand, wore his concern all over his face, from the wrinkled brow to the forced smile. He focused on the far-too-big FBI jacket Kate was wearing.

She took it off and wrapped it around her waist. When his eyes widened, she realized he had moved his focus to Ziggy on her hip. She wasn't helping the situation. "Hi."

Cody's gaze moved upward, seemingly taking the corners of his lips with it, giving her a sexy, secretive smile. "My shirt looks good on you."

She looked down at it. The Thirsty Cactus, Cody's bar. He gave it to her the first night they met when she ruined hers taking down a drunk patron. Coincidentally, it was also the first night they'd slept together. Heat built in her cheeks.

"Paxton Banks." He extended his hand, taking Kate out of the memory.

"Cody Stanton." He carried himself with an air of self-confidence just shy of smug. They shook, and Kate did everything in her power to stay planted where she was. The air tense around her, squeezing her.

She looked from Cody to Paxton and back. Kate had convinced herself it was Cody's athletic physique her body craved, but seeing him next to Paxton, Cody was a two-inch shorter, blonder, narrower version of him. Her stomach was emptier than the barracks at dawn. Her insides quivered in protest. Maggie was right. She had a type.

"How did you know I was here?"

"I told you not to go. So naturally, it's the first place I looked." Cody ran his fingers down her arm, making the hairs stand on end.

Kate wasn't the public-displays-of-affection type, and Cody knew it. Or at least she thought he knew since the time he got an elbow to the sternum for putting his arm around her at the bar.

He looked over at Paxton. "She runs head-on into danger, this one."

"I'm aware." Paxton didn't take his eyes off Cody. The muscle in his jaw went hard as stone.

"Paxton, why don't you go ahead. I'll catch up." She prayed he'd get the hint, but knowing Paxton he knew what she was doing, and wasn't going to let her out of his sight.

"I can wait."

Of course you can.

"How do you know Katie?" Paxton's negotiator voice was rigid.

She shoved her hands in her pockets to keep from fidgeting.

"Katie?" Cody raised his brows. "We go way back. And yourself?" His voice was cordial but cocky.

"Same."

They didn't have time for a pissing contest. Kate needed to get them away from one another. She gritted her teeth and turned toward Cody. "What are you doing here?" She squeezed the words past the could-this-be-more-awkward lump in her throat.

"I was worried about you." His voice lowered. "You sounded off on the phone. I wanted to make sure you were all right."

The guy was great in the sack, but she'd always felt like he wanted more than she could give him. Right now Kate had much bigger things to worry about. "That was very nice, but you didn't have to come up here. You must be exhausted."

Cody shrugged.

Paxton's phone rang, and a surge of relief washed over her.

"Excuse me," he said, taking a few steps away.

"So, you're FBI?" He pointed to the jacket around her waist. "Who's he, your partner?"

"No. And no." Kate took a step closer and lowered her voice. "You know how there's a lot of stuff about my job I can't really talk about."

"You never talk about your job. Ever. In fact, you change the subject every time it comes up."

"I do that." Kate glanced over her shoulder to make sure Paxton was still out of hearing distance. "But this is one of those things I can't discuss. I appreciate your help this morning, but right now is not a good time."

"Are you coming over later?" His voice was silky smooth. A reminder of how he got her into bed in the first place.

She heard footsteps behind her, and by the change in Cody's stance, she knew it was Paxton.

"Things are kind of messy right now."

"Yeah. I get it. You're working." Cody looked over her shoulder at Paxton, and only God knows what expression on his face. "I wanted to make sure you were okay. And you are. So, I'll go."

"Cody, right?" Paxton came up alongside Kate.

He nodded.

"Do you know where Katie lives?"

What kind of question is that?

Cody looked from Paxton to Kate and smiled. "I've been there a time or two."

"Good." Paxton placed his hand on his gun, and Kate prayed it would stay holstered. "Would you mind giving her a lift home? I have something I need to take care of."

"Is it for the case?" She turned toward Paxton. "I can ride along."

His jaw tensed. Something had pissed him off, but she wasn't sure if it was her or the phone call. "Was it Dupree?" Kate cringed, thinking about Senator Diaz making good on his threat.

"No. This doesn't concern you. Why don't you run along with your boyfriend."

Kate shot him a you're-a-jackass look, and before she could spit out her retort Paxton was walking toward his car.

Her. He was absolutely pissed at her.

After the most uncomfortable car ride with Cody to her house, she declined grabbing lunch because that would be even more awkward. He wasn't her boyfriend, despite what Paxton said. Kate used her dead laptop as an excuse as to why he couldn't come up, and got in her car and drove off to pick up a new one. It wasn't a lie. It also wasn't the whole truth. But what was the truth? Fuck. Who did Paxton think he was, giving her a disapproving look? She was an adult. She could sleep with whoever she damned well pleased. This is why she didn't date. It was messy and emotional and completely overrated.

Kate schlepped her new computer up the stairs of her place, careful of her back and shoulder, carrying her take-out bag in the hurt arm. She was tired, hungry, and smelled like a bonfire. She wanted to eat her Frosty and fries, hop in the shower, and take a nap. But showers were out of the question with the stitches in her shoulder.

She swung the door open, stopping at the entry, but her alarm didn't sound. Kyle was in her leather club chair, feet on her weight bench, with papers strewn all around him. Apparently a nap was out of the question too.

"Kyle?" She put the bags on the island and rested her hand on Ziggy. It looked scary when Paxton did it. "What are you doing in my house? What is all this?"

"Hey." He nodded at her over his shoulder. Oblivious to or ignoring her anger was anyone's guess.

"Don't 'hey' me." Kate cranked up her pissy tone. "How did you get in here?"

Kyle stood and put the loaner laptop on the chair. He brushed off his skinny jeans and tugged at his white T-shirt with neon orange finger smudges. "I used a lock pick, then overrode your security system with a reversing moss algorithm."

"This is a Cooper alarm system." She pointed to the keypad on the wall. "It's unhackable."

"Unhackable." Kyle laughed. "It's a simple eight-digit binary code. Any computer genius worth their salt could take that thing down in seconds. Two point seven by the way."

"Two point seven what?"

"Seconds. Jeez, keep up." Kyle crumpled a Snickers wrapper and placed it on the weight bench next to two others. "Oh. You're out of peanut butter-filled pretzels and Snickers bars. I didn't see a grocery list on the fridge or I would have added them. That's where I keep mine. But you might also want to add Cheetos because you're dangerously low."

"Now I really *am* going to shoot you for breaking and entering." *And pantry theft.* Kate pulled Ziggy out of the holster but left the safety on and the muzzle down.

"Whoa. Hold on a second there, Jill Valentine. I was doing you a favor."

"Jill? Favor?" Kate shook her head, trying to make sense of his ramblings. "Are you having a stroke?"

"Jill Valentine. Badass zombie killer. Resident Evil." Kyle dragged his hands through his hair, stopping at his temples. He made an exploding noise, flinging his fingers open wide. "Are you seriously telling me you have no idea who she is?"

Real explosions. Pretend explosions. Kate was getting tired of it all. "What I am telling you is to get out of my house."

"You haven't even seen what I found yet."

Kate took a step toward him. "What have you found besides my last friggin' nerve?"

"Look." Kyle grabbed the laptop and a few pieces of paper from the mess on the floor. He set them up on the island. "Senators Thomas and Gail."

"Wait. How did you know I was researching the senators?"

"Hellooo?" Kyle pointed to himself. "Genius."

"Kyle?" Kate placed Ziggy on the counter far from him. She probably wasn't going to shoot him, but she wanted to leave her options open. About the only thing he was going to threaten was her grocery budget and her patience. She snatched up a page, reading her own notes. "These are from my private client files. How did you get this?"

"I was able to restore a few items off your old laptop. Between that and the stuff I pulled off your cloud storage and the key logger on the laptop you borrowed last night, I was able to compare the two senators with a few others with similarities."

Kate wasn't sure if she should be angry or impressed. She took a deep breath, balling her hands into fists so tight she was afraid she'd pop a stitch in her shoulder. "How did you get into my *password*-protected files?" Her tone leaned on the side of exasperated.

"1B@dA$$Ch!ck is hardly a secure password. But I can help you with that later." Kyle snatched the crinkled papers back from her. "Now. Do you want to see this or do you want to keep asking stupid questions?"

"Fine, but this invasion of privacy discussion is not over." Kate tore open the fast-food bag, flipped the top off her chocolate Frosty and dipped a fry into it. She savored the salty-sweet goodness as the cold and hot hit her tongue.

Kyle reached over to take a french fry, but Kate slapped his hand. "Nope."

"Jeez, touchy." Kyle turned his attention back to the computer. "This is a narrowed-down list of state senators that voted similarly to Senator Thomas and Gail."

"I have a comparable list. It's like two dozen names."

"Twenty-one, to be exact. Senator Diaz is on there too." Kyle pointed to his name. "From your web search this morning."

"That's too many to investigate." Kate shoved another fry

in her mouth. "Too many enemies in too many places to narrow down the list."

"We need more information. That's where you come in." Kyle grabbed a pen. "Tell me everything you know."

"You've already *read* my client files. That's everything."

"I read through your fitness log too. You might want to focus on some negative training to increase your pull-up count. I read about it in a men's fitness magazine. I saved the link for you."

"Okay. Thank you. Now go home."

"You know what you need?"

"An electrified door and a shoot-first instinct?"

"You've got a pretty funny sense of humor. Dark, but funny."

"Go home, Kyle."

"Stress relief. Maybe a romantic comedy or a massage."

A massage did sound good, but in her condition it would only hurt. "Out." Kate pushed him toward the door. "Now."

"Oh, I forgot. I also put a tracker on the IP address that sent the threats. I triangulated the coordinates best I could but was only able to get it down to a ten- or eleven-mile radius. It's offline so no way to know where it is coming from. But as soon as they put that puppy back on a network, we'll be the first to know about it."

"Okay. Yup. You should go downstairs and monitor it." Kate shut the door on him. Why she bothered locking it was beyond her. She rolled her shoulder, working the stiffness. Maybe a half Percocet would help.

She took in the mess Hurricane Kyle left and sighed. Her phone chirped, and she pulled it out of her pocket.

Drinks? Maggie always knew the right thing to say.

Yes! Give me 15 min to change. Kate smelled her hair. *30 min. Look cute. We're going to The Thirsty Cactus.*

Kate looked down at her T-shirt and cringed. Like her day hadn't been awkward enough.

Chapter Ten

Kate did her best one-armed sponge bath, hair wash and style, and her simple makeup routine of foundation, mascara, and tinted lip balm. Finding something to wear, which didn't cling and show the bandages on her back and shoulder, was more difficult. She decided on a pair of black jeans, tank top with a burgundy oversized, v-neck sweater, and black leather knee-high boots. It wouldn't be Maggie's idea of *cute*, but she was feeling pretty good about it for Sunday happy hour.

By the time Kate pulled up to The Thirsty Cactus, her stomach was in knots. She'd left things a mess with Paxton, not correcting him about Cody. She left Cody's car awkwardly while trying *not* to make it awkward. And then there was the bomber going after senators, a situation she couldn't speak about. Kate rolled her head side to side to release some tension.

Loose gravel from the parking lot crunched under her heels, out of tune with the sounds from the bar. Kate walked past a Cadillac CTS, the color of pink only Maggie or a Mary Kay representative would request from the dealership. Kate paused in front of the door, the brass handle, the shape of a saguaro cactus, under her palm. She took a deep breath of cool air, yanked the door, and was greeted by the greatest of the eighties, the music of choice every night of the week. Her shoulders relaxed a little at the familiar sounds. It was one of the many reasons she liked this place. Of course, she also owned the building, was sleeping with the bar owner, her bar tab came out of the rent Cody owed, and they made decent onion rings, so there were lots of reasons to choose from.

She scanned the red leather booths with patrons huddled around the polished metal tables. It was more out of habit than necessity; she knew Maggie preferred the bar.

"You're late." Maggie swung on the stool, her fuchsia ruffled top dancing as she moved. "Cody made me pay for my own drink. Do you believe that?"

"Oh, the nerve of that man, not letting you put your whatever-the-hell-that-pink-thing-is on my tab." Kate cranked up her sarcastic tone, taking a seat at the stool next to her. "Doesn't he know who you are?"

"I know, right?" Maggie sipped her drink, pinky out.

"You look beautiful. New top?"

"Thank you. Yes." Maggie put her drink down on the bar. "Thanks to your testimonial at the last weapons expo, I had my best month of sales. I decided to treat myself."

Six years ago when Maggie suggested starting her tactical clothing business Kate was hesitant but supportive. In less than a year, Maggie had turned her passion for fashion into an extremely lucrative business, eclipsing profits at the dry cleaners. "That's great." She reached over and squeezed Maggie's hand. "Is Chris joining us to celebrate?"

"No. Chris isn't going to make the cut."

"Maggs, I'm sorry."

Maggie shrugged. "Some guys aren't comfortable with a woman making more money."

"His loss. You, my friend, are fabulous."

"I know." Maggie brushed her hair off her shoulder.

Kate caught Cody's eye at the other end of the bar. She

wasn't sure what proper etiquette was for whatever weird-ness they were experiencing, but a nod seemed the most casual. Because that was what they were, casual.

"Beer, Kate?" José, the youngest of Cody's bartenders, came around them carrying a bucket of ice. His bronzed arms flexed under the *Don't be a prick, have a drink* T-shirt.

"Yes, please."

He put a frosty bottle in front of her, his dark hair and eyes glistened under the pendant light. He turned and made busy with filling the ice bins. He was a good kid, hard worker, and didn't ask a lot of questions. She liked that about José. Kate tipped the beer back, chugging about half of it.

Maggie waited patiently for her to put the bottle down. "So, how was your day? How do you feel?"

The answer to both—terrible. Not that Maggie could do anything about either one of them sucking. "You know me, can't complain." She could, but Kate had the sneaky suspi-cion Maggie wasn't interested in any of it. "How's the jacket coming for Senator Gail?"

"Great. Should be done in a day or two." Maggie drained her glass and leaned in closer to her. "Are we done with the small talk? I want to hear all the dirt."

Her muscles tensed across her shoulders. That half a Percocet she took earlier must not have been enough. "All what dirt?"

"The you and Paxton dirt. I want all the juicy details. The good, the bad, and the naughty. Don't leave anything out."

And there it was, the true reason for this little bonding time. The stiffness spread down into her chest and back. Kate took a swig of her beer. "There are no *juicy* details. He's working a case that overlaps with one of my clients. The end."

"Okay, sister-friend, you can lie to yourself if you want to believe that's *all*, but I know better." Maggie looked around then lowered her head. "You are so in love with that man."

Lust maybe, but love? Her chest constricted more. Kate shook her head. "You're out of your mind."

"Really?" Her tone was all I-know-you-better-than-you-think.

She finished her beer, holding up the empty bottle to signal José. "Yup."

"Nope." Maggie waggled her finger at her. "The way you used to talk about him, the photo you carried in your wallet, and now the way you were acting the other day."

"I talked about him because he was one of the four people I was around for two years. The photo was of our special ops unit. And the other day was—" *Intense. Surprising.* "It was nothing. Just a friend helping a friend."

José slid her another beer and Maggie another pink martini glass. "Thanks."

"You're a terrible liar." Maggie laughed and snorted. "A friend?"

"Exactly."

"Like how you and Cody are friends?" She gave an exaggerated wink.

"No, that's different." She kicked Maggie's stool. "What Cody and I have is an arrangement. Paxton is just an old friend. When this case is over and our paths no longer intersect, life can go back to normal."

"You do realize nothing about your life is normal, right?"

"This coming from a girl who spends most of her days in a bomb shelter under a dry cleaner."

"Touché."

They clinked their drinks and took a sip.

Maggie played with the cherry in her glass. "Are you going to tell Dr. Lynda about all of this?"

Kate cringed at her therapist's name. A dull throb started in her temple. "No. The woman already wants me to journal about my combat boots and camouflage days."

"I've heard it's therapeutic."

"So is boxing, but I don't see her prescribing me an hour in the ring." Kate took another drink. "Besides, if I tell Dr. Lynda about Paxton, she'll go into how-does-that-make-you-feel mode. You know how much I hate that."

"Therapy only works if you're open and honest. I think you should tell her." Maggie cocked her head.

"Maggie, I would do anything for you. Anything. But there's nothing to tell."

"When are you going to see Paxton again?" Maggie's tone was softer, more concerned-sister.

Kate bit her lip. The way they left things at Senator Diaz's house, she really wasn't sure. "Tomorrow. Never. I don't know." Kate rested her good arm against the bar. "It's complicated."

"So, uncomplicate it. Call him."

"Nut-uh." Kate blinked to clear her blurring vision. "We're working together, and he thinks I'm dating Cody, and I punched him."

"You punched Paxton? When?"

"After he kissed me."

Maggie squealed and bounced around on her chair.

Kate winced at the noise, shushing her.

"Nothing to tell? I knew you were holding out on me. Did he pull you in close and wrap you in his arms? Was it magical?"

"I *punched* him in the face."

"You stress too much."

Kate held on to the bar with one hand and took another long pull from her beer. "That's what Kyle said."

"Who's Kyle now? Some new guy?"

"My neighbor." She pointed to the black tile floor. "Downstairs. Paxton invited the little hurricane hacker in, and now I can't get rid of him. I have a Kyle infestation."

"I'm not sure what all that's about, but he's got a point."

"No. No." Kate jerked her arm, sloshing some beer on her jeans. "You don't get to be on the little snack thief's side."

Maggie held her hands up. "I'm on your side. I'm always on your side. Team Kate one-hundred percent. But I think you put too much pressure on yourself. If your mom or my dad were here, what would they tell you?"

"Floss more. Curse less."

Maggie took the beer bottle from her hand and placed it on the bar. "No. Well maybe, but they would tell you that life is short. You need to live while you can."

"I'm supposed to what, then? Get hitched, buy a house with a little white picket fence, adopt a dog, squeeze out some kids, and live happily ever after barefoot in the kitchen?" Kate blew raspberries.

"Maybe not that—it sounds a little too Stepford Wives. But some version of it."

"That's what he wants. He told me himself."

"He did? When?"

Kate waved her hand. "I don't know. Maybe in Istanbul or Beirut. We were on the move a lot that mission."

"You're worried about a fantasy Paxton had eleven, twelve years ago? People change. Did you ask him what he wants now?"

She squinted, bringing her friend into focus. "No, Maggs, I didn't. And I'm not going to. He'll be gone in a few days. That's ridiculous."

"Why? Because you're scared he's going to want you."

I've wanted to do that since I met you. Kate remembered the way her lips tingled when he kissed her, igniting a little heat in her chest. "No. Because people don't change that much. Me, for example. I'm the same person I was back then."

Maggie snorted and slapped her thigh. "You are not the same person."

"I'm not going to lock up Ziggy, get a desk job that I hate, have dinner on the table by five, and join a knitting club or some bullshit. That's not me."

"I'm just saying I saw the way you looked at him and acted around him. Girl, whether you want to admit it or not, you've got it bad."

"You read too many romance novels." Kate picked up the bottle and sloshed more beer on her jeans.

"And you're a lightweight tonight. What's wrong with you?"

"Watch my purse." Kate stumbled off the stool.

Kate cleaned up in the ladies room. On the way out she got lightheaded, grabbing the wall to steady herself. A blurry, blond figure caught her around the waist. "You okay?" Cody's voice was concerned.

Kate let her eyes focus on Cody and bopped him on the nose. "Never better."

"How much have you had to drink?"

"I need a unicorn."

"Yes, you do." He helped her over to Maggie and propped her up on the stool. "Are you going to drive her?"

"I'm already three deep. I won't be driving anywhere"— Maggie sipped the pink concoction—"but I called her a ride."

"I've never seen her this wasted." Cody looked over his shoulder and back to Kate. "Keys. Both of you." Cody held his hand out.

Maggie pulled her key fob out of her pocket and pulled Kate's out of her purse. "Here. Now go. You're busy." Maggie shooed him away. "I've got this."

"You're sure?"

"Absolutely."

Cody grabbed a water off the bar, put it in front of her, and walked away. Maggie spun Kate's seat to face her, making her a little dizzy. She tucked a piece of hair behind Kate's ear. "You were in the bathroom a while. Did you puke in there?"

"No."

"Good. I don't have any mints." Maggie beamed over Kate's shoulder. "Remember. I did this because I love you. Someday you'll thank me. Now smile."

"Why?" Kate turned to follow Maggie's stare. Paxton stood at the entrance in a pair of khaki cargo pants and a bright blue polo shirt. He was like a preppy wet-dream. "You called Paxton." Kate glared over her shoulder at Maggie. "Traitor."

"Hi again." Maggie finger-waved and tossed her hair over her shoulder as he walked up. "Sorry to call you. She's trashed, the owner took our keys, and I didn't know who else to call."

"It's okay. I was on my way home from dinner."

"I can get a cab." They probably pulled him away from a date. He probably went on lots of dates. "I need my phone. And a phone number." She reached for her purse and slipped off the stool. Paxton caught her around the waist.

"It's not even eight o'clock on a Sunday, and she's lit."

"You know." Kate got woozy and grabbed Paxton's arm to steady herself. She squeezed a little, sliding her hand over his tight muscle. "I'm right here."

"I've never seen her get drunk on two beers. Ever."

"Katie?" His voice was softer. Paxton cradled her face between his strong hands. He lifted her chin so their gaze met.

She stared into the blue-gray abyss of his eyes. A battalion of stomping boots rattled in her chest. Her pulse picked up pace. "You have really pretty eyes."

His features softened. There was a glint in his eyes. He blinked and pulled away from her slightly. "Did you take a Percocet?"

Kate held up her hand, her pointer finger and thumb a little apart, squinting through the opening. "Half."

"I—I wouldn't have allowed her to drink if I knew she

was on pain killers." Maggie's tone turned worried. "I didn't realize she was hurt so bad. She said she was fine."

"Of course she did." Paxton straightened to face Maggie, and she missed how close he was. "She downplays her pain until she's gotten a concussion or dislocates a shoulder."

"How do you know that?" Maggie twisted on the stool to face him.

"Katie and I aren't that much different when it comes down to it." Paxton grabbed her purse off the bar. "I guess I understand her in a way no one else can." He lifted Kate up by the elbows, pointing her in the direction of the exit.

"That's so sweet." Maggie followed, holding the door.

Kate looked over at her friend. "Aren't you coming?"

"No. You're in good hands." She kissed Kate on the cheek as they ambled by.

Traitor.

By the time they reached her front step, Kate was feeling a little more sober and a lot more sour at Maggie for this setup she orchestrated.

Paxton's hands circled her waist, helping her out of the SUV. She was steadier on her feet, and she needed to put more distance between them. "You don't have to come up."

"I'm not going to dump you on the doorstep." He held the building door for her.

They climbed the steps, the only sound from the click of her heels on the metal. She should tell him she was sorry for the way she acted earlier, sorry for being an overall pain in his ass, sorry that Maggie called and bothered him when he was clearly out for the evening. Something. "Cody's not my boyfriend." Not an apology, but it needed to be said.

"Okay." He pulled her house key off the side of her purse and spun the lock.

Okay? Just okay. She had no idea what she expected him to say, but it was more than *okay.* She pushed the door and walked into her disaster studio.

"What happened here?"

"Kyle. Kyle happened."

"You two are developing quite the friendship."

"Huh. Friends don't eat friends out of house and Snickers."

"I don't really know what that means, but I'm going to take your word for it."

Kate pulled her good arm in her sweater and tried to maneuver it over her head. "Ow, ow. I'm stuck."

"Don't pull." Paxton put his hand up the back of her sweater. Even though she had a tank top between them, his muscular arm wrapped around her set her skin on fire. "Wait a minute. You're caught on the tape of your bandage."

He helped her get the carnivorous sweater over her head and handed it to her.

The cool air felt good against her heated skin. Kate smiled at him. "Thank you."

"That's the smile I've been waiting for." Paxton brushed his knuckles down the side of her cheek. "I missed it."

Her heart thundered up her throat. She always wondered about the things those hands could do. She turned away from the wickedly sensual touch.

"Sorry." Paxton shrugged. "It was nice to see you being you again. The Katie I remembered."

Why did he have to be so infuriatingly sexy? Kate rolled her hands into the sweater to keep from reaching out.

"Have you cleaned these yet?" He pointed to the gauze on her shoulder.

"No." Kate shook her head. "I—I'll get it tomorrow."

"Today is forty-eight hours. This dressing is mostly off already, and you can't reach your back." He headed for the bathroom. "Where are your medical supplies?"

"Under the sink. Red bag." Kate pulled the tape the rest of the way off her shoulder, tossing it and the gauze into the bin at the end of the island.

He came back with her kit, towels, and a washcloth. "Do you have distilled water?"

"Bottom of the pantry." She went to go around the island, but he stopped her.

"Sit."

His macho, take-charge maleness made her stomach sour. She was a grown-ass woman. Not some child he needed to help.

Paxton pulled out a stool for her. "Please, sit."

"O-kay." Kate did as he asked, watching him mix up a concoction of distilled water and mild antibacterial soap in a salad bowl. He dipped the washcloth in, wrung it out, and came up beside her.

"This looks good." He softly patted over and around the sutures, being gentle not to tug them.

Kate wondered for a moment how many times he had done the same thing for himself. How many stitches he had in his leg because of her. How long it had taken him to heal. All things she didn't know because she was a coward. She swallowed hard against the pain in the back of her throat.

Paxton blotted the area with the dry towel and proceeded to bandage her up again. "Good as new."

Kate peeked over to check out his handiwork. "Williams would be proud."

She wasn't sure if he smiled from the compliment or the mention of their former medical sergeant. Either way, it looked good on him, and she couldn't help smiling too.

"I'm going to do your back."

Kate nodded and pulled her hair off to the side.

Paxton pulled the other stool up behind her, his legs straddling her hips. Lifting the back of her tank top by the hem, his hands grazed her sides. She sat statue-still, focusing on steady breaths. He tucked the fabric into her hand holding her hair. Except for one or two of the band-aids, she didn't even feel him remove them. Only his masculine hands on her skin.

Kate bit her lip. He dunked the washcloth back in the water, wrung it out, and repeated the process.

She froze while every gentle brush set her insides on fire. The underlying sensuality of him taking care of her, touching her, was overwhelming to her senses and emotions. She wasn't sure if it was weirder that Paxton was sponge-bathing her in her kitchen or that she was getting turned on by it.

He blotted the dry towel against the area and applied a few fresh bandages. Paxton took the fabric from her hand and carefully slipped it down in place.

"Thanks." She slid off the stool, putting distance between them. She picked up the bowl, placing it in the sink.

"No problem." He moved to repack the kit.

"Don't worry about this stuff." Kate pointed to the medical supplies. "I'll clean it up with the rest of the house tomorrow."

"Are you sure?"

"Yes." The word came out louder than she expected. "I insist. You've already done too much. And I'm tired." Kate wrapped her injured arm around her middle to ease the searing need to be touched. Kate walked him to the door, holding it open.

"Goodnight." He leaned a little like he was going in for a hug.

Oh, God. She could not hold out one more millisecond if he put his hands on her. Kate quickly put her hand up to fist bump him. He straightened and met her halfway. "Goodnight," she said and closed the door behind him.

I'm an idiot.

Chapter Eleven

Despite her sloppy evening, Kate was feeling pretty good the following morning. That might have been the product of the ibuprofen and jug of water she drank before bed or the delicious Paxton-induced dreams. She spent half the day cleaning the wake of destruction Kyle had created the afternoon before.

She heard a knock on her door and turned the vacuum off. "Coming," she hollered. Kate grabbed the wad of dollar bills from the counter and flung the door open.

Paxton stood on her landing in his standard black suit and white dress shirt, carrying a messenger bag far too metro for his stature. "Uh, hi." She looked past him.

Paxton checked out the singles in her hand and smirked. "Were you expecting a stripper?"

Paxton as a stripper. Her heart responded in a quickening beat. She wondered for a moment if he had his handcuffs on him, and a little heat crept into her cheeks. She cleared her throat. "No. It's a tip for my grocery delivery."

"Grocery delivery? Isn't that for old people who can't leave their homes?"

"It's also for busy personal protection agents who don't

have time to grocery shop, but still enjoy eating." Kate opened the door wider for him to enter. "Plus with my shoulder, I figured it was better to not carry bags of groceries up the stairs."

"Wise choice." He eyed her *In my defense I was left unsupervised* T-shirt and jeans.

Kate shut the door and followed him. "What's with the man-purse?" She pointed to the messenger bag slung over his shoulder.

Paxton gave her an I-can-take-you look, increasing the heat in her face and neck. He put it on the kitchen island and pulled out three file folders. "Research."

Oh, goodie. Kate tossed the money in the fruit bowl, looking over at the labels. "These are for the senators?"

"Yes. I heard back from the lab this morning. The explosive components found at the hotel matched the dynamite found on Senator Gail's car."

For a brief moment, Paxton seemed to be in his glory. He really had a passion for the work he did. He probably had a lot of passion behind those powerful thighs and rock hard abs. Kate placed her hand on her breastbone, covering her ever-quickening heart. No. She needed to focus. "Is it warm in here? It's warm in here. I'm going to open the window."

"Are you coming down with something?"

Yeah, Paxton fever. And the only cure is a hot and sweaty night to get it out of my system. Damn Maggie for meddling last night. It didn't matter how good his hands felt on her. They were working together. That's it.

"Katie?"

She looked up at him. "Don't worry about me. I'm warm from running around here. Did they find any fingerprints or fibers or stuff?"

He flipped two of the files open to a lab analysis form.

"No fingerprints, but they're still working. At least we know they were the same material."

"We're looking for a neat-freak psychopath who hates senators and plays with dynamite. Does that help narrow down the list of suspects?"

"It might if we had a list of suspects."

"How about a list of possible victims?" Kate pulled the stack of papers off her windowsill. "Kyle was able to narrow the state senators down to twenty-one based on the commonalities of Senators Thomas, Gail, and Diaz."

"How did he get this?" He pulled the list out of her hand.

"I felt it was better I didn't ask. He's got some scary good skills." *I'd hate to think of what he's discovered about me.* Kate shuddered at the thought.

He gave her a disapproving look.

"It's all public knowledge. I didn't ask him to do it, but now that we have the list, it would be a good place to start figuring out who the next target could be." Kate pointed to the page. "Minus the three who have already been attacked, that leaves us eighteen possible targets to alert."

"Katie, you can't call up eighteen state senators and tell them you *think* they might be the next target of a bomber."

"Why not?" She dropped her files on the stool. "Wouldn't you want to know if you were on that list? I'd want to know."

"It would cause mass panic. For all we know, these could have been the only targets, and we won't even know if Senator Diaz is a part of the list until we receive the investigation report."

"So, we still have nothing."

"Not nothing." Paxton rested his hands on the folders. "We have pieces of a puzzle that need to be put together."

"I hate puzzles." The whole thing felt like a live version of a Clue game. *It was the terrorist in the possibly white vehicle with the dynamite.*

"You need to find the pieces to put together." Paxton opened the other file. "Every piece is relevant. Without them all, you are not seeing the whole picture."

Kate remembered when Paxton was putting together their missions. He would collect all the intel, map out their route, with plan B, C, and sometimes D contingencies, extraction points, all scheduled down to the synchronized-watch second. Kate was never a fan of the collect and plan portion of the mission. She wanted to be out there, doing something that mattered.

Kate pulled two mugs off the shelf, filled them with coffee, and slid one in front of Paxton. He smiled up at her. "Come on. We have a lot of stuff to go through."

"You're a total nerd."

"It's called an investigation for a reason. We investigate. Most of my time is spent looking at paperwork and filing reports." He pulled out the other stool for her.

Kate was hesitant after last night's awkward end to sit that close. She slid the stool a little farther out to put her pile of research on the counter between them.

"You want to start with voting results or backgrounds or group affiliations?"

"Voting, I guess." Maybe with Kyle's narrowed-down list, this would be easier.

Kate's door swung open, making both of them jump. Kyle strolled in carrying three bags of groceries, her Cheetos bag sticking out the top, already open. "I love these crunchy jalapeno ones."

Kate rolled her eyes and got up to close the door. Paxton shoved his files over for him to put the bags down. "Why do you have my groceries?"

"Dude man was on his way in when I was on my way up, so I offered to take them."

"Did you at least tip the guy?"

"I had my hands full."

Kyle went to put his hand back in the Cheetos bag, but she yanked it away from him. "Did you come up here just to eat my snacks, or was there a point to this visit?"

"Hey, I'm doing you a favor. These are empty calories. I'm saving you at least fifteen minutes off your workout. Maybe more."

"Oh, you're the hero in this situation."

"I like the sound of that." Kyle Superman-posed, then slumped back against the fridge.

"Well thank you for the help, but we really have a lot of work to do."

"Not so fast. I have a gift." Kyle pulled a folded up piece of paper out of his pocket and handed it to Kate.

She took it, examining the orange fingerprints. "What is this? A bill for your computer services?"

"Nah, the first one's always free. That's how the dealers get kids hooked." Kyle's gaze darted to Paxton and straightened up. "Not that I would know anything about that. It's just something I've heard."

Paxton raised his brow in a yeah-right glare.

Kate unfolded the page, careful not to get Cheetos dust on her shirt. "What is this?"

"Read it."

You will feel the pain of my loss. "Holy shit, Kyle, where did you get this?"

"What is it?" Paxton stood.

"*That* is a copy of an email sent to Senator Diaz on the same date and time frame as the other threats. From the same IP address."

"Look." Kate handed the letter to Paxton.

"You will feel the pain of my loss." Paxton narrowed his focus on Kyle. "Where did you get this? How did you get this?" He turned toward Kate. "How did he know about the threats?"

"He—"

"I hacked into Kate's client files, found out who she was researching, then hacked into the senator's email account and searched for the IP address which matched the other threats. Aaaand, you're welcome."

Paxton's facial expression froze somewhere between you're-going-to-jail and I'm-going-to-kill-you. "You illegally obtained confidential information. Used it to hack into a government official's email. And then thought it was a good idea to bring it to a federal investigator."

"I—"

"You know what?" Kate passed the Cheetos bag to Kyle, pushing him toward the door. "It might be time to go."

Kyle didn't speak; he stuffed a few Cheetos in his mouth and kept his head down.

She closed the door and walked back to the island.

"Katie, do you have any idea how many laws this kid broke?"

"I didn't ask him to do it. He just did." Kate didn't dare tell him about the breaking and entering. "He means well, and I understand what he did was wrong, but it's another piece of the puzzle. Now that we have it, doesn't that prove Senator Diaz was also targeted?"

"Stop. Katie, we can't use this in the case. I told you nothing illegal."

"Okay." She looked around, her gaze stopping at the garbage can. "We'll throw it out." Kate pulled the email from his hand, crumpled it, and tossed it in the trash. "We will assume Senator Diaz was targeted. We were going to do that anyway, right? That's why you brought his file." Kate pointed to the manila folder farthest from her with his name on it. "Then when the fire report is ready; the lab can connect the— the stuff that proves they are connected. We've already got an advantage. You could say we were acting on gut instinct."

Paxton gave her a disapproving look.

"If we still need the email, I'll call Senator Diaz's office myself and ask his aide for a copy. I'll go down there and sit in his office all day if I have to. If Kyle found it, they must still have it."

He glanced at the garbage, then the file in front of him. "Let's just get back to work."

After a tense and quiet hour of paper shuffling, Kate got up to stretch her legs. "How do you do this every day? It's maddening. Twelve voted to increase teacher compensation. Sixteen voted to legalize marijuana. Nine voted for tougher penalties for cop killers. Eight on here voted for tougher fines for littering. And the list goes on with little overlap."

He shrugged. "You get used to it."

Kate walked around the island, pulling the pictures of the victims off their files. These poor families were being ripped apart by fear and grief and there was nothing she could do about it. "It's unfair."

"What is?"

"This." Kate paced in front of the sink, anger knotting up her stomach. "This whole situation. I'm here highlighting voting records while Robbie's still in the hospital. Danica and Desiree are healing from bruises and a broken arm. Those poor girls are probably going to need therapy. And Jessie—"

"Hey, stop." Paxton walked over, placing his hands on her elbows to keep her from pacing. He smelled spicy and delicious. His closeness did nothing to soothe the emotions rioting in her. If anything, it made her feel worse. "You can't let it do this to you. We'll find something that connects them. It only takes one clue. One piece of evidence to blow a case wide open."

She forced herself to take a step back from him, immediately missing his touch. "We've been over and over the files."

"So we go over them again."

"These poor kids are hurt or killed because some whack job doesn't agree with something their parents did or said or voted on. How is that fair? It's not their fault, but they're the ones getting stuck in the crosshairs. And we're no closer to finding a suspect."

"Wait." Paxton turned and rifled through the files.

"We can't even alert anyone we think might be next."

"Wait, wait." He shoved everything else over, placing two pages in front of him. "Say that again."

"Say what again?"

"Say what you said again." He looked over at her, eyes wide and grinning. He was on to something.

"Um, I don't know. What did I say?"

"Kids are getting hurt…"

"Okay, okay. Whack job doesn't agree with their parents. It's not their fault, but they're the ones in the crosshairs. We're no closer to a suspect. We can't alert anyone."

Paxton smacked the countertop, making her jump. "Katie, that's it."

"What's it?"

"Look." Paxton pulled her closer to him, peering over her shoulder at the emails. Her nervous stomach rolled, and she pulled her injured arm across it.

"The threats? I've read them a dozen times."

"Look at them again. Where's the one Kyle found?"

She scooched past him, pulled the wadded up paper out of the top of the trash, straightening it out. "Here."

He put it at the end of the row. "What don't they say?"

"Who the killer is. When he's going to strike again. How much dynamite he's got. The next victim." She ticked them off on her fingers.

"Yes, but it also doesn't say *I'm going to kill you* or *you're a dead man*." Paxton picked up the first email. "Senator Thomas's threat reads *You will pay for the pain you have caused*. Senator Gail's says *Your double D's will look great in a casket*. For Senator Diaz, they wrote *You will feel the pain of my loss*."

"That still doesn't tell us anything."

Paxton turned to her. "They never say the senators themselves are in danger."

Kate took the emails from him. "But they were."

"Yes, but in all three situations, it's the kids who were the victims. When we were at the hotel you said Robbie would have been in the limo if he hadn't forgotten the stuffed bear."

"Rabbit."

"Doesn't matter." He flipped the page. "Double Ds—Danica and Desiree. The twins were in the car when the accident happened. If the blasting cap had worked, they would have succeeded. Jessie was in the apartment over the garage. If they wanted to kill Senator Diaz, they would have put the bomb in the house or waited until he got out there."

Kate's stomach churned a noxious mixture of fear and anger and disbelief, making her nauseous. She grabbed the counter to steady her. "The kids were the targets, not the senators?" Her voice was weak.

Paxton said something, but she couldn't make it out over the heartbeat pounding in her ears. How could she have missed that? She was protecting the wrong person. She should have been protecting Robbie, not the senator. Robbie got hurt because she wasn't good enough at her job.

"Katie." Paxton waved his hand, getting her attention. "How many of the senators on the list have kids?"

She ran a shaky hand down the names. A shiver lifting the hair on the back of her neck. "All of them."

Chapter Twelve

Paxton had been on the phone with the Phoenix field office for what felt like hours, filling in SAC Dupree on their discovery. Panic and anger clashed in her stomach at the thought of any more kids getting hurt. She needed to do something. She couldn't just sit here. With worries about mass panic out the door, he convinced Dupree to dispatch FBI protective details to the families on the list.

"Send me the address as soon as you have it." Paxton hung up and slid the phone in his pocket. The worry lines in his forehead were deeper than ever.

"I don't like that expression on your face."

"There are ten families in town, but the rest are all over the place. Some traveling for fall break, others have kids at boarding schools or college." Paxton raked his fingers through his hair. "Local and federal bomb squads have got their work cut out for them."

"Nothing has happened out of state or we would have heard something, right?"

"Right. We're only focusing on the ones locally, but we have alerted other agencies to be cautious."

"So, how—"

Paxton's phone chirped. He pulled it from his pocket, swiped the screen, and put it back, collecting paperwork for the files. "I have to go. I told Dupree I would meet him at the first location, and I have no idea when we'll be done."

Kate shoved her feet into her sneakers and walked over to her bed. "I'm going with you."

"I don't have time."

Kate pulled the bed skirt up, sliding out a navy duffel, slinging it and her purse over her shoulder. She met him at the door. "Ready."

"You still keep a go-bag?" He sounded surprised.

These days she used it more as a booty-call bag, but he didn't need to know that. It had a change of clothes, toiletries, and a handful of protein bars. All or none of which she might need. "Yeah, yeah. I need a different job. You can lecture me about it in the car. Let's go."

By the time they reached Senator Fitchner's home, the Bureau had locked down the area. SAC Dupree was stationed in a temporary command center made up of the FBI's finest folding tables and chairs in the middle of the street. The man was about as wide as he was tall, with a personality only a mother could love. He stood, arms crossed over his chest, staring at a live feed from the bomb technicians inside the home, sweeping for explosives.

"Sir, where are we on the search?" Paxton stood beside him, blocking the late-day sun from blinding Kate.

"Garage and car are clean. They just entered the home. I hope you're right about this, Banks." He didn't look happy, but that was just his face. Clenched jaw, intense stare, and always sweaty.

"Have them search secondary bedrooms first," Paxton said decisively.

Dupree picked up the walkie-talkie and relayed the order.

Kate kept her mouth shut, not that she knew the right words to say in this situation anyway. Her head hurt from weighing the pros and cons of the case the whole ride there. She hoped they were wrong, but that would leave them nowhere again. So she hoped they were right, but that meant more kids could be in danger.

"Where are the residents?" Paxton's tone was authoritative but respectful.

Dupree pointed to an FBI utility truck down the street with two agents standing guard. "The nanny and the kid. Senator Fitchner is out of town with her husband."

"Have you been able to reach her?" Paxton tucked his hand in his pocket.

"We've got her on the six forty-five out of Dulles."

Paxton jotted a note and put the pad back in his pocket.

"Will they be allowed back in the home?" Kate didn't realize she had spoken out loud until Dupree peered over his shoulder at her.

He lifted his chin in acknowledgment, but not approval of her being there, then turned back to the grainy picture in front of them. "That depends on what we find."

His ominous tone made her stomach even more uneasy.

"Sir." The radio crackled in Dupree's hand, sending a shiver up Kate's back. "It's affirmative."

She turned her attention to the live feed, squinting to make out the picture. The body cam focused on a black and white image of dynamite sticks tucked in the corner of a closet next to a basket of toys.

A chill started deep in her core, turning her stomach hard as ice. Her heart beat wildly, trying to send warmth to her shaking limbs. She was rooted to the spot, too uncomfortable to do anything but blink.

"I want everyone out now." Dupree's gruff order blasted the radio. "Fall back."

Paxton stood as straight as a flagpole. "I'll take them to the safe house."

"No." SAC Dupree's tone left no room for arguments. He

slammed the walkie-talkie on the table but didn't take his eyes off the screen. "I need you to catch the son of a bitch before they detonate another one of these bombs, and you can't do that if you're on lock-down in a safe house."

Paxton nodded.

"There are nine more homes to search. I need to know how to prioritize the goddamn list, and quick." Dupree rubbed the thinning spot at the back of his head. "This is a political and public relations nightmare. It needs to end. Now."

"Understood, sir."

Dupree turned to face Paxton. "Then go find me a suspect."

Paxton headed in the opposite direction of where they parked.

It took Kate a moment to realize he was on the move. She snapped out of it and jogged up alongside him.

"Where are we going?"

"We need to interview the nanny." Paxton headed for the truck Dupree pointed out earlier. "Maybe she heard or saw something in the neighborhood."

"Okay."

Paxton stopped short a few steps from the truck, turning to face Kate. He looked her square in the eye. "Do not. Under any circumstances. Tell her. What you just witnessed."

She couldn't even put it into a clear thought, let alone a sentence. Kate nodded.

Paxton turned, showing the agent his badge, and climbed into the vehicle. She followed him.

"Hi." He put his hand out to shake the girl's hand, and she flinched.

The twenty-something looked scared out of her mind. Her skin was almost ashen against her long, dark hair. A little boy, probably three or four years old, sat in her lap, playing with a stuffed panda bear.

"I'm Special Agent Paxton Banks, and this is Ms. Howard."

"Grace." She blinked at them. "This is Anthony."

Kate crouched down to the little boy. "I like your bear." She scratched its ear. "What's his name?"

He shrugged and buried his face in Grace's sweater.

Who would ever want to hurt this little boy? Why? Her heartbeat felt like a grenade launcher pounding against her ribs. They got lucky this time, but what if they aren't so fortunate next time? Her stomach clenched at the disturbing thought of there being a next time.

"We'd like to ask you a few questions."

Her gaze dropped to the little guy and back to Paxton. "Are you going to tell me what's happening?"

"Unfortunately, no." His tone was friendly. "Until the team is done investigating, we can't release any information."

Grace stroked the boy's hair, her hand resting over his ear. "Are we in danger?" The last word a whisper.

"No, ma'am, you're safe." His tone was reassuring, but it didn't look like she believed him. "This was only a precaution while the FBI was investigating."

"Is there a"—she looked down at the little guy —"b.o.m.b?"

"We're looking into that." Paxton pulled the notebook out of his pocket all nonchalant, like he hadn't just seen the true definition of evil. He conveniently avoided Kate's gaze. "Were you home this morning?"

"Yes, well, no. We left around ten."

"Where did you go?"

"I promised Anthony we would go to the zoo today. We weren't even out of the car when the FBI pulled in behind us. They wouldn't even let us go inside to use the restroom. We had to be escorted to the neighbor's house."

Anthony bounced the panda down Grace's leg. For a

moment Kate was envious of his childlike ignorance to what was happening around him.

"I'm very sorry." Paxton jotted a note. "This morning when you left or when you pulled back into the driveway, did you see any suspicious-looking people? Any vehicles parked on the street you didn't recognize? Anything at all out of the ordinary?"

"No. I don't believe so." She shook her head. "This is a gated community. It's very quiet and safe." She looked out the back window of the truck at the FBI agents moving about. "I need to call Susan and Malcolm."

"We've spoken with them." Paxton looked at his watch. "They should be getting on their flight in about forty minutes."

She shook her head, not focusing on anything in particular. "Are they going to let us back in the house soon? I need to start dinner."

"Agents are going to escort you to a safe house for the night as a precaution."

"Safe hou…" Her voice trailed off, and a tear slid down her cheek. She opened her mouth to speak, then closed it.

"When Senator Fitchner arrives they will bring her and Malcolm there to meet you."

Grace shook her head. "I can't—I can't do this."

Kate knew firsthand how scary it could be, swept off to a place you knew nothing about, with none of your things, where no one would tell you anything. She didn't have a choice, but the least they could do was make her feel like it would be an improvement over the current situation. "I know it sounds scary, but we aren't going to let anything happen to you. You and Anthony are safe, and we want to keep it that way. It's not going to be fancy, but at least it will have comfortable chairs and a bathroom." Kate motioned to the space in the van. "Would you be okay with that?"

Grace tipped her head and let out a tentative smile.

Paxton handed her his card. "If you think of anything. If you need anything. Please have the agents call me."

She squeezed Anthony closer to her chest. "I will."

———

By the time Paxton pulled up to Kate's building it was already getting dark. The bomb squad had defused the bomb, his team had collected security camera footage from the home and neighbors, and the crime scene team was collecting evidence to process. Her heart was heavy with grief for these families. She couldn't get the image of little Anthony's face out of her head. The fear in Grace's eyes when he said they were going to a safe house. The stress of this case was going to give her an ulcer.

What kind of psycho goes after innocent children?

Paxton put the car in park and rested his head back. She didn't know how he did it. He must be exhausted. A little niggle of disappointment hit her that he wasn't planning on walking her up. Not that he needed to or should. She was perfectly capable of getting herself into the house. She had tried to convince him of that the last few times.

Kate unbuckled her seatbelt and reached for the door. "Do you want to come up?" The words slipped out, and she clenched her fist. "I—I was planning on getting a pizza and going through my notes again."

"It's going to take a little while for the security tapes to get downloaded." He checked his watch.

"You know what, never mind." Kate pulled her bag off the floor and opened the door. "You have things you need to do. You're probably tired."

He cut the engine, stopping her half-way out of the SUV. She was unable to read the expression on his face. He was too good at keeping his emotions in check.

"You can't tempt me with pizza and take it away." The corner of his lips tipped up.

Pizza wasn't the only temptation. The warmth of his eyes. The softness of his lips. A desire blazed through her to reach out and run her fingers along the stubble on his jawline. Kate slid down off the seat. The light breeze played with her hair, sending goosebumps up her arms.

He angled toward her. "You want me to come up or not?"

Her body screamed yes, but her lips didn't move. As much as inviting him up scared the ever-loving shit out of her, Kate didn't want to be alone. Not tonight. She could call Cody. He would be just the distraction she needed to get her mind off this fucked-up situation, but she didn't want him.

She wanted Paxton.

"Katie?"

She swallowed back the hesitation. "Yes." Kate shut the door, not looking back.

They climbed the stairs in silence. When Kate opened her door she knew inviting him in was a mistake, but she was a professional. She could eat dinner with a colleague or an old friend. Friends eat pizza all the time. It would be like having dinner with Maggie. If Maggie were a frustratingly handsome man who made her heart rumble like a tank.

He hung his suit jacket on the back of the stool.

"What do you want? On your pizza." She added quickly, kicking off her sneakers.

"Whatever you're having is fine." He walked over to the window.

It was not very Paxton-like to be indecisive. She pulled the phone out of her pocket, pushed the app, and re-ordered her last order.

"Dinner in twenty-ish minutes." She slid her phone on the counter. She watched him loosen his tie, admiring the well-defined muscles in his back flex against the taut shirt fabric. What would she do if Maggie were there? Not gawk at her back, that's for sure. "Drinks." She pulled two beers out of the fridge and handed him one.

Paxton took a sip, staring out the window. With the city skyline lit up and the last hint of blush in the clouds, it was almost romantic. No. Romance was not part of a friendly dinner. It was brilliant or pretty or colorful. *Pull yourself together, Kate.* She stepped away, sitting on the barstool, giving them some space.

"This feels like the first time we were in Berlin."

If he meant awkward, then yes.

"Do you remember that mission?"

She took a drink of her beer. Reminiscing. That was totally something you do with a friend. "The exchange student?"

"That's the one." Paxton turned to face her. "We spent three days in a warehouse with no heat and a mangy cat with only one eye. That was the first time you and I went on a mission by ourselves."

Was he saying her loft was cold and barren, and Kyle was an unwanted stray? Well, the last part was accurate. "That mission went south quick. Our comms were down. We had to wait until the extraction site was clear. And I was pretty sure if I fell asleep the cat was going to eat my fingers."

"But we did all right." He walked over, resting on the other stool. "We improvised. Worked together to get him to the US consulate safe."

"We did." She watched Paxton's strong hands wipe condensation from the bottle. His fingertips grazed the label where the mountains had turned blue, and she wished they were on her.

Kate's pulse picked up, turning the rumble in her chest into a roar. She checked her watch. There was no way she could sit there in silence for sixteen more minutes. Small talk. She needed more small talk. "You know I haven't heard you mention anything about Claire or your mom. How are they doing?"

"My mother is getting remarried after all this time."

"No kidding. Good for her."

"Yes, and my sister is almost six years into her four-year degree."

"That's okay."

"If Claire would stop changing her major on a whim, she might graduate. She went from studying biology to business to yoga instruction."

"She needs to figure out what it is she's passionate about."

"Well, she better figure it out quick. Since I moved here she's been living on my couch and making me crazy. She's not driven like you, not focused."

Kate feigned interest in the back of her bottle, avoiding the compliment. "I'm not that driven."

He swiveled the stool toward her. "I've never seen you go after something and not get it. You trust your gut. I don't think there's anything you can't do."

"There are plenty of things I can't do."

"Like what?" He rested his arm on the counter, the muscles in his hand flexing and releasing.

Tell you how I feel.

Kate wanted to put it all on the line. Wear her heart on her sleeve. Dive in headfirst. All those cheesy, cliché gestures. But what then? She wasn't ever going to be the Katie Homemaker of his dreams, popping out babies and making pies all day. Putting her beer down, she moved her hands to her lap so she didn't accidentally touch him. "Pee standing up."

He gave her a be-serious look.

She let out a rough chuckle, rubbing her palms together unsure if they were wet from the bottle or nerves. "Relationships. They're lost on me."

"I doubt that."

She turned to face him. "It's not pretty."

"Maybe you just haven't met the right one yet. When that happens things will fall in place."

"Relationships are about trust and honesty. Even if I could tell a guy *what* I do, I couldn't tell him much else. I'm out with random men on a regular basis. Constantly in the line of danger. Most of my clothes are bulletproof. How do you explain when you come home with a black eye or a stab wound or"—she pointed to her shoulder—"shrapnel in your back and stitches in your arm? Normal guys would hop the first train out of Cuckooville."

"I get it. Trust me. I've been there. But the right guy will understand."

Kate rolled her eyes. "You sound like Maggie."

"He won't like it. He'll worry constantly about you getting hurt. He probably won't sleep until you're home safe. But he would see how much you care about your clients. And he would understand what you were doing, risking your own life to protect somebody else, is important."

Kate had a sneaking suspicion they had moved from hypothetical boyfriends to Paxton talking about himself.

"And if he doesn't, he's an idiot. And you should definitely punch him in the face."

Kate laughed, leaning in. Paxton closed the distance between them, their lips barely brushed. A zap of electricity between them sent a spark down between her thighs, igniting a time bomb of emotions. She stared into Paxton's eyes. And like that, he'd let his guard down, the dark desire staring back at her. It was raw and real and *not* something a friend would do.

Her front door opened. Kate watched Kyle in her periphery but didn't move.

"Why would you order mushrooms and black olives?" Kyle walked in carrying their pizza and mozzarella sticks, chomping on one or both of them. "That's a disgrace to pizza everywhere."

She glared over her shoulder at him. "Get. Out."

He put the box on the island with the oil-stained, white

paper bag. "Jeez. You could be nicer to me." He looked from Kate to Paxton, oblivious of the situation he had interrupted.

Was it a situation? Was this really happening?

"Kyle"—Paxton looked over at him—"I will let her shoot you tonight." His tone was sexy as hell.

Of course, he wasn't going to let her shoot him, but the fact that he wanted Kyle gone as much as she did put a smile on her face.

"Tough crowd." Kyle snatched the bag of mozzarella sticks, spun on his heel, and slammed the door behind him.

Paxton pulled back but didn't break eye contact. "Pizza?" The wanting in his eyes was too much. He wasn't asking about pizza; he was asking if she were sure this was what she wanted. Giving her a moment to get her head on straight. But pizza wasn't the hunger she needed to satisfy.

Kate licked her lips. "It's better cold."

Chapter Thirteen

Hot Paxton versus hot pizza? No contest. Kate leaned forward, brushing her lips against his, and the spark ignited again. Like a flamethrower, it warmed her down to her toes. She pulled back to gaze into his seductive, blue-gray eyes.

Paxton assessed her, making her stomach quiver with doubt. Had she overstepped? Read too much into his reaction? His soft, supple lips parted, begging her not to stop. This was a colossally bad idea. She said no kissing. It was her one stipulation working together. Against her rules and probably the FBI's.

Kate didn't care.

It felt too good to stop.

She slid off her stool between his legs, her thigh grazing his, and heat prickled through her, cranking her heartbeat up to holy-hell. She reached out to stroke the stubble on his jaw, the coarse bristles tickling her fingers. When he gulped under her palm, she realized how still he was. His white-knuckled grip on the stool back was tight enough to bend the frame. He was either holding back, unsure this was right or not sure she wanted this. Wanted him.

Kate slid her fingers down his arm, lingering a moment

over the tense muscles. Paxton loosened his grip, and she moved his hand to her hip.

She leaned into him farther, and his spicy cologne made her head spin. Masculine and mouth-watering. Kate planted a trail of kisses down the side of his neck, making Paxton groan. His other hand slid up her thigh to her waist, and he tightened his grip on her.

She inhaled sharply, and he pulled away.

"Katie, I don't want to hurt you."

His raspy tone excited her in a way she couldn't explain. Her heart beat like machine gun fire in her chest. "I'm not that fragile," she whispered. She stepped up on the rung of his stool and swung her other leg over his, straddling his thigh, bringing her to the perfect height to peer into his lust-filled eyes.

"I thought you were bad at this relationship stuff."

"This part"—Kate leaned in until their lips barely touched —"I'm pretty good at."

She kissed him hungrily, and the little bit of composure he held broke free—she knew it the moment he cupped her ass and squeezed.

He lifted her, and the stool crashed to the floor as he sat her on the island. He paused to pull the holster off his hip, setting it down on the counter before his gaze locked on hers once more, full of the same dark, burning desire that roared through her.

Kate wrapped her legs around his waist instinctively as if she'd done it a million times. He pressed his mouth to hers, the intensity in his eager kisses forcing her mouth open for his tongue to explore.

My God.

Her pulse pounded in her ears, emotions on the verge of short-circuiting. She wanted to scream and cry with every touch. And there were far too many clothes in the way. Kate grabbed his tie. Tossing it aside, she made quick work of his shirt buttons, yanking the dress shirt free from his pants. Her fingers trembled as she pushed the fabric back over his shoulders, letting it fall to the floor.

Kate grasped the hem of his undershirt. A thin layer of ribbed-cotton between her and Paxton, the only thing keeping her from what she'd wanted for years. Her hands stiffened. She'd seen him shirtless a thousand times. And yet this time. In this moment. It made her pause.

At her hesitation, he reached back, tugging the tank over his head. The fabric slipped through her weak grip.

She stared at his chiseled chest, his sculpted shoulders, his athletic arms, and every inch of him was more beautiful than the next. She'd memorized every muscle, every scar, every tattoo a dozen years ago, but her look-don't-touch policy was shattering in a moment of weakness.

Her hands roamed his skin, skimming across his taut abs, tracing the hard muscles and soft, dark curls across his pecs, his chest rising and falling erratically under her fingertips.

Paxton brushed her hair behind her ear and lifted her chin to look at him, his smoldering eyes undressing her. She was hungry for his lips. She wanted to kiss him until he groaned and gasped and moaned her name. Begged for more.

Grabbing the edge of her shirt, Kate pulled it over her head, cautious of her bandaged shoulder.

Paxton's gaze roamed her bare skin. Leaning in, he brushed gentle kisses across her neck again and again until he reached the hollow at the base of her throat. "Katie," he whispered.

She sighed. Her chickenshit nerves were too on-edge for words. The hairs on the back of her neck prickled with every kiss, and her stomach fluttered with anticipation of the coming ones. Feather-light and hot as the mid-July sun. Kate closed her eyes and focused on her breath, savoring the fullness of his lips.

This is really happening.

He released the clasp of her bra and carefully slid the strap over her arm.

Paxton gently caressed her breasts, and she gasped when he brought his warm lips down to them. *Fuck.* He flicked his tongue against the hardened nipple in a painfully tantalizing game before taking it into his mouth. His arousal fed her own —his cologne, his killer smile, the way his eyes drank her in as if he couldn't get enough of her. It was every moment, every touch, every glance lighting her body on fire, making it impossible to think.

She arched into him and took a ragged breath. She ran her fingers through his hair, sliding them down the back of his neck, and his muscles flexed under her palms.

He moved down her body, his mouth skimming her skin, his hands tracing her curves, stopping at the button on her jeans.

Her heart pounded against her ribs as fast as the throbbing between her legs. "Don't stop."

"I've never wanted anything or anyone the way I want you."

Kate couldn't help but smile at the admission. She hopped off the counter, unbuttoned her pants, and let them slide down her legs. Stepping out of them, she led him by the hand toward her bed, glanced over her shoulder at him.

"You drive me crazy," he growled, grabbing her hip and pulling her into him.

His erection pressed hard into the small of her back. He slid his hand around her and under her lace panties. His fingers didn't stop until he reached her clit, making Kate gasp. He stroked her soft, damp folds and massaged her swollen nub, leaving her breathless. Her skin burned hot and wet, and she pumped her hips against his hand, demanding more.

He hugged her tighter around the waist, and she melted into his chest, giving him a better angle.

"Yesss." Kate dug her nails into his arm as Paxton's fingertips worked in circles and short bursts, making every muscle tremble, twitch, and tingle until her legs damn-near gave out.

A sound, part weep, part whimper, slipped past her lips. *Holy fuck.* She shuddered, surrendering to the waves of pleasure, drowning in sensation as her climax tore through her. "Oh. Oh, fuck." Kate collapsed, but he held on to her.

She closed her eyes, licked her lips, and rested her head back against his chest. She was panting, so lightheaded she could barely stand. But Paxton's strong arms held her tight as he kissed her ear and neck while she caught her breath, his scruff enmeshed in her hair. Her massaging shower head was good, but this—this was orgasmic perfection.

"More," she demanded.

"More what?" His voice was a low rumble in his chest.

"More everything." She turned, yanking his belt free. She pushed him backward toward the bed, unbuttoning his pants while they walked.

Paxton curled his hands into her hair, pulling her into his heady kiss, and his pants fell around their feet. "Katie"—he rested his forehead against hers—"I want to, but I don't have anything on me."

Kate smiled, reached over to the nightstand, and pulled out a condom.

"Thank God." Paxton kicked off his shoes, stepping out of his slacks.

She admired the bulge in his boxers and his powerful thighs but froze when her gaze landed on the scars that covered his right leg like tank tracks driven by a drunk toddler. Her stomach cinched tighter than a pair of combat boots but not as tight as the lump of guilt in her throat. *I did that to him.* She gasped as tears burned behind her eyes. *It's my fault.* Raging lust turned to heart-rending remorse.

He reached for her, and she backed into the nightstand, knocking over her electronic charging station and lamp, but she couldn't care what parts of her life crashed around her. She disobeyed a direct order and almost got him killed. A sob ripped through her.

"Katie?"

She covered her chest with her hands, suddenly realizing how nearly naked she was.

"Katie, look at me." Paxton closed the distance between them. "Please, look at me." He lifted her chin. "I'm okay."

Tears flowed down her cheeks. The words stuck in her throat, and it was several seconds before she could answer. "You're not."

"I am." He wiped away her tears, replacing them with kisses.

"I'm so sorry."

"It was my choice to protect you." Paxton kissed the top of her head, holding her gently. "I don't regret that decision. I'll *never* regret that decision." He pulled away to look at her, and she missed his warmth. "I feel more whole here, now, with you, than I have in years."

He lowered his lips to hers. The kiss was slow and gentle, heat simmering through her veins, her body warming again to the delicious sensation.

"Let me show you how okay I am." His velvety voice coaxed her. His gaze was intense, full of emotion, and a determination she'd seen many times on missions. But now that determination was aimed at her, and it was intoxicating. His lips captured hers, passionate and persuasive.

She sighed as he took over.

He hooked his fingers in the edge of her lace panties, tugging them down over her hips, and she went limp all over.

"Oh," she whimpered, her sex flooding with heat and desire as he pulled his boxers down, revealing the beautiful length of his engorged flesh.

He sat on the side of the bed, pulling her to straddle him.

His chest was hard against her breasts. The cotton sheets were soft against her shins.

Reaching down, she stroked the rigid shaft with her fingertips, fascinated, as she allowed her nails to graze the sensitive skin.

Paxton let out a throaty groan, virile and carnal. Ripping open the package, he slipped on the condom. He rubbed the tip of his penis against her still-sensitive nub before pressing gently inside.

She lowered her hips, inhaling at the sheer size of him, then her body opened up to let him satisfy all those years of craving. She moaned and sank her teeth into her lower lip.

Fuck, he feels good.

He held her, gliding slowly out, then burying himself inside her again and again.

It was even better than she'd imagined it would be, his length and girth filling her, overloading her senses. She breathed him in, spicy cologne and the sharp scent of desire, both his and her own.

His lips found hers and the savage intensity of his kisses made her head spin. She hadn't felt this good, this right, this *whole* in her entire adult life.

With strong hands, he grabbed her waist and helped to lift and lower her.

She leaned back, gripping the edge of the bed, watching the pleasure their steady rhythm brought to play across his face. Paxton was better than okay. *He's exquisite.* An unexpected release of tension, over a decade old, escaped every cell of her body. The grief and regret and worry, leaving her giddy, relieved, and wonderful.

He locked eyes with her, and the world around them seemed to disappear. She wanted to make him feel as good as she felt.

Throwing her arms around his neck, she rocked her hips forward and back, burying her head into his shoulder. Kate's muscles twitched and tightened around him with every passionate pulse.

His muscular arms and chest flexed, and with every thrust, his grip on her tightened. "Say my name."

Her heart crashed into his. Beating together. She gulped back the emotions building in her throat. Even if it were for only a few minutes, Kate had everything she'd wanted for as long as she could remember. "Paxton," she whispered.

With a grunt, he picked up the pace, urging her hips to thrust harder, deeper. "Louder."

She closed her eyes and muffled a moan into his neck, kissing and nibbling below his ear. "Paxton."

"Again."

"Paxton."

"Oh, Katie," he cried out.

And for the first time since he showed up in her life, she didn't mind him calling her Katie. She liked the way it sounded in his ecstasy-induced, heat-of-the-moment tone. It excited and invigorated her.

Paxton's low groans became louder and more intense. His breathing heavy, his eyes glazed, his skin flushed.

Kate contracted the muscles between her legs. His eyes went wide and his mouth dropped open, but no sound escaped. Her thigh muscles burned, but she thrust her hips, bringing him to the point of no return.

"Oh, God. Katie." He grabbed her ass, thrusting with everything he had left. "Oh, K—Katie." He convulsed and collapsed against the wall behind the bed, holding onto her, both their chests heaving.

She brushed the sweat-soaked hair from her forehead and rested against him, listening to the tempo of his heart slowly return to its normal *ba-DUB, ba-DUB*. Savoring the warm contentment, she twirled her fingers into his dark chest hairs. Kate had never been so connected, so in sync, with anyone. Ever. "That was—"

"Incredible?" He placed a kiss on the top of her head.

"Unexpected."

"So you didn't lure me up here with the promise of pizza to take advantage of me?"

Did she? She lay there for a few moments smiling to herself, like a day-dreaming school girl. *She did. She lured Paxton Banks into her home and seduced him.* The realization turned the heat up in her cheeks. *Now what?* Her skin prickled and stiffened. She and Cody had rules. Clear expectations. But Paxton? Was she supposed to ask him to leave? Is that what she wanted?

He twisted to the side to look at her. "You didn't fall asleep on me, did you?"

Say something. She didn't meet his gaze. A phone buzzed somewhere behind her, and she looked over her shoulder toward the sound. Her charging station hung precariously over the edge of the nightstand by its cord, the lamp lay in a few pieces on the floor below it, and their clothes formed a breadcrumb trail from the island. "I think that's your phone."

"I'll call them back in a moment." He stroked her hair.

"It—it could be important." Kate slid off his lap, trying not to put any pressure on her shoulder or back. She took a few steps to the bathroom, pulled her robe off the door, and slipped into it.

Out of the corner of her eye, she watched him walk over to the kitchen trash can and toss the condom. "Are you okay?" He turned back, closing the space between them. All his glorious nakedness taunting her.

She cinched the belt at her waist. "I'm a little sore, but that's more explosion than—" She pointed to the bed, not looking at him.

He put his hand on her hip, his heat searing her skin through the thin fabric. "I mean are *you* okay?" The huskiness in his voice kindling the fire.

Stepping away from him, she followed their trail of

clothes. "Fine." Kate tucked her jeans under her arm and tossed his boxers at him.

He caught them in one hand and slipped them on. "Are you kicking me out?"

I don't know what I'm doing. I told you I'm not good at this. She closed her eyes for a moment and exhaled. "I'm not really equipped for overnight guests." She continued picking up clothes.

"No civilian, at least none older than a college student, should sleep in a twin-size bed."

She didn't have the nerve to tell him the reason she kept the single bed was so guests would have to go home.

He strutted over in his boxers, pulling her to him, and wrapped his arms around her waist. "*That* was the best team-work we've ever had, Katie." He kissed her ear and down the side of her neck, igniting heat between her legs. "I'm sure we can figure out some kind of sleeping arrangement."

Even with a pile of clothing between them, she could feel him harden. *Sleep? Who the hell would sleep?*

Chapter Fourteen

Kate sat on the floor of her loft with her computer in her lap, up against the weight bench, the senator's files scattered around her. Normally, the only sounds this time of day were the hum of her refrigerator and the clock over her sink ticking away, but today Paxton's heavy-breath sleep was a surprisingly welcome addition. She looked up over the screen at him, barely able to make out his shape in the dark. The street lamp from across the block cast an amber hue over the island and kitchen cabinets, but not bright enough to reach the bed.

By the time they'd gone to sleep, Paxton had followed up with SAC Dupree and his team. The bomb squad had searched three more senators' homes and come up empty. It was good news. She should be happy, but they weren't any closer to a suspect or a motive for attacking innocent children.

The covers rustled. "Katie?"

"Over here." She aimed the laptop in his direction so he could see her.

"What time is it?"

She looked down at the screen. "Three-thirty."

Paxton groaned and tossed the covers back. "I forgot about Howard hour."

"About what?"

Paxton shuffled toward her. "Where's the switch?"

"About four steps to your right by the bathroom." Light flooded the loft. She let her eyes adjust, squinting up at Paxton in the sweatpants he'd pulled out of his go-bag before climbing into her bed and holding up the covers for her to join him. "You can't name something after me and not explain."

He sat on the cold floor next to her, placing one of the files in his lap. "Is this my sweatshirt?"

There was no use denying it, the sweatshirt was three sizes too big and said FBI across the back. But admitting it smelled deliciously like him was not a discussion she wanted to get into. "It was on the chair, and I was cold. Don't change the subject. Howard hour?"

He rested back against the weight bench, his shoulder brushing hers. "You used to wake up an hour before the rest of us. We called it Howard hour."

Oh, right. It wasn't that Kate wanted to get up an hour before her team. It was the only time she had to herself in a unit of men. She could take a hot-ish shower and shave her legs without someone getting impatient that *the girl* was taking too long.

And here they were, years later, Paxton in her home, half-dressed and dangerously close to her. And how had she forgotten how dreamy his groggy-morning face was? Kate could pinch herself to make sure it was all real, but she didn't want to risk it.

"Did you even sleep?" Paxton rubbed her knee, sending hot trickles up her thigh.

"Some." *No.* She'd waited until Paxton's breathing rate slowed and his grip on her loosened before slipping out of bed. Another thing she wouldn't admit.

"What's going on here?"

"You said Senator McNahb, Baker, and Russo's homes were cleared last night. We can exclude them from the list."

Paxton shook his head. "It's not enough to make that determination. They might not have been on the target list, or we may have gotten to them first. We still need more evidence."

"And I think I found it. Hand me the voting page I was working on yesterday."

Paxton dug through the file in his lap. "This one?" He handed her the lined paper with handwritten scribbles from her research.

"I think I narrowed down the target list." She smiled over her shoulder at him.

Paxton leaned in toward her, looking more awake. "I'm listening."

"Voted yes to legalize marijuana." She handed him back the piece of paper with the senators' voting data.

He took it, reading down the page. "Senators McNahb, Baker, and Russo aren't on here."

"Correct." Kate angled toward him, her knee resting on his. "But Senators Thomas, Gail, Diaz, and Fitchner *are* on there."

"No. Fitchner isn't on here."

"That's what I thought too, but Senator Fitchner isn't anywhere on any voting records. So I started digging." She turned the laptop toward him, her browser open to the Clerk of the Superior Court website. "They have a marriage certificate listed for Suzanne Fitchner and Malcolm Spilner dated almost two weeks after she was elected. She must have continued to use her maiden name to not confuse her constituents, but changed her legal name. Suzanne Spilner is how she votes."

Paxton pointed to a name on the list.

"That's the only vote they all have in common." A jittery

excitement flooded her limbs, and Kate bounced her knee. "It's good, right?"

"All four of the senators who have been targeted are here, and the three cleared homes are not. It's a good place to start. Why are these highlighted?"

Kate pointed to the page. "Those five senators have kids out of town, which leaves us with four state senators who voted to legalize marijuana as our priority list. Senators Barron, Garsky, Lopez, and Turley."

Paxton tilted his head, staring at her with bright eyes. "You're better at this than I gave you credit for."

Her skin tingled at the commendation. She laced her fingers together to keep from fidgeting. "I can't tell if you're annoyed that I turned into the exact person you trained me to be or you're jealous."

"Impressed." Paxton rubbed circles on her leg with his thumb. "How did you come up with that?"

"I think better after an orgasm." The words escaped before she realized she said it out loud.

Paxton smiled. The sexy, sensuous grin, building in intensity, sent her temperature rising. "That would have been good to know two days ago." Paxton's tone had naughty written all over it, and her pulse quickened. He put the file and laptop on the floor beside them, leaned in, and kissed her, his morning scruff scratchy on her chin. "Maybe another one could solve the whole case."

It was a bit much to ask of an orgasm, but who was she to argue? Kate ran her hands over his shoulders, admiring the strapping, corded muscles. "If this is a dream, I'm gonna be pissed."

He laughed into the base of her neck, his whiskers tickling her. "Does this"—his fingers crept under the sweatshirt and her tank top, spreading warmth in every direction—"feel like a dream?"

God, yes. It all felt like a fantasy. Her entire life had been fugazi, completely out of whack, since he walked into that emergency room days ago. She sighed when his palms covered her breasts.

Paxton pulled away. "Did you hear something?"

"No." Kate rubbed his stubble, pulling him back into the kiss.

He stopped again, but that time she absolutely heard a knock. "It's probably some lost junkie. It happens sometimes. They'll go away."

When the third knock happened, Paxton was already on his way to the door.

The only person who would come here this time of night is— *shit.* Her chest tingled and tightened, making it hard to take a breath. Kate scrambled to her feet. "No. No. Don't answer it." She caught up to him just in time to see the look on Cody's face when Paxton opened her door.

Cody tilted his head to the side, taking in the two of them half-dressed until his eyes narrowed at Kate.

The heat that was building moments before all flooded her face. She wasn't ashamed, there was nothing to be embarrassed about, but the look on Cody's face made her stomach quiver like playing hopscotch in a minefield.

Paxton put his shoulders back and reached out to block her with his arm.

"Paxton." Kate pushed him aside.

He didn't take his eyes off Cody. The muscle in his jaw twitched, then hardened.

"Paxton." She tugged the door free from his grip, and a twinge of pain shot through her shoulder. "Why don't you call in what we found?" She placed her hands on his bare chest, pushing him back into the apartment. "They can redirect efforts to the priority list."

Paxton turned without so much as a glance at her.

Kate stepped out on the landing, closing the door behind

her. The cold metal under her feet sent a chill up her bare legs. "Cody, what are you doing here?"

"What am *I* doing here? What is *he* doing here?" Cody's tone was a little too jealous for her liking.

"He's an old friend I'm assisting on a case." But even as the words came out, she didn't believe them, either. There was always something more under the surface, and after last night, she didn't know if she could ever be *just friends* with Paxton.

"Kate, you have scruff burn on your face, and you're wearing the top half of his tracksuit. I'm not stupid."

Kate wrapped her arm around her middle, tipping her chin up. "What does it matter? We"—she motioned between them—"are not a couple."

His face twisted with exasperation, cheeks reddening, nostrils flaring, eyes bulging. "You're right. We're not. But I at least thought we were honest with each other. Here." Cody shoved Kate's keys at her, his movement rushed and clumsy. "You didn't come to get your car. I saw the light on, so I knew you were up." His voice got quiet. "I won't make that mistake again."

"Hey, don't be like that."

"I've asked you a dozen times to go out with me, but you've always got an excuse."

Kate looked up into his blue eyes full of pain. Pain she'd had no idea until this very second she had caused. For her, it might have been just sex, but his burning glare affirmed that, for him, it hadn't been. Tightness settled in her chest. She lowered her voice. "We had an agreement. Just sex."

"When a gorgeous woman wants to have sex with you, you take it. But I want more than a *you up* text." Cody straightened his shoulders. "Go on a date with me."

It wasn't a question or a request. It was a demand. "What? Cody. My life is—complicated."

"Fine. I'll make it easier on you." Cody turned and

stomped down the stairs. "Until you go on a date with me, all previous arrangements are null and void." He swung the door open and walked out without looking back.

A blast of cool air ripped through the entry, taking her breath with it. Kate squeezed the sweatshirt around her middle. She turned toward the door, hand on the handle, and cleared her throat, trying to wrestle down the you're-a-shitty-person feeling. How had she missed the signs? How had she not seen that coming? And how much of that had Paxton heard? She forced out a breath and went back into her apartment.

Paxton stood at the island in his slacks and shirt, attaching his holster to his belt. He didn't bother acknowledging her. The muscles in his face and neck were so rigid she was going to need the Jaws of Life to get him to open up and speak to her.

Shit. He'd heard all of it.

She slammed her front door harder than she expected and made herself jump. "Paxton—"

"I'm not doing this with you." His voice was sharp as a bayonet. "Not now."

The tightness in her chest clamped down harder, making her lightheaded. "You're leaving?" She grabbed the back of a stool.

"I have a job to do." Paxton pulled his tie off the island, avoiding her gaze.

She ground her other fist into her hip. "It's four in the morning. Where are you going?"

Paxton acted as though he hadn't heard her. He wasn't hard of hearing; he was a hard-ass. Somehow in that few minutes Kate spent on the landing with Cody, Paxton had gone back to his old self with no trace of the guy kissing her moments before. He finished knotting his tie and flipped his collar down. Just when Kate thought he wasn't going to respond at all to her *where-are-you-going* question, he cleared his throat. "The lab traced the explosives to a construction demolitions company." His words were as rigid as his jaw. He looked at his watch. "I want to be there when they open at five o'clock."

She dropped her arms to her sides, straightening her posture. "I'll go with you. I need twenty minutes to get ready. Unless"—Kate took a step forward—"I haven't been a valuable asset to the case."

He stopped mid-reach for his jacket, looking down at her bare legs. "Twenty minutes." His tone wasn't happy, but he agreed.

———

Nineteen minutes and fifty-two seconds later, Kate sat quietly in the passenger seat of Paxton's SUV as he wound his way through town before rush-hour traffic. The case files were on the armrest like a barricade between warring countries. The little hairs on the back of her neck lifted, pricking up to the top of her scalp. He hadn't said much since they left her place. Hadn't looked her in the eye either. She half expected him to leave while she was in the bathroom getting ready, but for some unknown reason, he waited.

She picked up the police report Paxton had her print before they left. If he was going to ignore her, she might as well read up on the demolitions company theft.

He cleared his throat after a few minutes. "Does he show up at o-dark-thirty a lot?" His tone was civil but serious.

"He doesn't usually show up unannounced."

"That's not what I asked."

I know. Kate didn't want to fight with him. They had finally gotten to a good place. She didn't want to screw it up, but lying to him wouldn't help. She dropped the paper in her lap, clasping her hands over the top of it. "Occasionally."

"You said he wasn't your boyfriend. Was that a lie?" His tone was negotiator calm.

"I didn't lie. He's not my boyfriend."

"But he wants to be."

"Yes. I guess." Kate blew out a breath. "We occasionally—"

"You're just fucking him." His curt voice attacked her.

Kate drew her head back quickly, making her dizzy. Paxton's rare use of profanity always took her off guard. Asking to come with him was a bad idea. She should have given him space to get his head straight.

"Is that what this is?" He didn't pause to let her respond. "So what, you're going to add me to the rotation? Do we pick days or take numbers like at the deli counter?"

"Stop it." Kate spat out. The heaviness of his words weighed down on her. Was she supposed to not live her life? Pine over a man who never gave her the time of day? "I've slept with exactly seven men before last night. Two in high school, one in the military, and four since. And yes, Cody happens to be the last one." *And that's over.*

"You told him I was a friend you were helping on a case." His jaw clenched tight. "Is that true? Is that all I am to you?"

"You want the truth?" Kate angled toward him. "Until you showed up in the emergency room I thought you were dead or hated my guts. Either way, I never thought I'd see you again. But here you are. Whatever happened between us last night was never supposed to happen. I don't know *how* I feel or *what* you are to me." Her voice quivered, but she couldn't hold it back. "I need to wrap my head around all of this."

Paxton stopped at a red light and turned toward her. Shock and anger and hurt played across his face, hardening his features in the dark cabin. "I'm an all-or-nothing guy. I won't settle for occasionally. I won't share you with someone else." He took a breath and let it out slowly. "I won't let you break my heart again."

Break his heart? Again? His words sliced her open like a knife to the chest. Could she have broken his heart and not known about it? Kate opened her mouth but closed it again. There was no apology she could offer which would suffice.

"You're either in or out."

Panic coursed through her veins like ice water, freezing her organs. Who throws out ultimatums before they've even had coffee? She wanted to say yes because she didn't want to say no, but that would lead her down a path she'd never been, never one she ever thought possible. Fuck, she wasn't equipped to make decisions like this. "What are you talking about?" She forced the words out past the glacier in her throat. "When did I break your heart?"

"Katie, when you left without saying good-bye"—Paxton dragged his fingers through his hair—"it destroyed me. It hurt worse than my leg ever did. I can't do it again."

Hot tears burned her eyes, threatening to spill over her lashes. She never meant to hurt him, physically or emotionally, and she'd done both. She really was a shitty person. "I didn't know that." Her voice was shaky.

The light turned green, and Paxton brought his focus back to the road. "Now you do."

"I—I need time. I need to figure all this out." Kate swiped her thumb under her eye, wiping a tear on her jeans. Her mother had always told her boys were a waste of time. She needed to be independent. She needed to be smart. She needed to trust her instincts. But she wasn't a kid anymore. And Paxton wasn't other guys.

So what do you do when your gut disagrees with everything you've been taught your whole life? When your brain can't formulate a logical answer? When you ached for someone? When you had more questions than answers? "Maybe, can we focus on the case right now? Call a truce. And we can discuss this when we're not trying to catch a terrorist?"

Paxton dipped his chin a fraction, and Kate took it as his agreement to postpone the discussion. But postponing it didn't mean she'd have an answer then, either.

She held up the police report in a poor attempt to change the subject. "This was filed a few days before the threats."

Paxton didn't answer for a few seconds. "The threats we know about. Yes."

"They steal dynamite and blasting caps, then threaten all the senators who voted yes to legalize marijuana. It doesn't even make sense. Does that sound like a terrorist to you?"

"Domestic terrorism comes in all shapes and sizes. Could be an activist group or lobbyists or a plain old nut job." Paxton turned down a side-street, looking up through the dark windshield.

"What do we know about this company?"

He shook his head. "Only what's listed there. It's a construction demolition company. They blow stuff up for a living."

"Do you think the robbery was premeditated or opportunity?"

"Don't know." Paxton scrubbed his hand across his chin. In their rush to leave, he didn't have time to shave, but she liked the scruffiness. "At the bottom is what they listed as stolen."

"Six electronic blasting caps and twelve sticks of dynamite."

"If the two detonated devices were set up like the ones we retrieved from Senator Gail's car and Senator Fitchner's home, we're still missing four sticks of dynamite and two blasting caps."

The thought of someone still out there, a threat to society and the senator's kids, made Kate's mouth go dry.

"The FBI bomb techs and local bomb squad are working

through the narrowed list of senators, but there could still be two bombs out there, so keep that quiet. We don't need mass panic to complicate things."

Like things weren't complicated enough?

Paxton pulled up next to a temporary trailer inside the barbed-wire-topped fence of a construction site. Kate stared at it through the windshield, the only defining features of the metal building were a few rust spots along the exterior. The small window in the door, not big enough for an adult to climb through, shined some light down on the cement block step.

Kate nodded and unbuckled her seatbelt. "Do you suspect this guy?"

"Everyone's a suspect." He pulled the FBI blazer off the backseat and handed it to her. "The construction foreman filed the report on the day he discovered the explosives missing, and he followed all the proper procedures, but you never know."

Kate slipped into the jacket, covering her tan sweater. She followed Paxton up the dimly-lit step to the trailer and entered when he held the door for her. The cramped, makeshift office was littered with rolls of building plans and stacks of paper. A file cabinet on the far wall housed an ancient coffeemaker, slowly dripping into the carafe. The smell of coffee mixed with dirt, dust, and destruction reminded her of their time in the military.

A burly man with more salt-than-pepper hair and beard looked them up and down, stopping midway on Paxton, catching a glimpse of either his badge or gun or both. He put his bagel down, wiping his hands on his Dickies. "You here about the explosions on the news?"

"What makes you say that?" Paxton's tone didn't hint at his thoughts.

"I didn't call the FBI, but here you are." He tugged at his hunter-green suspenders, which matched the Kraftview

Demolitions Company logo on his once-white shirt. "What else could it be?"

"Special Agent Paxton Banks." He put his hand out to greet him. "And this is Ms. Howard."

"Benjamin Conner." He shook their hands.

"Ms. Howard and I have some questions about the police report you filed two months back."

"Did you catch the son of a bitch who stole my supplies and put me behind on this job?"

"No, sir, but I'd like to." Paxton pulled out his notebook and pen. "What can you tell me about the day you got robbed?"

Benjamin walked over to the computer, pressed a few buttons, and a printer buzzed to life. "Everything was fine when I locked up for the night. Next morning, I had a hole in my fence and the explosives locker was busted open." He ambled around the desk and grabbed the pages. "Employee records to date, storage records, and inspection reports."

Paxton nodded. "That's very helpful."

"Employee records?" Kate took the printouts. "Do you suspect it's an employee who stole from you?"

"Has to be." Benjamin shrugged.

Kate's muscles stiffened up, drawing the list closer to her. "Why is that?"

"This wasn't some kids messing around or tweakers looking for stuff they can pawn. I have a couple of hundred-thousand dollars' worth of equipment and tools on-site. Nothing else was touched. They came through a piece of the fence that falls between two cameras, so we never got a good look at him. They cut the lock on the only construction container that had explosives. I don't keep dynamite on-site at all times, so they would have had to know when it was delivered and where it was kept. Then there's the obvious."

What more could there be? It sounds like an open-and-close case for an inside job.

Paxton finished scribbling something and looked up. "Which is what?"

"Dynamite is volatile. It needs to be handled carefully and stored properly. Someone who didn't know what they were doing would have blown themselves up before they hit the sidewalk. It's been two months, and I'm only now hearing in the news about explosions."

Ugh. Kate gulped and shook her head in disbelief.

Paxton slid Kate a sideways glance. "Is there anyone in particular you suspected? Anyone you fired right before it happened? Someone you got into a disagreement with?"

"Not that I recall." Benjamin scratched his beard. "All of my guys are background-checked and thoroughly vetted. That's why this was such a disappointment. Until this, we hadn't had so much as a Twinkie go missing off my desk. Police looked into it, but I never heard a thing."

Kate flipped through the papers, her eyes not focusing on anything in particular. "If you don't keep dynamite here regularly, how far in advance do you know about a delivery?"

"Depends on the municipality. Some you need to file the paperwork weeks in advance for a demolition. This shipment took about three months."

"Thank you for your time." Paxton put the notebook in his pocket and handed him a card. "If you think of anything else, please give me a call."

"I'll do that." Benjamin pulled a tack from the corkboard behind him and jammed it into the card. "You be careful. Anyone willing to steal dynamite is desperate, and desperate makes them dangerous."

He got that right.

Chapter Fifteen

Kate and Paxton sat at the back corner table of Gino's Coffee House. It was her and Maggie's favorite place to hang out in high school. Nothing had changed—from its stark-white walls to its dark-wood countertop to the pop of pale-yellow accents. Nothing had changed, except Kate.

She inhaled the freshly brewed, liquid heaven that wafted around them. She never imagined she'd be sitting here with Paxton, nibbling a still-warm cheese danish. Paxton hadn't touched his pastry, and if he didn't pay attention, she was going to take care of it for him. That probably wasn't wise if she was trying to stay in his good graces. Since her early-morning visit from Cody, the tension between them was as thick as the cream cheese in their baked goodies, and he still hadn't met her eyes.

She pressed her thumb into the crumbs on her plate, licking them off. Kate flicked the back of the employment log Paxton had his nose buried in. "What do you think?" She lowered her voice. "Was it an inside job?"

He dropped the papers on the table, rubbing the backside of his hand along his jaw. Deep lines of concentration creased his forehead. "Benjamin's got a point. There are too many factors that someone would need to guess at or get lucky on for it not to be."

"He said they were all vetted, so something would have turned up if they had a criminal record, right?"

"You would think so, but there's nothing in the police report." Paxton took a bite of his pastry, then wiped his fingers on the napkin. "We need to narrow down the list."

"How? Prioritize it by job title? Tenure?"

He sipped his coffee. "Most people who steal from companies don't stay long after the job's done. It's a guilt thing. If we look at the people who were fired or who've quit between the town's approval and a week after the theft, we're left with"—Paxton flipped to the last page—"two people before the theft and two more in the week following."

The milk steamer hissed and spittled, bringing Kate's attention to the barista behind the counter for a moment. "Four? That's not bad. Does it say why they left?"

"No." He ran his finger down the list. "Only name, address, hire, and termination dates."

Kate drained the rest of her coffee cup, scanning the morning crowd from their table by the rear exit. The too-long line of caffeine-dependent workaholics snaked clear through the quaint cafe. It wasn't nearly that busy when they'd gotten there earlier. "Then we go down the list, working backward from the theft?"

"My thoughts exactly." Paxton tossed a few dollars on the table and shoved the papers in his bag. "We should go."

Kate's cell phone dinged. She fished it out of her purse to see a text from Maggie. *Senator Gail's blazer is done. Dropping it off today.*

Thank you, Kate texted back with a thumbs-up emoji.

Paxton wrapped his danish in the napkin. "Everything okay?"

"Yes." Kate shoved the phone back in her purse. They exchanged polite smiles, the kind you would provide a passing stranger on the street, not the kind you'd give to someone you'd slept with only hours earlier. Her stomach soured. "Maggie is going to deliver Senator Gail's blazer today. Not that she needs it now."

"We don't know what she'll need if we don't catch this guy."

Kate nodded. She didn't want to think about that.

He motioned to the door. "After you."

After forty-five minutes of sitting in rush-hour traffic to the west valley, Kate and Paxton visited the home of Peter Lyle Mykels, who left the construction company one week after the theft. The house was dark and quiet, but Paxton knocked for the third time anyway.

Kate checked her watch. It was already a little after seven o'clock. If Peter was still in construction, he would be long gone for the day. She stepped off the walkway and through the yard, sticking close to the side of the house.

"Where are you going?" His exasperated whisper was full of reproach.

"Shh." The landscape rock crunched under her shoes as she side-stepped a barrel cactus. She stopped at the first window, cupped her hands around her eyes, and leaned in. "Nothing."

"Is the place empty?" His tone carried a tinge of this-just-got-interesting.

"I don't know. I can't see through the blinds." She pointed to the garage door, heading back toward him. It had a slim pane of glass at the top. It was probably designed to be a decorative accent, but it would double as a confirmation if a vehicle was inside. "Come here. Give me a hand."

"Katie, no." Paxton crossed his arms over his chest. "Nothing illegal."

"Relax. I'm not breaking in." *Just playing Peeping Tom.* She walked past him to the driveway. "And I seem to remember you used to love shoving me in air ducts and down maintenance shafts." She waited for him to warm to the mention of their past experiences working together. "Oh,"—she snapped her fingers—"and a dumbwaiter in Istanbul."

"I didn't love it. You were the only one on the team who would fit."

She jumped up, trying to look into the tinted glass, and pain shot across her back when she landed. "I need a boost to see inside."

Paxton didn't move. His face, stern with disapproval.

The man was exhausting. How had she worked with him for two years in the Army? Kate rubbed her temples to ward off the slight throbbing that had started. "Fine. Pull the car up, and I can climb on the hood."

"That's a government vehicle." He pointed at it like the fact meant something.

She clenched her teeth then looked back, narrowing her eyes at him. "You want to know if he's in there or not?"

He blew out a breath, checking the street over his shoulder. A flash of satisfaction rippled through her as he walked over, but the tightness across his jaw revealed his discomfort. "Quickly." He spun her away from him, wrapped his hands around her waist, and lifted her.

It was the first time he'd touched her since that morning and it already felt too long ago. She put one hand on the garage door and the other on top of his to stabilize herself. His skin under her palm sent a warmth through her, prickling out in every direction. How was it possible that his simple touch could bring such a reaction?

"Anything?" His impatient tone brought her attention back to the garage.

The place was full but organized. "Tool bench. Sawhorses. Lots of boxes. No car."

When he put her down, he pulled his hands away immediately, and she bit her lip to suppress her disappointment. Kate was grateful to not be facing him. She didn't want to know if he was still mad. If he was still hurt. If the flush in her cheeks would out her that she wanted him to touch her again. She stepped away and tugged her sweater in place. "This is a dead-end. We—we should go to the next house on the list." Without a look back, she walked to his SUV.

Ten minutes—and even fewer words spoken—later, they pulled up to the second home on the list. There was a man standing in the driveway next to a red motorcycle. "Shit, is he leaving?"

Paxton had barely put the SUV into park when they were out the doors headed toward him. "Excuse me," Paxton hollered over as they walked up. "Are you, Jason James Marino?"

The man pulled out a helmet and gloves from a black saddlebag trimmed with silver rivets. "Who's asking?" The man glanced over his shoulder.

Paxton pulled his badge off his belt, holding it up for him to see before returning it. "I'm Special Agent Paxton Banks, and this is my associate, Ms. Howard. Are you, Jason James Marino?"

Paxton stopped in front of the bike, and Kate took a few steps to the side. The man turned toward them, his almost-black hair curling over the collar of his leather jacket. His hands were weathered far beyond his years, likely from hard work, but he looked in good shape otherwise.

"JJ Marino. Yea, that's me. What's this about?" His dark eyebrows furrowed.

"We'd like to ask you a few questions about the theft at your former employer, Kraftview Demolitions Company." Paxton's tone was friendly but professional.

"You got a warrant?"

"No sir, just a few questions." He handed JJ a business card.

"I need a lawyer?"

Paxton pulled his notebook out of his pocket. "Not unless you want one."

JJ scoffed and shoved the card in his pocket. "No warrant. No lawyer. No thanks." He swung his leg over the bike, resting into the seat. "The last time the cops were here to *ask* about the KDC theft, they tore my house apart. I told them I ain't stole nothin', but they did it anyway. Broke one of my daughter's cheerleading trophies."

"I'm sorry to hear that." Kate wrapped her arm around her stomach, giving him a friendly smile. "Do you know anything about the theft?"

"Just what I heard."

"Which is what?" Paxton stood at attention.

"Someone broke in and stole a shipment of explosives. Cut a hole in the damn fence and got away. Conner, the foreman, was going apeshit."

Paxton jotted a note. "Any idea who did it?"

"Naw, man. By the time I got there, the cops had the construction yard on lock-down. They were questioning everyone. I didn't even know what was stolen until the police showed up here with a search warrant."

"Why'd they search your house?" Paxton's negotiator tone was comforting, but his expression was stoic.

He shrugged. "Everyone's a suspect, I guess."

Kate paced a few steps to stand in front of him. "Were you involved?" She watched JJ's face carefully for any signs he could be hiding something. He didn't break eye contact. Didn't redden around his nose and cheeks. Didn't raise his eyebrows or drop his jaw. Her gut wasn't giving her any indication she should be wary.

He glared at her, then slid the key into the ignition. "Look, I've got a kid in high school with her sights set on an Ivy League education. I need the money, but I wouldn't be stupid enough to think I could get away with stealing and selling sticks of dynamite. And it wouldn't do my daughter any good if I was locked up or blown up."

He was telling the truth, or he was a damn good liar. Either way, it meant they had a lot more work ahead of them. "Why'd you leave the company?"

"I was fired. Too many mornings I came in late." JJ zipped up his jacket and slipped his helmet over his head. "And if I don't leave now, I'll be fired from this job too."

Paxton didn't move from the front of the bike so Kate stayed put. He looked up from his notes. "Do you know Peter Mykels, John Scott, or Jesus Garcia?"

"Know *of* them, but I don't *know* them." He shoved his hands in his black-leather, fingerless gloves. "Garcia was a decent worker, but his English sucked so we didn't talk much. I didn't bother with Mykels. That cranky, old son of a bitch was always so negative. John Scott was one odd character. I kept my distance from him."

A niggle of apprehension settled in her gut. Kate glanced at Paxton, but he paid her no attention. "What does that mean?" Kate shifted her weight, resting her arm on her hip. "Odd how?"

"He had a loner weirdness about him. He ate his lunch in his car by himself. Always sat by himself in the back of the meetings. He kept his head down, got his job done, and left."

Paxton looked up from his notes. "Do you think any of those guys are capable of something like this?"

JJ shrugged. "A man is capable of doing anything he puts his mind to."

Too true. And if his mind was set on hurting innocent kids, how were they going to stop him? Her stomach hardened and muscles tightened straight out to her fingertips. She opened and closed her fist a few times. They had to find this guy.

"Thank you for your time, Mr. Marino." Paxton nodded and stepped toward Kate, getting out of JJ's way.

He turned the key, and the rumble of the motor vibrated through her. JJ nodded back at them, flipped down the visor on his helmet, and took off down the driveway.

"I'm not getting a mad-bomber vibe from him." Kate looked over her shoulder at Paxton, who was watching the bike glide down the street. "What do you think? Innocent until proven guilty or just innocent?"

Paxton put the notepad back in his pocket and checked his phone. "Innocent for now."

"Who's next on the list?"

"Jesus Garcia is next, but John Scott's address is closer and based on JJ's loner comments, I'd put him higher on the persons of interest list." Paxton started toward the SUV.

Kate followed him and checked her watch again. "Think we can catch him before work?"

"Only one way to find out."

"We could use the lights and sirens." Kate's voice was hopeful.

"No." Paxton shook his head, opening the door for her. "Protocol dictates that's for emergency situations only."

"Paxton, this is an emergency. I have a good feeling about him."

"We have no proof this guy is our terrorist. If he is, and he's there, it could spook him. Sirens and lights can make a dangerous situation worse."

She'd made a living of making dangerous situations worse. This thing with Paxton was proof of that. Kate stood there looking at him until he finally met her gaze, the passion she'd seen this morning replaced with wariness. Wariness about her. About the case. Her gut clamped down tight like a tourniquet, stopping blood flow to her extremities. She needed to prove to him she was trustworthy.

Chapter Sixteen

They pulled up to the home of Johnathan Anthony Scott, with its immaculately kept lawn and colorful flowers in the pots along the walk. In the summer they would not have survived a week, but in the fall the flowers would thrive. Kate followed Paxton to the front door. He knocked and stepped back in line with her.

A middle-aged woman answered. Her curly, red hair was cut above the collar of her black uniform, with a crest Kate couldn't place. "May I help you?"

"Good morning, ma'am, sorry to bother you." Paxton handed her a business card. "I'm Special Agent Paxton Banks, and this is my associate, Ms. Howard. Is John Scott here?"

"No." She rested against the door with her elbow. "Why?"

"Do you know when he'll be back or where we can find him?"

The woman scoffed, a pink flush flooding her freckled cheeks. "I'd like to know that myself." She crossed her arms over her chest. Her body language screamed angry, but the dark circles under her eyes and pained stare told a different story. Worry, maybe?

Kate eyed the thin, gold band on the woman's ring finger and stepped forward. "Are you Mrs. Scott?"

"Yes." She fidgeted with the button on her blouse. "What's this all about?"

"Your home is listed as John's last known address. You don't know where he is living now?" Paxton's tone was friendly.

"No." The woman shook her head, her gaze dropping to her shoes. "He left a few months ago."

Left? Kate's stomach fluttered, and her breath quickened.

"Ma'am, may we come in and ask you a few more questions?" Paxton took a step forward. He must have picked up on the same word Kate had. *Left.*

She checked her watch. "I've got some time before my shift, but not unless you're going to tell me what this is about."

"We're following up with some employees of the construction demolition company where your husband worked."

"Were they robbed again?" She looked from Paxton to Kate and back.

"No." Paxton shook his head. "It's the same one from two months ago. We have additional questions."

"I don't know how much help I'll be, but come on in." She ushered them in. "Like I told them last time, I don't know anything about a robbery, but I know John wasn't involved."

Kate looked around the small living room filled with neutral-colored furniture. Bland on top of boring covered in blah. *Who knew there were so many shades of tan?* The only real color in the room was from the book jackets organized by size, largest to smallest, on each shelf, and a wall covered with meticulously spaced photographs.

Paxton pulled out his notebook. "Mrs. Scott—"

"Cassandra."

Paxton nodded. "Cassandra, how do you know John wasn't involved?"

"He would never do something like that." Cassandra rested her hip against the back of the couch. "It's not in his nature. The police turned our house inside out and didn't find any tools, even though I told them they wouldn't. Besides, what would he do with demolition equipment at home?"

She has no idea what's been taken. A heaviness settled in at the thought.

Paxton jotted a note. "When was the last time you saw John?"

"He hasn't been home in about two months." Cassandra clutched the cross around her neck.

"Did you file a missing person's report with the police?"

"Of course." She touched the cross to her lips. "I also called every hospital, funeral parlor, and police station in the valley."

He could be three sheets to the wind, holed up in a mistress's house, face-first in a ditch somewhere yet to be discovered, or—or maybe he was on the run. Kate pressed her lips together to keep her thoughts from escaping.

"Has any money gone missing from your bank accounts, or have any charges been made on your credit cards that would indicate where he is?"

"Not a one. But…"

Kate and Paxton both stopped and stared at her.

"But I thought I saw him a few weeks ago. Or at least I think it was him. I couldn't get close enough."

Paxton's brows raised a fraction. "What do you mean you think it was him?"

"The guy I saw had a walk with a shuffle, like someone with a bad back. John walked like that on account of his years in construction. By the time I turned around at the next light, I couldn't find him."

"Where were you when you thought you saw him?" Kate looked over at Paxton, but he kept his head down, writing.

"Crossing the street by the pharmacy up here." Cassandra

pointed toward the road.

It's possible he's still in town.

Paxton looked out the window where she pointed. "Does he have any friends or family in the area he could be staying with?"

She shook her head. "We moved here from Texas when he took the job at the construction company almost two years ago. We don't have family in town." Cassandra slid her cross back and forth on the chain. The whine of the metal friction made the hairs on Kate's arms stand up. "When he disappeared, I reached out to anyone we knew. Friends in town. Family back home. No one had seen or heard from him."

Kate crossed the room, taking in the photos displayed. "Is this John?" She pointed to a picture of Cassandra in an emerald green gown and a gentleman dressed in a tuxedo.

"Yes. That's his parents' anniversary party."

Their wedding, a trip somewhere tropical, Cassandra holding a baby, the two of them in ketchup and mustard costumes. So many photos. She obviously cared for the man, or she would have taken the photos down. *If he had up and left me without a word, I would have used them for kindling by now.*

"Who's this?" Kate motioned to a picture of them and a little boy at the Grand Canyon.

"That's Simon, our son."

Paxton walked over to the picture. "Has he had any contact with Simon?"

Cassandra straightened, dropping the crucifix on her chest. "He was killed almost a year ago."

Killed? Kate's heartbeat slowed, draining her emotionally like a leaking wound. *When? How? Why?* Kate pressed her lips together, forcing her questions down with a gulp. Her focus narrowed in on Cassandra's bottom lip. It moved, but no sounds escaped.

"We're sorry for your loss." Paxton dipped his chin. "May I ask what happened?"

Cassandra picked up a picture from the end table and ran her finger over the glass. "He had just turned nine." She took a shaky breath. "John got him a new bike for his birthday, and he was out riding it." She sniffled and put the frame down. "I was getting the cake ready when we—we heard the car tires screech. I called an ambulance when I saw the bike in the road"—her voice cracked—"but it was too late."

Kate put her hand over the ache, building in her chest like she could stop the pain with a little pressure. It was bad enough saying good-bye to a parent, but a child? She couldn't imagine.

"Did they catch the driver?" Paxton pulled a tissue out of his pocket, offering it to Cassandra.

"He stopped." She wiped under her eye and blinked up at the light. "He claimed it was an accident. Never saw Simon, but he was high as a kite when he climbed out of the car."

High?

"High on—marijuana?" Paxton tilted his head, studying her.

Cassandra nodded. "John wasn't the same after. I guess neither of us was, but he wouldn't get help. He was so angry, lost touch with a lot of people, stopped sleeping, became depressed. I—I tried to get him to go to therapy with me, but he refused. Then one day, he didn't come home. I thought maybe he needed space from me, this house, all the pain, but he never turned up."

Paxton scribbled something in his notepad.

People don't vanish. He was planning on leaving and stockpiling cash for his escape, or he was getting help from someone. She looked over at Paxton, his face not giving away any clues to what he was thinking. Kate pointed to a picture of John and Simon in fluorescent orange hunting vests with rifles. "Is that your cabin? Would John go back there?"

"No. They rented it for the weekend."

"Were the guns rented too?" He turned toward Cassandra.

"Those are John's. I made him keep the guns in a locker out of the house." Her tone turned agitated. "I'm not really sure what any of this has to do with a theft at his old work."

If the annoyance in her tone bothered him, Paxton didn't let it show. "We're following up with everyone who was employed at the time of the theft."

"You said that, but I already told you. John's a good man. He would never steal anything." Cassandra checked her watch. "Is there much more? I need to leave soon for work."

Kate pulled her cell phone out. "Would you mind if I take a few photos?"

Cassandra let out a heavy breath. "If you must."

She snapped a few pictures of the family photos on the wall before walking back to Paxton. "Did he take anything with him when he left?"

"His thermos of coffee he took every morning. He kissed me on the head, got in the car for work, and never came home." She glared at Kate. "When I called the company, they said he hadn't been to work. Wherever he went, it wasn't there."

Kate chewed on her bottom lip. He lied and left.

Paxton didn't budge from his spot. "What was he driving?"

She looked from Kate to Paxton and back. "If I tell you, will you leave?"

Kate nodded. Paxton did not.

"He had an old, white Corolla. Mid-two-thousands."

A white car? Hadn't Senator Gail said a silver or white car rammed them?

Paxton pointed to his business card in her hand. "If you hear from John, please let me know. We'd love to speak with him directly."

"Sure." Cassandra dropped it on the foyer table and held the door for them.

"Thank you for your time." Kate followed him out and

walked toward the car. The quiet between them was stretched further than the driveway. "Do you believe her story?"

The muscle in his jaw tensed. "Yes, I think she was telling the truth."

"But?"

"Opportunity. Skill set. Motive." He opened the SUV door for Kate. "John Scott just became our first suspect."

"What do we do now?" Kate climbed in the vehicle. "Watch the house?"

"If he hasn't been back in two months, chances of him coming back now are slim, especially if he's in hiding. Still, I'll have someone canvass the area. You snapped a few pictures?"

"Yes. I'll text them to you." She pulled out her phone while he walked around the car, hitting send on her pictures of pictures.

"We should show them at the pharmacy since she thinks he was headed in that direction. Maybe they've seen him," Paxton said, getting in the vehicle.

Kate nodded.

There were two pharmacies in close proximity to the Scotts' home. Not one employee at the stores recognized John from the photos, but that didn't mean he hadn't been there.

"I'll drop you off at home and head back to the office." Paxton checked his phone. "I need to brief the team on every-thing here. Put out the BOLO on John and his vehicle. Check on the bomb sweep."

Kate's mind meandered. *Where would I go if I were on the run with dynamite in a damaged car?* Somewhere secure, temperature-controlled, easy to get in and out, and away from people.

"Hey, you still with me?"

"Yes." Kate stared out the window. "I'll..." She caught a glimpse of a storage unit facility, craning her neck as Paxton drove past.

"You'll what?"

"Turn around."

"Why?"

"Turn the car around." Kate's voice was louder, more demanding.

"What did you see?" He pulled into a parking lot and out the other side.

"Cassandra said she made him keep his guns in a locker outside of the house, right?"

"Yes."

"Do you think she meant a self-storage unit? A storage locker?" Kate pointed to the sign up ahead of them. "It's down the street from their house, and near a pharmacy where she thought she saw him."

"You think he's living in a storage unit?" Paxton pulled into a parking spot in front of the office. "Katie, where would he even go to the bathroom?"

"Oh, please. The world is your urinal." She shared space with Paxton and the guys for two years in the military. She knew firsthand they didn't need indoor plumbing. "I don't know if he's living there, but it can't be a coincidence. If he has a unit, they could have a current address." Kate shrugged, and a twinge of pain shot through her shoulder. "It's something we should verify, right?"

He put the vehicle in park. "We're here. Let's go ask."

As they walked in, Kate checked out the massive metal gate next to the building, at least nine feet tall and two car-lengths wide.

"Welcome to Valley of the Sun Mini Storage." The lanky young man behind the counter stood to greet them. His straggly brown hair flopped over his brows, and he swept it aside. "Are you in the market for a storage unit?"

"Not exactly." Paxton pulled his badge off his belt, presenting it.

He leaned over the counter to check it out. "FBI?"

"Special Agent Paxton Banks, and this is Ms. Howard."

When he smiled and stood upright, he looked like Shaggy from Scooby-Doo. "Marcus Hessler. Employee of the month."

"Marcus, Ms. Howard and I have a few questions."

"About what?"

"Someone that might be renting a storage unit from you."

Her hands shook when she pulled the phone from her purse. Kate clicked the screen on and turned the picture of John and Cassandra toward Marcus. "Do you recognize this man?"

Say, yes. Say, yes.

"What did he do?"

Paxton shook his head. "He didn't do anything."

"Then why are you looking for him?"

Paxton pointed to the image. "His wife filed a missing person's report."

"That's sad."

"He was last seen in this area. Do you recognize him?" Paxton's voice was more commanding.

"Nah." He scratched his chin. "We have four-hundred eighteen units. That's a lot of people coming and going, but most don't stop in the office. They drive straight through the gate." He pointed out the window overlooking the storage locker area.

Kate put her phone back in her pocket. Four-hundred eighteen possibilities. That would be the worst game of hide-and-seek in history.

"If we gave you his name, could you check your records to be sure?" Paxton motioned toward the computer.

He shook his head. "I'd help, but it's company policy. No warrant. No records."

"Really?" Kate sugar-coated her tone and client-smiled at him. "You can't just look?"

"We take client confidentiality very seriously. Especially with credit cards on file, identity theft is a real concern." He pointed to a four-drawer file cabinet on the far wall. The key dangling out of the lock. *Yeah, really secure.*

"That's understandable." Kate placed her hands on the counter. "But see, *we* don't need to look at the records. We only need to know if he has a unit. *You* could look and give us a simple yes or no."

"Sorry. Company policy." He shrugged. "The job's shit, but I can't pay my rent without it, so I can't afford to lose it."

Come on, dude, give me something. This has got to be the place. It's the only thing that makes sense.

"Do you have the manager or owner's business card?" Paxton pulled one of his out.

"Yup." He traded cards with Paxton.

"If you will let him know I'll be reaching out I'd appreciate it."

"Sure thing." He put Paxton's card in his pocket. "I'll tell him."

"Does your security system record?" Paxton pointed to the black and white screen over the only desk.

"Yup. Twenty-four-seven. Three-sixty-five. Every entrance and exit."

"And how long is the video stored?"

Marcus shrugged.

Kate squinted at the television, straining to make out the pictures from their angle. "Have you seen an older, white Corolla come through here?"

"All kinds of cars and trucks come through here, but I don't pay much attention to the ones who go through the gate. If they have a code, they have a unit. They come and go as they please."

This guy was useless. They would have been better off questioning the cartoon Shaggy. "One last question." Kate rested her hip against the counter. "I don't have a garage at my building. If I wanted to rent a space for a car, do you have anything big enough?"

"Sure." Marcus smiled and handed her a trifold brochure. "Our ground floor, twenty-feet by twenty-feet, temperature-controlled units would be perfect. You just roll the door up and drive right in."

Kate nodded and tapped the brochure on the counter. *Just roll the door up and drive right in.*

"Thank you for your time." Paxton turned to open the door and let her through first.

She forced herself to keep calm, but her insides shook. Kate waited to speak until they climbed in the SUV. "How long will it take to get a warrant to search their records?"

"Based on what?" Paxton started the car but didn't put it in gear.

"Based on John Scott appears to be a worthy suspect. He's been seen in the area."

"It's all circumstantial. We have no evidence he stole the dynamite or has a unit here or at any storage company, for that matter. No judge in their right mind would let us root around files and security footage hoping and praying to find evidence."

"We could stake out the gates in case he shows up."

"No."

"Paxton, you have to trust me. I have a good feeling about this. You heard Marcus; they have units big enough to store a car. Temperature-controlled."

He held up a hand to silence her. "Katie, I'm sorry, there isn't enough evidence."

She pointed inside the gated area. "What if we got a bomb-sniffing dog to take a walk through there and see if he can pick up the scent of the dynamite."

"You *cannot* kidnap a K-9 officer."

"Not kidnap. Borrow. Dogs love to go for a walk."

"Look, I know you want this to pan out. I do too, but until we have more evidence, there is nothing we can do."

Fine. Then more evidence is what we'll get.

Chapter Seventeen

On the way to dropping Kate off at home, Paxton got a call
from the office and had to turn around. He held open the
door of the FBI field office for Kate, then followed her in. The
small, barren lobby always gave her an unwelcome queasi-
ness. Kate looked down at her casual clothes. Not what she
would have worn had she known they were going to stop,
but she wasn't going to wait in the car.

"I'll get you a visitor's pass, and we can head up to brief
the team."

Kate gazed over her shoulder to find him watching her,
and trepidation tingled from her tummy to her toes. She'd
been through the check-in process several times as a linguistics consultant, but this was more than being locked in a room
with a voice recording. It was strange and stressful and stim-
ulating. She'd never been this involved in a case before, but
she enjoyed the challenge. Or maybe it was the company.

"Kate, how are you?" The young man at the check-in desk
stood to greet them. "I don't have you on the list today."

She smiled at the familiar face, calming her stomach. "Hi,
Andrew. I don't have any translations today. Just observing
with Special Agent Banks." Kate handed him her driver's

license, avoiding Paxton's assessing eyes. Now was as good a time as any for him to know she'd worked with the FBI before.

Andrew wrote down her license number on the visitor log, gave it back to her, and slid the paperwork toward Paxton to complete.

"How did Jeremy do on his French final?" Kate leaned on the counter, letting the friendly banter distract her.

"Aced it, thanks to you."

She had several small jobs she worked when she didn't have a personal protection client on the books, dry cleaner, bartender, cater waiter, valet, receptionist, and tutor, to name a few. The tutoring was by far the easiest and most fun. "Your brother worked his butt off. All I did was help him with pronunciations."

Paxton put his identification on the counter, signed the clipboard, and pushed it back toward Andrew. "That should do it."

Andrew matched his credentials to the paperwork and handed it back. "Looks good, Special Agent Banks." He gave Kate a visitor badge. "Hey, come see me when you're ready to check out. I'll try to get my mom to send over her cauliflower casserole recipe for you."

"You got it. Thanks." Kate tapped the desk.

Paxton walked toward the elevator, slipping his badge back on his belt. When Kate came up alongside him, he pushed the up arrow. "When were you going to tell me you've worked with the FBI?"

"You knew I had top-secret clearance." She clipped the guest pass to her sweater. "When were you going to ask?"

His unreadable face opened up to a smile and knowing eyes. The elevator dinged, and he motioned for her to enter.

"Paxton Banks, did you investigate me?" She let a heavy heap of mock-surprise into her voice. Of course, he did. He wouldn't be a very good agent had he not.

He pushed the button for the fifth floor without looking over at her. "I may have done a little digging after SAC Dupree agreed to this—arrangement."

"And?"

"And what?"

She turned toward him. "And what did you find?"

Paxton adjusted the messenger bag on his shoulder to straighten his jacket. The elevator dinged, and the doors opened to a flurry of activity. "We can discuss it later. With that other thing."

The other thing? Oh, yes, the are you "in or out" discussion. Can't wait. Kate followed him into the bullpen. The island of cubicles in the middle of the room with offices flanking on all sides should have made it feel dark, but the low partitions and glass office walls let in all the light. It was a better view than she was used to as her accommodations while transcribing. The soundproof shoe closet she usually visited had fluorescent bulbs and drab gray paint.

"Banks." SAC Dupree's voice boomed across the space, quieting the group. "Tell me you have something."

"We do."

He headed straight for them, stopping a few steps short of flattening Kate. "I'm listening."

Paxton's shoulders inched back. "John Scott. He was an employee of the demolitions company until two days before the theft and hasn't been seen since." He projected his voice to those standing around. "His son was killed by a driver under the influence of marijuana, and we surmise he is taking out his grief on the state senators who voted to approve the legalization of sales. That's why he's targeting their kids. He had knowledge of the dynamite delivery, the skill set to handle it properly, and motive."

Dupree gave him a slow nod, letting the news soak in. "Listen up, people." He cleared his throat, turning toward the staff, and the floor quieted. "Special Agent Banks has a suspect. It's all hands on deck." Dupree side-stepped to let Paxton address the room. "Banks, what do we need to catch this guy?"

Kate watched the rest of the team turn their attention to Paxton. She stood a little taller, proud of her participation in the investigation. For a moment it felt like the old days, working together for the greater good, and they were pretty good at it.

"I need another special agent to run down the other two former employees of the demolition company." Paxton handed Dupree the employment list from his bag. "I want to be positive they had nothing to do with this."

"Done." Dupree shoved the papers toward a woman on his other side. "Carlson, dot the i's and cross the t's." She nodded, and he turned back to Paxton. "What else?"

"Analysts." Paxton pulled the notebook out of his pocket, tearing out a page. "I need everything on Johnathan Anthony Scott. BOLO on him and his vehicle, bank and credit card statements, cell phone records, police report from the son's death, list of friends, relatives, or enemies who could be helping him. We need everything, and we needed it yesterday."

All this time Kate had thought Paxton loved giving orders, but it was more than that. He was a natural-born leader.

He made eye contact with her for a second before focusing back on the team. "If the police report from the theft is correct and crime scene analysis of these incidents are accurate, he's still got enough dynamite for another two bombs."

"We will *not* let that happen." SAC Dupree crossed his arms over his chest.

"When we spoke with the wife, she indicated he wasn't in his right mind. He'd grown depressed and angry. We'll want to bring Psych in on this."

"I'll make a call." Dupree punctuated his agreement with a nod.

Kate clasped her hands so she wouldn't fidget. "And a police presence around his last-known address."

SAC Dupree looked at her like he didn't realize she was standing there. "What's this now?"

Paxton let out a breath. "The wife thought she saw someone who looked like him in the area but wasn't sure. It's a Hail Mary at best, but no stone unturned."

Kate's cell phone rang in her pocket. The sound broke the silence, and a rush of embarrassment heated her face. She pulled it out to see Senator Thomas's name on the screen. She moved to decline the call but stopped with her finger hovering over the button. Panic rippled through her, sending her temperature ticking up. *What if something happened?* "I'm sorry, it's Senator Thomas."

"My office is open." Paxton pointed to a door behind her and fell back into his briefing.

She nodded, swiping the screen. "Senator?" Her voice was quiet until she found Paxton's nameplate and stepped into his space. "Is everything okay?"

"Yes." He sounded better than he had the last time they spoke. Giddy, almost. "I wanted to let you know they are going to bring Robbie out of the medically induced coma tomorrow."

He's going to be okay. Her muscles went to jelly, and she placed her hand on the desk to support herself. Kate ran her fingers over the papers and files stacked perfectly on the corner of the desk. "That's wonderful, sir." She picked up a picture of a teenage Paxton, his wide smile putting his braces on full display, holding a baby girl, no doubt his sister, Claire, with his parents behind him. The family image made her heart ache for her mother. "Best news I've heard all day."

"It's quite a relief."

The midday sun splashed through the windows, gleaming off something on top of the file cabinet. She picked up a bronze hunk of mangled metal about the size of her palm attached to a wooden base. She held it up to read the engraved plate *Stronger every day*. It was the ugliest motivational junk she'd ever seen.

"Kate, are you still there?" Senator Thomas's voice brought her back to reality.

"What? I'm sorry."

"I said do you have a suspect yet?"

Kate turned the piece of junk this way and that. "I'm at the FBI now. We've uncovered a few leads the team is investigating."

"Thank you for doing that. I know it's not part of your job, but"—he sighed—"it means a lot to me that you would follow it through."

"Absolutely, sir. I want to get to the bottom of this."

She heard a noise and spun, almost cutting Paxton with the jagged edge of the metal. He caught her wrist, taking it from her.

"Senator, I have to let you go, but congratulations."

"Thank you. Keep me posted."

"I will, sir. You as well."

Paxton placed the memento back on top of the file cabinet. "Congratulations?"

She nodded, turned the ringer to vibrate so she wouldn't be embarrassed again, and slipped the phone into her purse. "They are waking Robbie up tomorrow."

"That's great."

"Yeah." Kate pointed to the metal scrap. "What is that?"

"A piece of the shrapnel they pulled out of my leg." His voice was nonchalant.

Kate's eyes welled up like he had struck her with the ragged thing, blurring past and present. Memories so vivid flashed before her eyes. Rolling him off of her, checking his wounds, pinned down by gunfire, shrouded by pieces of market tables and plumes of dust and debris. The ringing in her ears so loud the voices of her team didn't register in their comms.

Paxton put his hands on her shoulders, making her jump. "Hey, Katie, come back to me."

Kate gasped and pulled away from his touch, trying to keep what little composure she had left. Anxiety and anger knotted her insides so tight her skin felt stretched. "Wh—why would you keep that?"

"I don't know." He shoved his hands in his pockets. "I was going to toss it after I got out of the hospital, then when I got through rehab, but it had too many memories attached to it. Claire thought it would serve me right as a reminder that what doesn't kill you makes you stronger, so she had it dipped and mounted."

Kate turned toward the windows, willing her hot tears to stay hidden. She blinked, staring across the Deer Valley airport. *Shit.* The only way she could start making up for all the hurt she had caused him was to help him solve this case. But she couldn't do that sitting in an office feeling sorry about her past. "You're busy here." Kate took a step back toward the door. "I can find a ride home. I've got some things I need to follow up on."

Kate climbed the steps to her building, opened her door, and stepped into the silence. A drastic difference from the FBI office. She'd racked her brain the whole taxi ride home how she was going to prove what she knew in her gut. John Scott had to have a unit at the storage company. It was the only thing that made sense. She just needed proof for Paxton to get a warrant. But how was she going to get proof? Legally?

She slid her purse on the island. A bright green sticky note stared back at her from the fruit bowl. *Need animal crackers and*

Cool Ranch Doritos. Kyle was going to bankrupt her. Kate yanked it off an apple, crumpling it.

"Kyle." She looked down at the wadded paper. "If he can hack my computer and break into my house to eat all my snacks, he could easily get the proof we need from the storage company."

She tossed the garbage on the counter and raced down the steps. "Kyle?" She banged on the door. "It's Kate. Open up."

He swung the door wide, his dark, messy hair flopping over his forehead. Kyle pulled a sucker out of his mouth, leaving a blue tint on his lips. "Yeah?"

"The other day you said you were able to put a tracker on the IP Address from the threats and you triangulated something."

"Sure, but it won't do you much good." Kyle's voice lacked its usual enthusiasm. "The computer is offline, and I could only get the tracking down to about a ten-mile radius."

Ten miles? Ugh. Scottsdale alone was eleven miles wide. That was a lot of ground to cover. "Where? Show me?"

"I don't know if that's such a good idea. Paxton didn't seem too happy with me the other day." Kyle shoved the sucker back in his mouth and hung his head. "Besides, if they are using a VPN and a different IP address, the information can be hundreds of miles off."

Hundreds? Shit. "Look, Paxton will get over it. Kyle, please, I need to know what area you found."

"It stretched from Papago Freeway all the way up to Glendale Avenue and a few miles in each direction of Black Canyon Freeway."

The Scotts' home, the pharmacy, the storage unit. All of it fell in that area. But so did thousands of other businesses and residences. It didn't matter. This was it, this was the confirmation she needed. She smiled at Kyle. "What do you know about storage facility security systems?"

He shrugged and slurped on the sucker at the corner of

his mouth. "It depends on what they're storing. They have cameras, motorized gates, sometimes dogs, barbed wire, silent alarms, trip wires, electrified fencing—"

"What would I need to patch into their security cameras?"

"What brand and model is it?"

"Don't know."

"Is it a wired system or wireless?"

"Don't know."

"How many cameras?"

"Don't know."

He let out an annoyed breath. "What *do* you know?"

This is the first day in almost a week without an explosion hurting innocent people. "The cameras cover the entrances and exits. They are always recording. The screen in the office is black and white."

"None of that is useful." Kyle tugged on the hem of his T-shirt, pulling it over his PAC-MAN belt buckle.

Kate swore under her breath. "What would be useful that I can get without tipping off the employees by asking too many questions?"

"Without the model number or the way it's set up to transmit and record, we can't do much of anything from here." Kyle ran his hands through his hair, making it stand up in places. "I'll have to go on-site to connect."

That would work, but would Paxton approve? "Is it legal?"

He shrugged. "Probably not."

"No." Kate shook her head. "You could get caught." *And Paxton would have my head.*

"I could pose as a security salesman, ask all the questions, and get out." His tone picked up enthusiasm.

"No." Kate shook her head again. "You can't be involved in this. It has to be something I can do." She clenched her teeth and released. "And it has to be legal."

"So *you* pose as a security system saleswoman. I'll give you a list of questions to ask."

"That wouldn't work. The guy there has already seen my face. He knows I don't work for a security company."

"Well, aside from setting up your own cameras on public property, there is nothing more you could do."

"That's it." Kate slugged him in the arm. "I'll set up my own cameras." For the first time since she met Kyle, he had proven to be more than just a rock in her boot.

Kyle crossed his arms, rubbing the spot where she hit him. "Do you know how?"

"You point the camera at whatever you're watching and turn it on. Easy."

Kyle scoffed and pulled the lollipop out of his mouth. "Okay, but do you know how to set the cameras to transmit the picture to a recording device like a laptop?"

"No, but you could show me."

"And what about troubleshooting an error if you encounter one?"

"No, but—"

"Don't say I can show you."

"Why?"

"Because there are thousands of factors. I could never teach you everything I know about electronics like you could never teach me everything you know about being a badass." Kyle shoved the lollipop back in his mouth and rested his hands on his hips. "You need to take me with you."

Kate shook her head. "Yeah, I don't think so."

"It'll be an adventure." Kyle clapped his hands. "We could have code names. I'll be Batman, and you could be Robin."

"No." Kate shook her head more vigorously. "Absolutely not."

"Fine. You can be Batman."

"No. *I'll* be going alone, and *you'll* be staying home."

"Lamest. Code names. Ever."

"They're not code names." Kate's voice was louder than expected. She balled up her fists and released them, letting out a cleansing breath. She didn't have time to stand there and argue with a twenty-two-year-old man-child. She had cameras to buy and bad guys to catch. "You aren't going."

"But I'm your backup."

"No, you're not. You're just some guy who breaks into my loft and eats all my groceries."

"Give me three reasons why I can't go?"

She ticked the reasons off on her fingers. "You're not trained to pull off a mission. I don't do backup. It's dangerous."

"You came up with those too fast." Kyle huffed. "Then I'm not going to tell you how to clear a four-a-nine error."

"That's fine." Kate threw her hands in the air. Why did she even bother mentioning it? "I'm pretty smart. I can figure it out on my own."

"How much you know, there's no such thing as a four-a-nine error. I made it up."

Kate turned toward the stairs. "Forget it. I'm sorry I asked. I'll figure something else out."

"Wait." Kyle ran out after her, grabbing her wrist and stopping her on the first step. He released his grip when she glared at him. "What if I stay in the car? We could use walkie-talkies. I have all the equipment anyway. Pleeeease. I really, really, really want to go."

Her conscience teeter-tottered like a lopsided Jenga tower. Paxton needed that evidence, and she needed to get it for him. She would set up a few cameras and see if they could catch anything suspicious. It was all perfectly, kind of, legal. Once they had it, Paxton could get his warrant and stop this guy before he hurt someone else. Kyle would stay in the car where it was safe. No harm in that. Right?

"What do you say, partner?" Kyle put his hand out. "Do we have a deal?"

"We're not partners." Kate turned toward him, pushing his hand away. "But we have a deal under one condition."

"Anything." Kyle's eyes beamed with excitement.

"You have to promise you won't ever tell Paxton about this."

"What if he asks me?"

"Lie. You were home all night playing video games. This conversation never happened. And you know nothing about storage units."

"But he's the FBI. I'd be lying to a federal agent."

He picked a bad time for honor and integrity. Kate rested her hand on the railing. "Everything we're doing is legal. You either want to go or you don't."

Kyle made a motion with his hand like he was zipping his lips and flung an imaginary key over his shoulder.

She rolled her eyes. It was a bad-fucking-idea to let him come along. She knew it in the pit of her stomach, but what choice did she have? It was the only way they were going to get what they needed, and he could navigate any issues with the cameras far quicker than she could. *Get in. Get the cameras up. Get out.*

Kate let out an audible breath. "Make sure the walkie-talkies and cameras are charged. We leave at midnight."

"You won't regret this, Robin."

Kate cringed, turned, and walked up the stairs. "I already do." *Batman.*

Chapter Eighteen

Kate hadn't said more than two words since Kyle got in her SUV dressed like a nerdy cat burglar with a backpack full of electronics. He hadn't stopped talking. Whether it was nerves or the massive amounts of her stolen snacks coursing through his veins, he was more anxious than normal. Or was this normal? She'd only spent short bursts of time with him in the building until now.

Kate turned off the exit ramp, stopping at the light before the storage facility. "Why don't we practice being quiet since we won't be able to talk when we're there?"

"Quiet. Sure. I can be quiet." Kyle unzipped his backpack, pulled out a package of pretzels, and proceeded to crunch his way through the bag.

Kate held back a groan. He was basically an okay kid, but silence was not his strong suit. She checked her watch. Almost twelve-fifteen. In another thirty minutes, she'd be on her way home to monitor their cameras so Paxton could get his warrant.

They hadn't stopped John Scott, only slowed him down. Even if he wasn't living there, he could be storing his car or the dynamite. She put her hand on her stomach to calm the unease that had been there for days. They needed to stop this domestic terror nightmare.

She turned off the lights as she crept closer to the storage place, angling the car across the street where their cameras wouldn't capture her license.

Kyle pulled a camcorder out of his bookbag. "There are four cameras already set up to connect to the laptop. As soon as you turn it on, I should see what you are seeing." He put it back in and zipped it closed. "They only have a ninety-six-hour battery, so if you don't get what you need in the next four days, you'll have to replace it."

Kate nodded, taking the bag from him. "I don't know if we have that long."

"What are we looking for?"

Kate hesitated answering him. She reached into the back seat, removing Ziggy out of her purse. She secured him in the holster at her hip and covered him with her hoodie.

"You can trust me."

She couldn't share details of the case. "Anything out of the ordinary. I'll know it when I see it."

"If you tell me what we're looking for I can write an algorithm to alert us when whatever or whoever gets captured. Otherwise, you're stuck watching days of footage to catch it on your own."

That would be fine, but they didn't have days. They needed the evidence now. She rubbed her palms on her dark jeans. "A white Toyota Corolla. Older model."

"That should be easy enough. Not many of those rolling around town." He pulled his laptop off the floorboard, flipped up the screen, and started typing. "License number?"

Paxton probably knew that by now from filing the BOLO, but asking would tip him off. "Unknown."

"Arizona license plate?"

"Probably—or Texas." She slipped her arm through the backpack, making sure it didn't catch on her bandage.

"Are you sure you're up for this?" He pointed to her shoulder. "You were in rough shape a couple of days ago."

"Don't worry about me. I've been in worse situations than this." Kate leaned forward and slipped her other arm in the strap. "Just stay in the car."

Kyle nodded and handed her a walkie-talkie.

She got out of her SUV, clipped the comm to her jeans, climbed on the hood, up to the roof, and pulled out one of the cameras and a bungee cord. High-tech she was not, but it would get the job done. Maneuvering closer to the palm tree, Kate wrapped the bungee around, secured the ends, and shoved the camcorder through. She pressed the power button and the little red light glowed.

"Robin, we have picture." Kyle's voice blasted through the walkie-talkie at her hip.

She jumped, making her lose her balance and crack her hurt shoulder into the tree trunk. "Shit."

"A little to the right. Over." Kyle directed her from the video feed.

She turned the volume down, then did as he ordered.

"Right there." Kyle's chomping came through loud and clear. "One down, three to go. Batman out."

Kate turned the volume down more. He was enjoying this too much. She slid down on her butt, hopped off the hood, and walked behind the other cars on the street. Climbing on top of a box truck at the back gate, she followed the same procedure.

"Down a little bit. Over."

Kate tipped the camera.

"Coming through all clear, Robin. Over."

The easy ones were done. The other two were going to be a problem. Kate climbed down, debating her options. There were no cars parked on that side of the street she could climb on, and even if she could, she stared up at the storage company camera, which would provide a perfect view of her.

No, she'd have to go through their parking lot and get behind the cameras.

She pulled the walkie-talkie off her hip. "I'm headed inside the gate to catch the other angles."

"I thought you said they had to be on public property?"

"They do, but I'm not a spider monkey. I can't shimmy far enough up a palm tree to get the angle we need without getting caught. If I go through the parking lot and climb on the roof of the building, then I can attach them to the palm trees along the street. I could aim them to catch cars leaving and cars on the street." She let the button go, turned the volume down again, and clipped it back on her jeans.

Kate secured the backpack and adjusted Ziggy holstered at her hip. She crossed the street, headed for the main entrance. Once there, she stared up at the nine-foot-tall fence she'd examined earlier in the day. Hugging the building, she slipped into the shadow of the awning, out of their camera's view. She couldn't squeeze through the rails, so she'd have to go up and over.

Kate stepped on the bottom rung, wrapped her fingers around the bars, and pulled herself up. The stitches at her shoulder tugged, throbbing against the taut skin. She wrapped her sneakers on either side and pushed up. It was like climbing the rope in basic, only the rope had more grip and she hadn't had seven stitches in her shoulder then.

She slid her good arm up, pulling herself and pushing with her legs when a noise stopped her. Her heart pounded in her chest like a platoon of boots. Kate slid down a few inches, looking around. She'd requested a police presence in the area, but she didn't want to get caught by one.

"Psst." Kyle stood under the camera on the street-side of the gate. "Psssst."

Her chest heaved. "You almost gave me a heart attack," she whisper-hollered. Kate dropped down to put her feet on the rail. "What are you doing out of the car?"

"You looked like you needed help."

"What I *need* is for you to stay in the car."

"I tried the walkie-talkie, but you didn't answer."

Kate twisted the knob. "I turned the volume back up. Now. Go back to the car."

"Hurry up. I'm bored and out of snacks."

Hurry up? Kate stepped down on the asphalt to face him. "If you keep interrupting me, it will take even longer."

"If I open the gate, would that help?"

"You can do that?"

Kyle gave her a smart-ass, of-course-I-can smirk.

She looked up at the fence then back at Kyle. Her shoulder was still throbbing from the palm tree and her first attempt at scaling the gate. The sooner they could place the other two cameras, the sooner they could get out of there. She checked her watch. Twelve-forty a.m. *Get in. Get the cameras up. Get out.* "Okay, but then you go right back to the car."

He headed for the keypad, staying on the backside of the camera. Kyle popped the back panel off, attached a cord from his phone, and started typing.

Kate looked around, checking the area. "Are you sure you know what you're doing?"

The gate buzzed and started sliding open. "Voila." Kyle held his arms out, Vanna White-style.

"Kyle, you are scary good."

"I know." He shoved the phone in his pocket. "But it's nice to hear once in a while."

"Now, close the panel up and go back to the car." Kate hugged the wall and headed for the other side of the parking lot. The shoulder strap of her bag got caught on the sales office doorknob. When she pulled, it clicked open. She stood still, listening. No alarm. She peeked through the window at the security panel. No lights. *Kyle must have shut down the whole system, not just unlocked the gate.*

Unhooking the bag, she caught a glimpse of the file cabinet. The one Marcus said they kept files in. The one that could prove what she knew in her gut. Pushing the door open wide enough with the tip of her shoe, she slid in. She let her eyes adjust to the dark space, illuminated only by the snow-filled screen of the non-working security feeds on the other side of the office. Kate pulled a penlight out of her pocket and headed for the file cabinet.

She crouched down and yanked the drawer labeled *S-Z*. Locked. The sound of metal jingling stopped her. *They couldn't be stupid enough to keep the keys here.* Kate felt around the back of the cabinet until she wrapped her fingers around a keyring. "Bingo." She pulled them out, jammed a key into the lock, and turned until it disengaged.

Finger on the button, she popped open the bottom drawer. Rummaging through file names, she looked for Scott, John. *Nothing.* "Shit." She went back a few more files in case they were filed incorrectly. *Setter, Shielder, Simon.* She put her hand on the drawer to close it and stopped. *Did that say Simon, Scott?* John's Scott's son was named Simon.

Kate pulled the manila file out. *Client name Scott Simon. Unit three-twenty-six. Size twenty feet by twenty feet.* "That's big. Big enough to hide a car." She continued reading down the agreement. *Temperature-controlled. Ground level.* "It would be cool and easy to move the dynamite." *Payment type, cash.* "That's got to be him. That's got to be John." Kate reached into her pocket to pull out her phone but realized she had left it in her purse.

Bang.

The sound cracked through the air, and her heart leaped into her throat, pounding out nine-one-one. It could only be one thing.

Not the gate shutting. Not the door slamming. Not the backfire of a car.

Gunfire.

"Fuck." Kate dropped the file.

Scrambled to her feet.

Pulled Ziggy from the holster.

She looked both ways out of the office. The path was clear to the still-open gate.

She took off running. Head down. Staying in the shadows. The backpack and camera equipment inside slammed against her sore, scratched back.

She ran until she reached her SUV, yanking the driver's door.

No Kyle.

She jerked the back door open and stared into the emptiness. "Fuck." She gulped down breaths.

She spun on her heel, facing the building, searching for movement.

Nothing.

She threw the backpack on top of her purse and pulled the walkie-talkie off her hip. "Kyle?" she whispered. "Kyle. Answer me."

Nothing.

Silence was not normal for Kyle. Her stomach dropped like a drone airstrike, the weight making her knees weak. Something was wrong. Very, very wrong. A nauseous rush of regret hit her.

A car started in the distance, echoing off the building.

Kate sprinted back toward the main entrance, through the gate, and caught the tail lights of a light-colored sedan exiting the back of the facility.

"Shit." Kate holstered Ziggy and took off up the aisle of storage units after the car. She pushed her muscles as hard as she could, but not fast enough to catch up. Had the back gate been closed, it would have slowed them down, but she was unable to make out the license plate before it turned up the street. She doubled over, placing her hands on her knees, catching her breath.

A siren wailed in the distance, sending her adrenaline into

overdrive, the hormone feeding her muscles and anxiety. She ran to the end of the units, looking around. She needed to find Kyle and get the hell out of there.

"Kyle!" she screamed at the top of her lungs. Her voice bounced off the storage units, unleashing a rush of panicked heart palpitations.

She ran to the end of the next aisle, the one the car came out. Kate blinked into the darkness, trying to focus her eyes on anything out of the ordinary. She advanced down the row of storage lockers. When she noticed a large shadow on the ground, her feet fused to the pavement. Her veins turned to ice, and a cold sweat racked her body, making her shake uncontrollably. She blinked rapidly, trying to make out the shape. Kate reached for the penlight, but she must have left it or lost it along the way. "K—Kyle?"

The lump groaned, and Kate flinched.

Kate knew he was in trouble by the way he lay limp. She forced her stiff legs forward, falling to her knees on the asphalt beside him. Her heart and her conscience hitched. The breath left her chest like someone had landed a hurricane kick to her gut. She gasped for air.

"Please, Kyle." Kate placed two trembling fingers at the base of his neck. His thready pulse allowed hers to beat again. She patted his shoulders, arms, chest, looking for some kind of reaction. "Kyle, we have to get out of here." Her voice was shrill. She stopped when she reached a wet pant leg. It didn't smell like he pissed himself. It could only be blood.

"Fuck." She pulled her hand away, the movements jerky and awkward. Her stomach was harder than armor-forged plates, the pressure in her abdomen and chest unbearable.

The sound of sirens got closer, and Kate prayed they were headed directly toward her. She couldn't see a thing. There was no way she could move him without knowing how badly he was injured.

"I told you to wait in the car." She felt around his thigh for a rip in the fabric and gagged when she reached wet flesh. She tore off her hoodie. "I told you I didn't need any help." She shoved the sweatshirt under his leg and wrapped it around his thigh, tying the arms tight in a knot over the exposed flesh.

She pressed down with both hands and Kyle whimpered. Whimpering was bad, but it meant he was alive.

"I told you—" A tear slid down her cheek. She wiped her face on the shoulder of her T-shirt. "I told you it wasn't safe."

Red and blue flashing lights came up from behind her, the headlights illuminating Kyle's pale skin. The blood on the pavement. A lot of blood. The result of her life's bad choices. "I should have stuck to the plan. If I didn't go into the office." Kate's voice cracked. "This is all my fault." An image of Paxton flashed through her mind, the way she held pressure on his leg wounds in the Humvee racing toward base, and it was gone. *I can't do this again.*

"Help!" Kate screamed when she heard the cruiser's door open. "Please. He's been shot," she pleaded through sobs.

Kate heard the muffled police radio behind her.

"I'm sorry." Kate pushed against his leg harder, hoping to stop the bleeding. "I'm so sorry."

"Show me your hands." A male voice behind her sounded.

"Hurry. Please." Kate squinted over her bad shoulder at the blinding headlights. "He's lost a lot of blood." She blinked against the spots in her eyes. "He needs an ambulance."

The steps behind her were slow and steady. "Ma'am, I need to see your hands."

"If I move this kid bleeds to death." Her tone was sharp. "Get an ambulance."

"An ambulance is on the way." He was closer, almost directly behind her.

Kate looked down. "You hear that?" Her voice was softer.

"The ambulance is on the way. Hang in there. It's going to be okay."

The police officer came around the other side of Kyle, facing her. He met Kate's gaze, then glanced down to the gun on her hip, leveling his gun at her. "Step away, and put your hands on your head."

"Can't do that." Kate shook her head. "I didn't shoot him." She looked down at her bloody hands and back up at the police officer, tears running down her cheeks. "I was on the other side of the place when I heard the shot. I rushed over to help."

"If you didn't shoot him, who did?"

"I—I don't know," Kate sobbed. She lifted her right hand up where the officer could see it. "I'm going to take the holster off my hip and slide it over to you."

He had his weapon trained on her chest. "Nice and slow."

"Don't shoot. The safety is on." She pulled Ziggy in the holster off her belt, placing it on the ground. Kate swung her leg out, kicking him away from her. "My name is Kate Howard. I'm a personal protection agent. That's my gun, but it hasn't been fired."

She put her hand back on Kyle's leg with the other one increasing the pressure. "This is Kyle Moss. He's my neighbor. I forced him to come with me. He had nothing to do with this."

"Ma'am put your hands behind your head. I won't tell you again."

"You can arrest me when the EMT gets here to take over." Her tone was not one to be messed with. She glared at him, daring him to be stupid. "I am unarmed. I'll cooperate with anything you want me to do, but *not* until Kyle gets help."

The officer stepped forward, kicking Ziggy farther away.

This was a code red fuck-up of epic proportions. Kate's chest constricted like a zip tie pulled tight, cutting off blood flow, oxygen, and rational thought. She never wanted to feel like this again.

Again.

Kate looked down at Kyle. He always looked young, but now, he looked more like a kid than ever. She desperately wanted him to say some stupid, overly-excited, little-brother-like thing. "You need to hang in there, okay? Hang in there. Help's coming."

He didn't murmur. Didn't moan. Didn't move.

Chapter Nineteen

Kate sat on the bench in holding cell A at the Phoenix Police Department. Concrete floors, metal benches, and iron bars. Luxury it wasn't, but it was what she deserved. After three hours of giving her statement and getting processed through booking, she had nothing better to do than reflect on her poor life choices. And there were more than enough to choose from.

Waiving her right to an attorney, she took the blame for everything but shooting Kyle. Although she hadn't shot him herself, it was still her fault. He shouldn't have been there in the first place. Her stomach churned like a Humvee doing donuts in the desert. A gritty, raw mess of a situation, stirring up a cloud of regret.

Kate picked at the threads of her torn jeans, dried blood having hardened the fabric from her knees to her ankles. Kyle's blood. She put her feet up on the bench, tucked her injured arm around her, and rested her head on it. She knew better than to close her eyes. The only image in her head was Kyle. Limp, pale, blood pooling under his thigh. It was a different picture than Paxton bleeding, but the reckless-disregard-for-human-life feeling was the same.

All of it her fault. That was something she could never forgive herself for.

"God, please let him be okay. I swear if you get him through this I won't complain about him eating my snacks ever again."

A door squealed and heavy footsteps came toward her. She gulped against the cannonball in her throat when Paxton came into view. Her chest squeezed, poking at the pain in her heart. He was a sight for sore eyes, but the hard set of his jaw and his intense stare relayed his disappointment and anger in her.

Kate felt like she was on the wrong side of a claymore mine, waiting for it to explode. She pushed her sore muscles to sit up straight, not brave enough to talk first. The quiet—so dense, so disturbing—between them triggered a sudden onset of nausea.

"What were you thinking?" His tone was one-hundred-percent Captain Paxton Banks, like the first day she met him with zero room for pleasantries. "You almost got Kyle killed, and you could have cost me this whole case."

She was suddenly grateful for the bars separating them.

Kate knew this would cross his desk, but she thought she'd have more time to formulate her explanation. But what was her explanation, other than recklessness? "I declined my one phone call." She forced her shoulders back. "What are you even doing here?"

"A shooting at a facility on the FBI's radar sends up red flags."

His black suit and crisp, white shirt looked fresh, but she took in the puffiness under his eyes. She couldn't tell if he was exhausted from not sleeping, from being woken up at this ungodly time, or being worried about Kyle and his case.

"Breaking and entering. Property damage. Identity theft. Resisting arrest." The severity of his tone was making the charges sound even worse. "And SAC Dupree is adding impeding an investigation to the list." Paxton's jaw muscles were pulled so hard the pressure could have formed diamonds.

There was absolutely nothing she could say that would make any of this better.

"Kyle is in surgery for a gunshot wound they suspect you for. They're testing your gun. Even if you didn't shoot him, if he doesn't make it, they will add felony murder to the charges." He paced a few steps in front of the cell. "What the fuck were you thinking, dragging him into this?"

Kate flinched at his use of the F-word. Making excuses for her actions would get them nowhere, but perhaps what she learned would help in the investigation.

Kate took a deep breath. "Unit three-twenty-six is rented by a Scott Simon. It's the reverse of Simon Scott, John Scott's son. It's temperature-controlled to not damage the dynamite, at ground level, and big enough to live in or park a car where no one can see it. And it's being paid in cash six months at a time."

"Are you kidding me?" Paxton's gaze narrowed. "I can't use illegally obtained information in an investigation."

She loved and hated his affinity for rule-following, but the black-and-white, Boy Scout-ness was getting old. This wasn't the time to ignore pertinent information. "You're willing to overlook hard facts that could easily solve this case, just to keep your nose clean?"

Paxton crossed his arms over his chest. "Right and wrong isn't a suggestion. It's the law."

The tightness in her chest crept up her throat, threatening to cut off her air supply. It didn't matter that she did it for the right reasons—she was wrong. She was never going to live up to Paxton's expectations. Kate swallowed hard against the agonizing awareness. "There are camcorders on the palm trees covering the two main gates." Kate wrapped her arms around her middle. "They are on public property.

The one at the back of the storage facility should have caught the person leaving who shot Kyle. They were both feeding to the laptop in my car towed to impound." She rested back against the block wall. "Perfectly legal. No warrant necessary."

"That's *all* you have to say for yourself?" He looked at her like she was exactly where she deserved to be. She was a danger to herself and everyone around her. An animal behind bars.

He was right.

"Everything else is in the police report and my written confession, Special Agent Banks." She placed hard emphasis on his name. "You're welcome to read them." She closed her eyes and put her head back, but didn't hear any movement. Kate resisted the urge to open them to check.

"I never should have allowed you in our unit. I should have stood my ground then, and I should have challenged SAC Dupree when he allowed you to be involved in this case."

Kate sat up, pressing her hand to her breastbone. Her pulse was weak. Her pride weaker. "So what?" Her tone was strangled. "You—you wish you never knew me? Is that it?"

"It's my fault you are what you've become." He pointed to her blood-soaked jeans. "I turned you into this."

"Who or what I am has *nothing* to do with you."

"I'm not going to stand by and watch you destroy your life and everyone's around you."

"So go," Kate hollered and pointed in the direction he entered. "There's the door. No one's stopping you."

"This was a mistake. You. Me. Working together. All of it." He shoved his hands in his pockets and took a deep breath. Kate watched as he struggled to keep the expression on his face neutral, but she caught the downturn of his lips and furrow of his brow. "I'm out."

I'm out?

His words hit her like a dirty bomb, shattering her hopes and shooting shards of shrapnel into her heart.

I'm out.

The words dug in deep with their ragged edges, destroying everything in their path with no chance of survival.

I'm out!

If the words were meant to maim and destroy her, mission accomplished. Kate dropped her chin a fraction and pulled her elbows into her sides. All those years wondering what if, and it was over before it even started.

Kate picked a spot on the bars below his chin to focus on. "Good. That makes two of us." She squeezed her arms into her stomach, forcing the words out. Her voice was not as steady as she'd have liked. Tears pricked the corners of her eyes. She rested her head back against the block wall so he couldn't see how his words hurt her. She was not going to fall apart in front of Paxton. She couldn't. "Please leave me alone."

After a few moments, his footsteps led away and the door slammed. Kate held her breath until she was lightheaded and weak, but she couldn't stop the tears from coming. Pent-up air exploded out of her with it, a tremble that seemed to dissolve her bones. Her body buckled in on itself, and she sobbed until her throat hurt. *Every time they worked together. Every time they rescued each other. Every look. Every touch. Last night.*

Every. Single. Moment.

A mistake.

"Howard?" A man's voice startled Kate awake.

She forced her eyes open and put her feet on the floor to keep from falling off the holding cell bench. Pins and needles raced up her legs, and she winced. "Yes." Her throat was dry and raspy from crying and lack of sleep. Kate grabbed the sleeve of her T-shirt to wipe up the smeared mascara she surely had under her eyes. She checked the clock on the far wall—just after seven a.m.

"You made bail." The officer jammed a key into the lock, and the sound of the door sliding open was like angels singing.

"I didn't call anyone." Kate stretched her legs out in front of her. The movement sluggish and sore.

He shrugged. "Someone did."

"Are you sure?" Kate looked around, but she was the only one in the holding area.

"You're Katherine Howard?"

"Yes."

"Then I'm sure."

Maggie had no way of knowing where she was, she and Cody didn't have that kind of relationship, not that they were speaking, and Kyle would still be in the hospital. The thought of Kyle on the ground bleeding made her heart ache again. She recalled Paxton's disappointed look when he'd stood where the officer was. He wouldn't have posted bail. He made it perfectly clear that he was out.

Kate scrubbed her hands over her face like she could wipe it all from her memory.

The officer stood at the open cell. "You coming or not? I don't have all day."

"Yes." Kate nodded. "Yes, sir." She stood and walked toward him, her back and legs stiff and tingly from the metal bench, following him down the hall and out the door.

She collected her belongings from the clerk and walked out the door they brought her in. This time without handcuffs.

Maggie stood to greet her, hands on hips, her hair flowing over the shoulder of her bubblegum-pink sweatsuit. Even at this time of day she was put together. An unexpected release of tension escaped Kate's shoulders, and her eyes welled up. The one person in her life she could always count on, who was always there for her. She was grateful to see Maggie, but a shot of disappointment hit her that it wasn't Paxton.

But he was out. Out of her work, out of her heart, out of her life.

"Do I need to keep mama away from the news today?" Maggie's tone was dry and tired.

Kate shook her head, and a tear tumbled over her lashes. She'd gotten an innocent kid shot, and for the second time in her life she'd lost Paxton. This time for good.

"You look like hell." Her tone softened, pointing to Kate's ripped, bloody jeans. "Are you okay?"

She let out a heavy sigh and the tension snaked its way back into her shoulders, weighing her down. She wasn't okay, but Kate nodded anyway. "It's not mine."

Maggie opened her mouth, but Kate put her hand up to stop her. She just wanted to go home, get out of these clothes, and sleep. "I'll pay you back."

"I know you will. I'm not worried about it. I'm worried about you." Maggie shrugged. "When were you going to call me?"

"Sometime this morning."

"So you voluntarily spent a night in jail?"

"It's not really voluntary when they slap cuffs on you and shove you in the back of a cruiser."

Maggie looked around. "Those are some serious charges."

"I know." Kate rubbed at her stiff neck, but it did nothing to reduce the tension. "Look. I'm exhausted. I stink. I've got someone else's blood caked under my fingernails. Could we do this later?"

"Yeah, let's go. This place gives me the creeps anyway."

Kate took a step forward. "Wait, how did you know I was here?"

"Paxton called."

"I'm sorry, Maggs."

"He wouldn't have had to call if you'd done it yourself." Her tone was matter-of-fact.

"It was late. I was going to call you after I knew you were up."

Maggie took the clear plastic bag of belongings from her. "He's worried about you."

I'm out. His words were stuck on replay like an old, broken cassette. The destruction of the bomb he dropped on her was still fresh. Kate headed for the door but stopped. "He didn't say that."

"Don't be silly." Maggie scoffed. "He's more bullheaded than you are, but he wouldn't have called if he wasn't."

"It's the Boy Scout in him. He can't help himself. Trust me. He doesn't care if I live or die."

"Paxton is head over heels for you. A blind, deaf, mute person could figure that out."

"Stop." Kate spun back toward Maggie and put her hand up. An avalanche of anger saturated her tone. "We're going to walk out of these doors, and I don't *ever* want to hear his name again."

"Look at me." Maggie reached out to take her hands. "You spent the first part of your life not knowing Paxton existed. Then he came into your world and it hasn't been the same since." Maggie squeezed her hand. "You need to choose if you want to spend the rest of your life wondering what could have been or take a risk and see where it leads you."

Kate pulled her hands back. "I don't have to wonder. He's *done* with me. He's *out.* His words. And I'm done with this conversation."

"Nu-uh, sister-friend." Maggie waved her finger in Kate's face, her tone matching in pissyness. "You're not a quitter. You're Kate frickin' Howard. You jump in front of bullets, you run toward the chaos, you spend your life protecting everyone else. Now you need to stand and fight for you."

"Maggie, there's nothing to fight for." Her voice was louder than she expected. "I just want to go back to my normal life."

"You're my best friend, and I say this with love. You're being a pussy."

"You know what?" Kate grabbed her bag out of Maggie's hand. "Maybe I don't want to fix it. Maybe I like my life the way it is. I didn't have closure before. Now I do. Maybe I want to finally move on."

"Fine." She brushed her hair off her shoulder, crossing her arms over her chest. "I'll drop you off at home. We can talk about this later."

"Don't bother." Kate turned the bag to check her watch through the plastic. "I'll get a ride to impound and get my car when they open." She flung the door open and walked out.

Two hours and two-hundred-fifty bucks later, Kate climbed the steps of her building. She was exhausted and filthy and wanted to sleep until her court appearance. She opened her door and threw her keys and purse on the counter. Her cell phone was completely dead, a fun little fact she didn't discover until after she left the jail, so she put it on the docking station.

Her mother would have been appalled at the way she had treated Maggie, and with a dead phone, she couldn't even send an apology text for being the world's worst best friend. None of this was her fault, but Kate had let the festering sore in her heart ooze all over her. Kate wanted everything to return to normal. Uncomplicated, uninterrupted, unattached.

She could move. Change her name. Cut her hair. But even a lobotomy couldn't make her forget Paxton Banks. She'd been trying since the moment they locked eyes halfway around the world over a decade ago. Her heart wouldn't allow it.

Kate walked into the bathroom to clean up and found a suit in a clear, plastic dry cleaner bag hanging from her closet. The steel gray one Paxton had tried on at Maggie's. A sticky note attached to the hanger. She pulled it off, reading Maggie's handwriting. *This would make a good apology gift.*

"She really can't help herself." Tossing the note in the trash, Kate stared at her reflection in the mirror. Puffy eyes. Dark circles. Blotchy skin. It was so Maggie to try to fix things. But some things couldn't be fixed. She was broken beyond repair.

Kate washed up and tossed her blood-stained and torn clothes in the trash. She donned a fresh T-shirt and jeans, with a flannel shirt for warmth. Her cell phone buzzed that she had messages, and Kate ran over to her nightstand, pressing the voice mail button.

You have two new voice messages. First message left at twelve-oh-two a.m. "Katie"—Paxton's voice came through the speaker. He sounded far happier than he was when she had seen him at the jail. "Sorry it's late. We found something. I'm on my way to meet Judge McCallister to get a warrant. Call me back."

"Warrant? Twelve-oh-two a.m.?" Her stomach hardened like body armor plates. She was still with Kyle on the way to the storage center at that time. "No. No. No." Why was her phone on vibrate? Then she recalled the call from Senator Thomas at the FBI and why. If she had just turned the ringer back on, she never would have been in this position.

Second message left at one-forty-seven a.m. "Katie. You didn't call me back, and now your calls are going straight to voice mail. I'm a little worried. Would you call me when you get this?"

Kate went to delete the messages, her finger hovering over the button. No good would come from replaying them, from hearing his voice. He certainly didn't want her to call him now. He was clear about that. She blew out a deep breath and pressed the delete button.

Kate clicked her message app to text Maggie and realized there was a new message from Paxton at twelve-thirty-eight a.m. *Got the warrant. Call me.* The words made her dizzy and nauseous.

She paced around her studio apartment, settling at the island, the silence threatening to unravel her sanity. A week ago, her home was her sanctuary. A space she could relax, revive her soul, escape the world around her. She used to love the quiet of being alone. Now, it was deafening and depressing.

Paxton's words replaced the tick-tock of her clock. *I'm out. I'm out. I'm out.*

Kate picked up the crinkled note on the countertop. *Need animal crackers and Doritos.* Kyle's sloppy penmanship brought tears to her eyes. She covered her face with her hands, hoping to keep the sob stuck in her throat from escaping.

Kate shoved the note, phone, and her keys in her pocket, slung her purse over her shoulder, grabbed the suit off the door, and headed for the car. She needed to put everything back to the way it was. Before Kyle and Paxton invaded her life.

Chapter Twenty

Kate stood in front of the Phoenix FBI Field Office bracing herself to withstand whatever clusterfuck she was about to face. She clutched her purse and the suit close to her chest. "Get in there. Drop off the suit. Get out." She swallowed hard, looking up at the fifth-floor windows, which reflected the mid-day sun. Hopefully, they didn't have orders from SAC Dupree to shoot her on sight. Or from Paxton, for that matter. She eyed the Kevlar suit Maggie altered for Paxton, then tugged at the hem of her flannel shirt. She should have changed into her own bulletproof clothes.

Her insides were cold and quivering, tingling all the way out to her fingers. Kate took a deep breath, put her shoulders back, and marched into the lobby. Her head held high, she walked up to the desk with the dry cleaning bag slung over her arm. *Get in. Drop off. Get out.*

"Hi." She greeted the gentleman at the desk with her best client-smile. "I need to leave this with you for Special Agent Paxton Banks. His name's on the tag." Kate laid it across the desk. "Thanks."

He stood, smiling down at her. "I can't accept deliveries, but I can call his office."

"No need." Kate's voice hid a hint of panic. She waved her hand. "It's just dry cleaning. I don't want to bother him. He's probably not even here anyway. I need to leave this and get going."

"I saw him this morning." The man picked up the phone before she had time to continue her protest. "Special Agent Banks, you have a delivery at the front desk." He nodded, tipping the alterations ticket in his direction. "Mr. Chen's Dry Cleaning." He locked eyes with Kate. "Yes, sir." He hung up the receiver. "He'll be right down."

Kate nodded her acknowledgment, and mixed feelings surged through her. Paxton obviously knew it was her the way the agent looked at her, and yet he agreed to come down. Why? Her stomach was harder than a cement barrier. What if they were going to hold her for some charges? What if Kyle didn't make it? When she called the hospital earlier to check on him, they refused to release any information because of the investigation. *Fuck.* A burst of heat exploded out of her chest. *This was a mistake.* She eyed the entry door, turning most of the way to face her car, which was parked across the street. If she made a run for it, she could get out of there before—

The elevator dinged, and she knew it was too late. Kate closed her eyes, taking calming breaths. *You can run from Paxton. You cannot run from the FBI.*

"If you've come here to apologize it's a waste of time." Paxton's tone was dry.

She deserved that after what she had done, but no matter how angry he was with her, she was a thousand and twelve times more disappointed in herself.

She rubbed her palms together to keep from shaking and let out a quiet exhale, hoping to dissipate the heat in her face. Kate opened her eyes and turned toward him. He was still in the black suit from early that morning, the newspaper tucked under his arm. No riot gear. No gun drawn. No handcuffs visible.

"Maggie insisted I give this to you." She pointed to the garment.

Paxton stopped next to the desk, his slacks not as fresh-pressed, his tie not as tight, his disappointed stare still firmly in place. But there was more behind his eyes. Pain? Worry? "I can't take that. It's too much."

"Wear it. Don't wear it. I don't care. But you have to take it." Kate shoved the bag toward him. "It can't stay at my place, and if I bring it back to Maggie I'll never hear the end of it."

"I'm supposed to take this and forget the stunt you pulled?" He slung it over his arm.

"It's just a stupid suit." Her voice was louder. *Get in. Drop off. Get out.* She spun on her heel to leave.

"I have something for you too."

"I don't need anything from you." She kept walking to the door.

"The lab cleared your gun."

Kate stopped short, hand on the handle. All she had to do was push and be on her way. She was twenty, maybe twenty-five, steps from her car and returning her life to normal. Her attention shifted to Paxton's reflection in the glass, and she shook her head.

"The slug they dug out of Kyle's leg didn't match."

"Of course it didn't." Her tone hardened. She turned back toward him and crossed her arms. "I didn't shoot him."

"Procedure requires us to confirm it."

Procedure. He loved that word. But it wasn't her problem anymore. He wasn't her problem anymore. "When can I get Ziggy back?"

Paxton handed his badge to the agent at the desk. "Could we get Ms. Howard a visitor's badge, please?"

Kate cringed at the formality of his tone. He'd called her Ms. Howard before, but this time it was different. Distant.

"Yes, sir." The agent pulled the log off the desk, jotting down his badge number. He handed it back and addressed Kate. "License, ma'am."

Kate debated walking out the door, but she didn't want to leave Ziggy behind. She pulled the license out of her wallet and walked over to the agent. She needed to get this over with, and then they never had to see each other again. *Get in. Drop off. Pick up. Get out.*

The agent placed her license and visitor's badge on the counter.

She took them, following Paxton to the elevator.

When it dinged and the doors opened, Kate walked to the back, keeping her space, and faced forward. She wanted to ask him what they discovered, what piece of evidence led them to a warrant, and what they found with it and where. But Kate knew Paxton wouldn't share any of it with her. Not now. Despite the fact that the elevator was moving up, she had a sinking feeling in her stomach. She stayed silent, staring straight ahead at the space where the doors met.

"I convinced them to drop the resisting arrest charge." He cleared his throat. "And since Kyle is expected to make a full recovery, they aren't going to pursue felony murder charges."

Relief rippled through her, and she slumped against the elevator wall. *Kyle was going to be okay.* The thought cooled her anxiety. It was far too generous of him to help her after what she did. She didn't deserve his kindness.

Kate opened her mouth, but the elevator opened before she could formulate a thank you. She followed him down the hall to his office. "You didn't have to do that."

"I didn't do it for you. Keeping pressure on that wound was the right thing to do. You saved Kyle's life."

Even though it was still her fault he got hurt.

Paxton dropped the newspaper on his desk and hung the suit on his chair. The Diaz file lay open, and he collected his paperwork into it. "And because the cameras you offered up caught some interesting footage, I convinced SAC Dupree to drop the impeding investigation charges."

"Interesting footage?" When Paxton didn't answer, she nodded. She was off the case so he had no obligation to tell her anything. Kate gulped down the lump of remorse in her throat. "Did you catch the guy who shot..." Kate couldn't bring herself to say Kyle's name out loud.

"Not yet, but because of your video we have an idea who we're looking for." A light, almost giddy feeling replaced the sinking feeling from before. At least they would catch the guy who did this to Kyle. He unlocked the top drawer of his desk and pulled out Ziggy and her holster. "I believe he belongs to you."

The fact that Paxton said "he" instead of "it" made Kate smile. She took Ziggy, attaching the holster to her belt. "Thank you." She fixed the flannel shirt to cover him. With Ziggy at her side, she felt a piece of her was the same—the old Kate—like maybe she *could* go back to the way things were before.

"I was there when Kyle got out of surgery." He rested his hand on his gun. "The hospital is on your way home. I'm sure he would appreciate the company."

Paxton was a good guy to be there for him. Kyle was like the annoying little brother you didn't want, but he hacked his way into your life. And your pantry. Kate looked out the window, her car parked in view. She wondered for a moment if he had seen her pull up and watched her give herself a pep-talk about going in the building. "Yeah. Maybe."

"He had a totally different story to tell than the one you gave the police."

Shit. Her pulse kicked up a notch. Kate needed to keep him from getting in trouble for any of this. It was the least she could do. "Oh?"

"He claimed the plan was his, all the equipment was his, and he was responsible for taking down the security and unlocking the gates and doors."

"Th—that's ridiculous. You can't believe someone all hopped up on heavy-duty pain meds." She avoided looking him in the eye, but Kate knew that Paxton knew she didn't have the skills to hack into a security system or the know-how to set the cameras to remotely record on the laptop.

"And then he told me he was Batman and you were Robin, so his whole confession was retracted." He huffed.

Kate nodded, unable to formulate a verbal response. She rubbed her palms together to ease the twitchy feeling in her limbs and cleared her throat. "That's probably best. Sounds like he was really loopy." She turned to leave, forcing one last look over her shoulder. She didn't know how to say good-bye to Paxton Banks, so she didn't.

"Hey. Ka—" Paxton came around the desk and caught her elbow. He looked down at her with those steel-blue eyes, not giving away a single thought, and a piece of her died inside. "Last time you looked at me like that you disappeared."

Would disappearing be so bad? They could both go on with their lives. Kate moved her arm, and he let go. What did it matter? He was *out*. He hadn't called her Katie once, and just then he stopped himself. Don't think she hadn't noticed.

"Remember, you're on bail. You can't leave town."

She glared up at him. "If you think so little of me that I'd run from the law, you don't know me at all, Special Agent Banks."

"Sorry. I meant—"

"Good luck on the case." Kate spun and walked out of his office. *And your life.*

Kate stopped at the convenience store for an iced tea, a box of animal crackers, and a bag of Doritos. She sat in the parking lot of the hospital for almost twenty minutes trying to convince herself to go in. It wasn't working.

She opened the bag of chips, staring up at the building, wondering which window was Kyle's and if his Spidey-sense was tingling because there were snacks in the vicinity. The thought made her smile. She checked her watch—almost two o'clock. She could check on Robbie while she was there, but telling Senator Thomas she was taken off the case was too mortifying after how appreciative he was. She could go to the bar, but she wasn't in the mood to deal with Cody. She could go home, but she didn't want to be there either. The last time she was there with Paxton, they'd slept together.

Her vision went blurry, and she wiped a tear from the corner of her eye. Kate rested her forehead against the steering wheel. She had to be radioactive to ruin everything around her so badly. The thought made her nauseous. She threw the bag of chips on the passenger seat, wrapping her arms around her stomach.

A loud knock made Kate gasp. Her heart jumped into her throat, racing. She looked around and stared out her side window at an older, Native American man in a security uniform.

"Ma'am, are you okay?" He eyed her suspiciously.

Kate nodded. "Yes, thank you. Everything's fine," she hollered through the glass. She tried to smile but didn't have it in her.

Either his face was frozen that way or he didn't believe her. He put his hand on the walkie-talkie at his hip. "Do I need to get a doctor?"

She started the car. "No. Just tired. Thank you for check-ing." She put the car in drive, pulled out of the parking spot, and pointed the car south. Kate ended up at Mr. Chen's Dry

Cleaning. She let herself in the back door, into the pressing area. She turned the machine on, waiting for it to warm up.

"Who's there?" Mrs. Chen's voice was surprisingly loud over the clothes dryer. "I have a gun."

No, she didn't. Maggie hid it for everyone's safety after a kerfuffle with their fabric distributor over the difference between lilac and lavender lace. But just in case, "It's Kate."

"Margaret not here." Mrs. Chen shuffled up beside her, her scowl a direct contradiction to the bright, over-sized flowers on her dress.

"I know. I saw the van was out for deliveries."

Mrs. Chen pulled her glasses up, watching the steam come off the press. "What you do?"

Kate motioned to the slacks stacked on the table. "Nothing. You look like you're behind." Kate wasn't in the mood for a lecture. She felt bad enough already.

Mrs. Chen put her newspaper down on the table next to the supplies with a yeah-right huff. "You only press when you in trouble."

Kate yanked a pair of slacks off the pile, placed them on the machine, taking special care of the pleat lines, pulled the handle down, and released. "I'm not in trouble." She put the other leg down and repeated. "I felt like helping out."

Mrs. Chen took the pants, slipped them on a hanger, slid a bag over them, and hung it on the rack. She would always take the extra help. "Same when you were a kid. D in algebra. You press. Skip class. You press. Back delivery van into parked car. You press."

"Technically, Maggie backed the van into that car. I just stole the keys." Kate set up the machine and repeated the process.

"You need to apologize."

Kate hung the pants. "An apology isn't going to work. Not this time."

"Mr. Chen always said, *you do right, and all work out.* You apologize. You do right." She punctuated it with a nod, and her glasses slid most of the way down her nose.

"He also said, *everything happens for a reason.*" Kate put the pair of pants on the rack with the others. "Maybe this was supposed to happen. Maybe we're not supposed to be together."

"Oh"—she *tsk-tsked*—"*boy* trouble."

Kate didn't bother denying it. She wanted to ignore it for the next decade. She'd done it once. She could do it again.

"You need to decide what most important"—Mrs. Chen pointed to her chest, flattening a giant yellow flower covering her heart—"in here. Focus on that."

Easier said than done. "What if I don't know what's most important? What if I don't know anything anymore?"

"You know. Too stubborn to listen." Mrs. Chen patted her chest again, then pointed to the dry cleaning tag on the next pair of slacks. "Mr. Reddy likes extra starch." She turned and shuffled away.

Kate grabbed for the starch can, but stopped, catching the newspaper headline. *Valley Teen to be Honored at Future Leaders of Tomorrow Lunch.* She picked up the paper, staring at a picture of Jessie Diaz. The same one Mrs. Diaz had clung to in the ambulance.

She unfolded the paper, reading down the story. *Nineteen-year-old Jessie Diaz will be honored at the Future Leaders of Tomorrow Luncheon Friday in a moment of silence. Diaz was killed earlier this week in a garage fire, cause still to be determined by the Phoenix Fire Department. Diaz was set to receive a humanitarian award for his time spent in homeless shelters teaching children to read, along with fellow members Peter Hurla, Janay Barron, Lorena Jones, and Nicholas Turley.*

Kate's vision went fuzzy, and a chill slicked its way up her spine. "Barron and Turley?" Those were the last names of senators on the list who voted to legalize marijuana. *What are the odds these kids are related?*

"Shit. Shit. Shit."

Dread spread through her, heating her blood, and Kate broke out in a sweat. If John Scott was going to make a move, that was where he was going to strike. She was positive about it. Off the case or not, she wouldn't let anyone else get hurt. There was no way she could do any of this on her own. As badly as she didn't want to call Paxton, she had no choice. Informing him was the least she could do to prove she once had been worthy of his trust. Of being part of the investigation. He was her only option.

Kate dug her phone out of her pocket and pressed Paxton's number. She paced a few steps while it rang. "Come on, come on. Pick up." When his voice mail clicked on, Kate redialed him.

"This isn't a good time." Paxton's pissy tone greeted her.

"The Future Leaders of Tomorrow Lunch." Kate blurted out.

Paxton groaned. "I don't have time for this."

"That's where he's going to strike. You have to cancel the event. Evacuate the hotel. Call in the bomb squad. Alert—"

"Stop." His tone was firm, final. The silence that followed said everything Paxton couldn't.

The Diaz file on his desk. The newspaper.

He knew.

Kate's muscles tightened and tingled to the point her skin felt stretched thin. She shook the twitchy feeling out of her hands.

"You are off the case. It's none of your concern."

"None of my concern?" She raised her voice. "I swore an oath to protect this country from enemies foreign and *domestic*."

"I'm not kidding. Stay out of it. FBI has been alerted to arrest anyone without a viable reason to be on-site. If you show up, they're going to drag you back to jail."

"Anyone without a viable reason. Got it." Kate ended the

call, shoved the phone in her pocket, and shut off the press. Every hotel downtown utilized valet services for large events and State 48 Valet, which she'd worked for before, was one of the largest. Kate nodded to herself. She'd have a viable reason.

Chapter Twenty-One

Kate adjusted the sleeve of her maroon State 48 Valet company blazer, a touch tight across her shoulder with her bandage. She locked the door of the Mercedes she'd parked and walked out the side of the parking garage. The downtown Phoenix street was quiet for midday Friday, with only a few people around the bus stop across the way. If she had to guess, at least two of them were FBI waiting to pounce if John Scott was spotted.

She checked her watch, walking up the sidewalk toward the hotel's valet stand. Almost eleven o'clock. The guests for the Future Leaders of Tomorrow Luncheon would be arriving shortly. Kate needed to keep her head on a swivel without drawing any unnecessary attention for a little while longer. She rubbed her sweaty palms on her black slacks as she dipped under the freestanding umbrella, shading the valet booth. "The first floor is almost full," Kate said to Leon, her manager. "Here you go." She held out the key fob for him to lock in the box at his knees.

"Huh? What?" Leon looked scared enough he might puke. His deep-brown eyes were hooded by his thick, dark eyebrows, which looked severe in comparison to his paler-than-usual skin tone. He was only a few years older than Kate, but the crinkle in his forehead added at least a decade. He was not handling this well.

When he didn't take the key, she put it on the stand in front of him.

"Kate, are you sure I'm not going to get arrested? I shouldn't have let you talk me into this. They said not to swap out any employees after the background checks." His normally jovial smile had been replaced with thin lips.

Persuading Maria to switch shifts with her was easy when Kate offered her an all-expenses-paid spa day at The Phoenician Resort. But Leon was a different story. It had taken her the majority of the day Thursday to track him down and convince him to let her have the shift. The FBI wouldn't tell him why the extreme measures, and it wasn't Kate's place to share, but he was right in thinking it wasn't good. She didn't blame him for worrying, but he couldn't change his mind now.

"Leon"—Kate put her hand on his arm—"I swear it will be okay." The only person in danger of getting arrested was Kate, and it was a risk she was willing to take to protect innocent people. "We've been parking cars for an hour. Don't you think if the cops were going to arrest you they'd have done it by now?"

"I guess." He shrugged and his forehead smoothed out a little. "But the agent said—"

"Am I still an employee on the books for the company?"

"Yes."

Kate hated seeing him this nervous. She took a valet ticket off the stand and shoved it in her pocket for the next car. "Did you hand over my file with the rest of them?"

"Of course"—he ran his hand through his thinning hair —"but Maria is supposed to be working, not you."

"In the years we've worked together, have I ever let you down?"

"No." The corners of his lips turned up a fraction.

"See." Kate patted his shoulder, giving him a bright smile. "It'll be fine. I'm going to park some cars and keep a low profile like I always do. There's nothing to worry about." As the last word hit her lips, she caught a glimpse of Paxton coming out the front door of the hotel and heading in their direction.

Fuck. Her pulse picked up at the sight of him, out of fear or pain she didn't know. Kate crouched down on the far side of the valet stand like she was tying her shoe.

"What's wrong? Why'd you make that face?" Leon looked down at her, at Paxton, then back to her. "Are we getting arrested?"

Maybe.

"Are you Leon Garcia?" Paxton's negotiator tone was in full effect.

"Yes, yes sir." Leon's voice was shaky. She hoped he wasn't going to piss himself while she was downstream.

She faked tightening her laces so she didn't look like a grown-ass chickenshit to anyone watching.

"I'm Special Agent Paxton Banks. Why don't you take five while I talk to your friend here."

Leon made a choking sound like maybe he'd swallowed his tongue, turned, and ran for the parking deck.

Kate brushed off the top of her sneaker and stood to meet Paxton's what-do-you-think-you're-doing-here stare. He was wearing a gray suit with a white shirt and black tie. It fit him perfectly, unlike the boxy black ones he'd been wearing all week. Kate couldn't help but stare. He looked and smelled amazing. She ached for him, but Kate kept her facial expression in check as best she could. He was out. Her heart knew it, but her body hadn't gotten the message.

Paxton cleared his throat and crossed his arms over his chest. His eyes, more gray than blue, were not playing games. "Where is Maria Sandoval?"

"Spa day." Kate took the key off the top of the stand and hung it in the cabinet below. "She's a hard-working mom. I thought she could use the day off."

Paxton shook his head.

"How'd you know I'd be here?" Kate narrowed her eyes at him. "Are you following me?"

"I graduated from the Kate Howard School of Been There, Done That."

Kate scoffed. He knew too much about her because he wrote the handbook.

"And your employee file stands out, especially after getting arrested the other night." Paxton straightened, shoulders back, head high, jaw tight. "I don't know what you think you're doing here, but you need to go before SAC Dupree sees you."

"I'm working." Kate motioned to the logo on her jacket. "I have a *viable* reason to be here."

Paxton ducked under the umbrella and took two steps toward her. The heat rolling off of him was stifling. She forced herself to stay planted where she was and looked up, meeting his gaze. "Oh, you're working all right. My nerves, my patience, and my willpower not to arrest you."

"No. I'm actually working. I've been an employee of State 48 Valet for almost three years now. Since the FBI took over protective detail for Senator Thomas, I need to do something to pay the bills." Just as she'd practiced in the mirror that morning.

"Who do you think you're kidding? I was the one who taught you to hide in plain sight. You're interfering with an ongoing investigation."

"By parking cars? I doubt it." Kate pushed her ponytail off her shoulder. "Don't *you* have a job to do?"

"Yes." He put his hand out, palm up. "Now, hand it over."

She knew he wanted Ziggy, and he could keep on wanting. "Hand what over? What are you talking about?"

"Him. Hand him over or I'll frisk you right here."

The thought of Paxton's hands on her sent a wave of heat through her. She patted her hip and smirked. "No weapons on the job. Company rule."

Paxton shoved her sneaker with his boot. "So, ankle holster."

Kate hated how well he knew her, how easy it was for him to get her hot and bothered, how badly she wanted to kiss him. "I have a concealed weapon permit. Unless you are here to arrest me, I will not be surrendering that right." She stood taller, looking up into his eyes. "And you can't really expect me to be out here without protection."

His jaw clenched so hard she would have sworn she heard a few teeth crack. "You shouldn't be out here at all." His voice was louder, less controlled.

"I'm exactly where I'm supposed to be." Kate held on to the stand to give herself strength. "I'm guessing we're at code orange for terror attacks. You, Special Agent Banks, should be inside doing whatever the hell they pay you to do. You said you were *out*." She moved her hands in a shooing motion away from the valet area. "So go be out."

He let out a ragged breath. "You are the most frustrating human being ever put on this planet." He rested his hand on top of the valet stand too close to hers. "I'd be all in if you weren't so *you* about everything."

I'd be all in if you weren't so you? She pulled her arm away from him, dug her fist into her hip, and cocked her head. "What the hell is that supposed to mean?"

"I value rules. You like to break them. I follow orders. You take them as a suggestion." Paxton's jaw hardened then released. "You have a real bad habit of doing the opposite of what I ask you to do." His tone was quieter. He let out a breath, softening his features. For a moment, the apprehension settled around his eyes. His gaze dropped to her lips, and when he looked up, the interrogator face was back. "I hate that you're out here. It's dangerous and disturbing and distracting."

Distracting? The word lodged in her throat. *I'm distracting?* His words from the day when he first kissed her rang through her head. *I couldn't afford to be overprotective of the girl on my team. Not thinking straight. Showing favoritism. Looking soft.* He was doing that. That exact thing all over again, here, in front of the FBI. Kate gulped back the lump of fear in her throat, tipping her chin up. "You don't have to like it or agree with it. It's my choice to be here."

The silence between them stretched like a rubber band, straining to the point of snapping. Paxton groaned, the sound something akin to giving up. "*Stick* to parking cars. *Stay* out of the way. And *keep* Ziggy holstered." He tugged on his jacket sleeve. "Bulletproof material or not, I don't feel like getting shot today." With that, he turned and marched back up the sidewalk and through the front door without a backward glance.

She smiled to herself. That's why he looked so good. He was wearing the suit Maggie tailored.

Kate spent the better part of an hour parking cars after Paxton confronted her. The FBI had closed off the self-parking section to minimize foot traffic in hard-to-view areas, so when Kate noticed movement through the stanchions of the parking ramp, she stopped to get a better view.

Shoving the car key in her pocket, she watched from the ramp between the first and second floors. A man was walking away from her toward the back of the building. She took a few more steps down the ramp, watching him from the next support column. She could see the employee entrance he was headed toward. Kate knew it was locked. The building was on FBI lock-down, and she had double-checked all five floors herself when she arrived earlier.

A shudder crept up her spine as she craned her neck to see more. The man was wearing a white waiter's coat and black pants. Kate was tempted to pull Ziggy out of his holster, but she'd most likely just scare the waitstaff sneaking back into the building from a smoke break. Kate hoped the guy would turn around so she could see his face, but no luck. She started down the ramp again, watching him, but something about his walk sent the hairs on the back of her neck on-end.

Kate picked up the pace when she hit the ground floor of the parking deck. She came around a row of cars, and an uneasiness in her stomach sent a shiver through her, pricking all the way up to her scalp. Something was wrong. She pulled her phone out of her pocket, looking at the image she had taken the other day of Cassandra and John Scott. This man was heavier than the picture of John. His hair was longer, but the color was about right.

The guy kept walking toward the employee entrance, not waning, not wavering. He was on a mission. And if all that hadn't sent up a red flag, Kate realized he was limping, a slight shuffle, leaning heavier on his left side. Was she being paranoid? Cassandra mentioned John had a limp from a bad back. "Hey, excuse me," Kate hollered, jogging in his direction.

He swiped a key card against the security pad at the employee entrance and grabbed the handle.

Kate swallowed the please-be-wrong lump in her throat. "John?"

The man pulled the door open and stared over his shoulder at Kate. His hair, uncombed. His face, unshaven. His uniform, unironed. But it was the manic sheen in his eyes which made her heart sputter and stop, his sallow skin highlighting the dark, depressing, sleep-deprived bags under his eyes.

Her chest heated and her lungs burned like a flare, incinerating her from the inside out, catching her fight-or-flight up in the flames, fusing her feet to the cement.

It was John Scott.

Chapter Twenty-Two

His eyes were wide and unblinking. Kate's stomach squirmed and squeezed under his unsettling stare, but she couldn't turn away. John Scott looked older, fatter, and scruffier than the images she'd seen at his home, but it was him. The jawline, the eyes, the bridge of his nose—all the same. She had zero doubt about it.

"Go home, young lady," he said, letting the door slam behind him.

Kate jumped at the sound, sending her heart back into motion ten times its normal rhythm. "Fuck." Kate raced forward, yanking on the handle, useless without a key card. "Fuck, fuck, fuck!" He was right there, their main suspect, and she let him get away. She fumbled to turn on her phone and pressed Paxton's number. She didn't wait for him to speak when she heard it pick up. "John Scott is in the building. I repeat, John Scott is in the building."

"Are you positive?"

"Affirmative." She spun toward the entrance of the parking deck, not waiting for an answer, pushing herself forward on stiff limbs.

Paxton relayed the information to his team. His voice

commanding.

"Where is he?"

"He came through the parking deck. North side. First floor employee entrance." Kate stopped at the sidewalk and looked right, toward the front of the hotel. "He's wearing a white waiter's coat and black slacks."

Paxton relayed the details. "There. That camera there. Where is that?" she heard him say with a pinch of panic lacing his voice, but couldn't hear the answer over her heart pounding in her ears.

Two guys who had been sitting at the bus stop ran across the street and in the front door. "Leon"—Kate waved her arm away from the building—"get out of here," she hollered.

He took off past the entrance. When he turned up the next street, she ran the opposite direction, toward the back of the building.

"Was he carrying anything?" Paxton sounded like he was on the move.

Her mind whirled. He'd had his arms out like he was carrying something, but there'd been nothing there when he turned. He was awkwardly stiff. Kate paused at the steps next to the loading dock and yanked Ziggy out of her ankle holster. A decade-old memory flashed through her mind. A young girl, tears streaming down her face, walking gingerly through the Afghanistan market toward her and Paxton. Her arms out at the elbow.

Realization ripped through her, incinerating the memory like napalm and sending fire through her core.

John couldn't put his arms down.

Kate gasped, sucking in air. He wasn't fat. He was carrying something bulky under his coat.

"Katie?" Paxton's voice brought her back to the loading dock. "Was he carrying anything?"

"He *is* the bomb."

"Say again?"

Going in there was a bad idea. Sitting on the sidelines was worse. She ran up the stairs two at a time. "He's wearing a vest. John Scott is the bomb."

"Katie, get out of here." Paxton sounded winded. "Do it now."

"No." She clicked the safety off Ziggy and tried the door handle. Locked. "We can't lose him."

"Get out of here. That's an order."

"He's got four sticks of dynamite and two detonators left, and he's ahead of us." Peering through the slender, vertical window on the door, she couldn't see anyone, but that didn't mean it was empty. She caught a glimpse of the inside lock, close enough she could reach.

"Katie—"

"I'm headed through the loading dock. Meet you in the middle." She turned off her phone and shoved it in her pocket. Kate didn't have a plan, but protecting people was what she did. And she did it well. *Get in there. Stop him from hurting anyone else. Get home safe.* She lined up the butt of Ziggy's grip with the window, turned her face away, and rammed him into the glass a few times. Glass shattered and fell around her.

Kate slid her arm through, ripping her jacket on the jagged edges, and turned the lock.

She inched the door open and held Ziggy to the side. She listened for a moment before proceeding. Hugging the bay doors, she crept toward the main building with a watchful eye on the stacked crates across the way. Kate checked back over her shoulder and around her, clearing her path until she reached a stairwell. She waited.

No movement. No footsteps.

She advanced through the fire door into the kitchen, startling a girl folding napkins. She grabbed the girl, putting her hand over her mouth. "Did a man come through here? Older? Brown hair? Scruffy beard? A limp?"

The girl shook her head and a tear fell down her cheek.

"I want you to go out the loading dock and get far away from here. Okay? Don't look back."

The girl nodded and Kate let her go behind her.

Kate progressed through the kitchen. She checked low to ensure he wasn't crouched under the prep tables and around rolling racks of utensils and dinnerware. She used the reflection on the polished appliances to see the angle from the other side. The kitchen was eerily quiet for a hotel hosting a lunch, and her stomach clenched tighter than a cadet's grip on their M16.

Kate came down the service corridor behind the meeting rooms, following signs for the event space. There were too many places to hide, but John Scott wasn't hiding. He was on a mission. When she reached the door labeled Ballroom B, her heart pounded out a warning against her ribs. She took two deep breaths, listening for movement before she pushed the door open, clearing the entrance.

No music. No food. No people.

She walked into the space, empty except for some chairs and tables stacked along the wall. *What the hell?*

Kate turned back down the service corridor. The door to Ballroom A was ajar. She peered into the opening. The room looked like it was in the middle of being set up, or maybe torn down. Round tables filled the room, draped with black linens that reached the floor. Chairs on racks flanked the sides. A bar on the far end and a podium closer to her. She blinked rapidly to make sure she was seeing things clearly. *Where was everyone she'd parked cars for?*

In the middle of it all stood John Scott. With his rigid posture and pinched expression, he looked as confused as she felt.

Something in his hand.

Jacket open.

Dynamite strapped to his chest.

Her pulse pounded in her ears. *Get in. Stop him. Get home.* She pushed the door open with her foot, stepping into the room. Kate extended her arms and pointed Ziggy at John's back, loosening her grip to ease her shaky hands. "Turn around slowly and get your hands up."

"No. No. No." He paced, turned, and muttered, not looking at her. "No."

Kate counted four sticks of dynamite, one with a silver metal top she assumed was the electronic blasting cap from the police report, strapped to a fishing vest with duct tape. The makeshift bomb vest had wires coming out the tops of the sticks, but she couldn't see if they led to each other or out under the waiter's coat.

Paxton came through the main door of the ballroom, opposite of where she had entered, gun drawn. He caught her eye for a moment before all attention was on John. "John Scott, put your hands where I can see them."

John tugged at his hair with his empty hand. "No. They're here." He looked from table to table. "They have to be here."

"It's over, John." Paxton's negotiator voice was calm and commanding as he approached them. "No one else gets hurt."

"It wasn't supposed to be like this. This way." John stumbled over his words. "It was supposed to end today." John turned, looking directly at Kate. Eyes narrowed. His lips curled into a sneer. She'd pissed off a lot of people in her life, but no one had ever looked at her with such hostility. Such hatred.

Kate stood taller, securing her stance.

"You—You did this. You took them. You messed this up." His voice got louder with every accusation.

Paxton laid his gun on a table. With his hands up he slowly weaved around the tables and stopped between John and her. "Katie, get out of here," he said, facing John.

What was he doing? He's going to get himself killed. Her chest constricted so tight, she worried she might pass out from the pain. Kate took a step over, putting John back in her sights. "Not happening."

"You stay there." John pointed at Paxton. He took a few short, quick breaths, backing away. "I have the blasting cap programmed to this phone. I push one button, and we're all dead." He swung a phone in the air, making Kate's whole body tense.

She couldn't get a good look at it, but from what she could see it was a nothing-special, old flip phone with the buttons on the inside. As long as he kept it closed, they were safe.

"John, listen to me." Paxton took another step toward him, and Kate followed as though they were tethered. "You don't want to do that."

"Don't—don't come any closer. I'll do it." He took another step back, and Paxton took a step toward him.

Kate's throat closed up like one of those sticks of dynamite was lodged there. Was Paxton out of his mind? She couldn't breathe, couldn't swallow, couldn't bear to watch Paxton get hurt again. That suit would stop a bullet, not a bomb. It was no more effective on explosives than the flack jacket he was wearing in Afghanistan.

"No." John hit himself in the head with the heel of his free hand. His motions were twitchy and unhinged. "Stay where you are. I—I mean it."

"John, I know you're angry and hurting, but you need to hand me the phone." Paxton took another step, putting his hand out. He was barely an arm's length away. "Please."

Kate gulped air and followed John's erratic pacing, like a pinball bouncing between the tables. She kept Ziggy trained on his head.

"Nononononono," he babbled. John took a few steps backward toward the partition wall separating the ballrooms. He looked in both directions at the exits. As much as she didn't want to kill anyone, she'd put a bullet in his brain before she'd let him escape or detonate the vest. But dynamite was unstable, and that could also trigger it.

His breath quickened to the point of hyperventilating, and he let out a whimper.

He was escalating.

"Katie, turn around and get some distance from here." Paxton's order was grave.

I'm not leaving you. Kate shook her head at his back, unable to say the words.

John stared at nothing. His gaze was distant and distracted. "They have to pay for what they did. They have to." John hit himself in the head again and again. "I didn't mean to shoot that kid. It was an accident."

Heat flushed through her body. Kate's head snapped up and her tense muscles quivered. "He shot Kyle?" The words, barely a whisper, burst past the lump in her throat. Her voice as raw as the pain in her chest. Kate slid her finger down over the trigger.

Paxton took another step closer to John. He was almost within arm's distance again. "Why don't you put the phone down, and we can talk about it. I know it was an accident."

Kate caught movement from the bottom of the partition door. Boots. Lots of them. Ready to storm the room.

"He—he came out of nowhere. It was dark." John looked up, suddenly aware of how close Paxton was to him. His gaze narrowed. "Get back." He flipped open the phone, his thumb hovering over the buttons.

A sensation of dread seeped into her bones, the pressure forcing from the inside out. She had to get the phone away from him. But how?

Paxton took a step back, putting his hands up higher. His right fist closed—a stop hand signal. "I'm unarmed. I want to help you. Will you let me do that?"

How he always seemed calm during negotiations like this she couldn't imagine. She focused Ziggy on the point between John's eyes. Chances of her making the shot and not getting them blown up were slim. Even if she dropped him right there, the dynamite could ignite. There was no way of getting to Paxton before it detonated. *Fuck.* Her muscles quivered and her stomach lurched. She wouldn't hurt him. Not again. There was no way to save him. No way to protect him.

John swung the burner phone in the air. "You let me go do what I came here to do, and you can both walk out of here."

"We're all walking out of here. We're going to get you the help you need." Paxton angled facing Kate and mouthed something.

Cosmo?

"No one can help me." John's face began to redden and a bead of sweat broke out across his forehead. "You can't bring my son back."

"You're right. We can't." Kate tried to keep her voice light. She shrugged her shoulders, hoping Paxton would know she didn't understand what he was saying. "But taking innocent lives isn't going to fill the void of losing your son. Cassandra needs you. Don't make her bury you too."

He paced along the partition wall he'd backed himself into like a caged animal. He was so focused on his mission he hadn't noticed the door in the wall. "No." He wiped his arm across his forehead, breathing heavy. "I can't—I can't do that. They have to pay. They took him from me."

"No." Kate's voice was steadier than she expected, her tone was ten shades of not-fucking-around. He stared at her, distant and cold. "Those children didn't do anything to you. They didn't take your son. That driver made a mistake. He got high and got behind the wheel, and he took your son from you."

Paxton mouthed it again.

Kokomo?

Kate shrugged and took a few steps closer. She was still a table's width away from Paxton. "My mother was taken from me when I was thirteen, lung cancer. She didn't smoke a day in her life. The man who later raised me, the only father I ever knew, was taken when I was twenty-one, heart attack. He was the healthiest person I'd ever met." Kate's voice wavered. "Life's not fair. We don't get to choose when our loved ones leave us. We have to do the best we can with the time we have."

Paxton turned to face her. "Katie, do not shoot *him*." He looked down and back at her.

She knew she couldn't shoot him. Couldn't wrestle the phone away from him. Couldn't do anything but try to reason with a man skirting sanity. There were no positive outcomes. They were in a lose-lose situation.

"Katie, when are you going to learn to listen." Paxton looked down and back up quickly. "Do. Not. Shoot. *Him*."

The way he said *him* sent a surge spidering through her fingertips. Paxton couldn't possibly be asking—no, ordering —her to shoot him. He looked down at the suit again. Maggie's suit. And back to her. The reality of his request hit her like a boot to the bowels, making her dizzy and queasy.

Was John's crazy rubbing off on him? She couldn't shoot Paxton.

Could she?

John let out a burst of laughter, so disturbing and deranged, she knew she didn't have a choice. Kate carried a 9mm, the Kevlar suit jacket could easily take the shot. She'd seen it herself when they were testing the fabrics on the mannequin in Maggie's shop. Provided she didn't miss. She shook off the thought.

Paxton's features softened, and he gazed at her with such trust and admiration her heart ached. "Katie, for once in your life." The steely harshness of his voice gone. "Obey an order."

He had a plan. He had to have a plan. He was Paxton Banks. Stubborn, scrupulous, and serious. He always had a plan.

A bead of sweat dribbled down her back, trickling through her shoulder blades. Her nerves were like razor blades under the surface of her skin.

Finger on the trigger, Kate focused Ziggy's front sight on Paxton's abdomen. John a blur in the background, pacing and muttering to himself. She aimed for his jacket pocket, adding a second layer of protection covering his seventh and eighth ribs. Farther from his heart. Still too close for comfort.

She wanted to say so many things. *I understand. I trust you. I'm sorry.* The muscles in her tight shoulders burned from the pressure against her stitches. Kate took a ragged breath, and with her exhale blurted out, "I'm in."

She pressed the trigger back.

Bang.

The shot echoed in her ears, and the bile in the back of her throat threatened to emerge.

Time slowed.

Her heart hit the ground before Paxton did.

The rush of air that escaped him sounded like *Kosovo*?

In a flash, she remembered their mission to Kosovo. The heiress kidnapped for ransom money. Paxton shooting the trigger out of the hostage taker's hand.

She gasped, bringing John back into focus. He stood, staring down in shock at Paxton, lying at his feet. The phone was too close to the vest. And what if she hit it and the blasting cap still went off. She needed to trust Paxton's plan.

"John!" Kate screamed.

John jumped at the sound, throwing his hands out wide.

Kate aimed at the phone's screen and fired, shattering it.

"No. No. Nooooo!" John cried holding the remaining piece of the phone in front of him.

Paxton made a groaning noise and rolled toward John, too preoccupied with his failure. He jammed something in John's calf—"Now,"—he yelled and rolled away.

Agents filed through the doors on either side of them and

behind John, grabbing both arms, securing him and his home-made bomb vest. His words slurred, teetered, and his eyes fluttered before he went limp all over, collapsing into the agents' hands.

Kate rushed to Paxton's side. "We need a medic over here." He let out a grunt when she rolled him on his back, and a syringe fell out of his hand. Kate pulled open the jacket with only a marred black, spot on the pocket, ran her palm over his ribs, and he let out a painful groan.

No blood.

A sigh of relief escaped, releasing a few tears as well. "Are you okay?"

He lifted his head. "You shot me."

"You ordered me to." Kate wiped a tear from her cheek. "It didn't pierce the skin. Probably cracked a few ribs though."

"Because you shot me." He grabbed her hand, lacing his fingers through hers.

Kate watched over her shoulder, the bomb techs securing John's vest. "Pax, where are the kids?"

"Safe." He winced, scrunched his face, and put his head back down. "We bused them up the street. We needed John to think they were in here."

They were never in danger? "And me shooting you?" Kate tightened her grip on his hand. "What was that? Plan B?"

"Plan B was the sedative. But I couldn't get close enough to give it to him." He chuckled and groaned. "You were plan C."

The EMT wheeled in a stretcher, heading in their direction.

"How'd you even know that I'd get in here? That I'd shoot?"

"Katie,"—he kissed the back of her hand—"I knew you'd do all the wrong things for all the right reasons, and you'd never let me down."

Chapter Twenty-Three

Paxton lay bare-chested on an emergency room gurney at St. Joseph's Hospital, his shirt, tie, and jacket draped over the end of the bed. On a normal day, Kate would have enjoyed the view. Today, she stared at his abdomen where the bullet—her bullet—had hit him. The pain in the back of her throat fought against the tightness in her chest. His skin was raised and red, the area larger than her fist. It was going to leave one hell of a bruise.

The ER doctor, who had stitched her shoulder up a week earlier, mulled over his imaging results. "A fracture in the lower ribs could have punctured your liver, kidney, or spleen."

She grimaced and bit her lip, holding her breath. *Please let him be okay. I can't do this again.* She turned toward the doctor to focus on anything other than Paxton.

"You got lucky, Special Agent Banks." The doctor peered over the tablet at them. "I don't see anything that would indicate injury to your internal organs or blood vessels."

The tightness loosened a bit as she exhaled. "Then he's okay?" Kate shoved her hands in her pockets to keep from fidgeting.

The doctor pushed a few buttons on the tablet then looked over at her. "He'll need to take it easy for five to six weeks. No vigorous activities, but he can walk around and perform his normal daily routine."

"Thank you." Paxton sat up, wincing in pain.

She cringed every time he made that sound. Kate took a deep breath and closed her eyes. She had done that to him. She'd hurt Paxton again. Kate opened her eyes and turned toward him. "Would you let me help you?" Kate reached for his hand, pulling him slowly to a seated position, then gingerly helped him swing his legs over the side of the gurney.

"I prescribed something for the pain." The doctor took a few steps, stopping at the triage bay curtain. "I don't recommend taking it if you'll be driving or operating heavy machinery, but it might help you get comfortable enough to sleep."

"I appreciate it." Paxton nodded, and the doctor slipped out, leaving them in awkward silence.

Her adrenaline had long worn off, and she was fighting a week's worth of exhaustion. Kate grabbed his white dress shirt off the pile. She slid it up his arm on his injured side so he didn't have to bend or twist. It was the least she could do after all this.

"You're awfully quiet." His voice was soft, and his breath was warm on her cheek.

Avoiding his gaze, she moved to his other side. She was sure when he'd been whisked off to the hospital she'd never see him again like when they were in the Army. That was the plan, but when he grabbed her hand as the EMT wheeled him away, she followed. She should have let him go. Kate told herself that she would stay until she knew he was okay, but she was just prolonging the inevitable. "You know, I thought about that moment a lot. You, laying there in the Army hospital bed. What I would have said or done if I was brave enough to go back."

"What would you have done?"

Kate held out the shirt for him to slide the other arm in. When he didn't move, she looked up into his blue-gray eyes. She shrugged and looked away. "Doesn't matter now."

"It matters to me." He groaned, sliding his other arm into the sleeve.

Kiss him. Say good-bye. Go. Kate fixed his collar and leaned in to kiss him. Her stomach fluttered like a dust devil spinning up a cloud of emotions. The light brush of their lips, keeping her *good-bye* hanging onto her tongue for dear life.

Paxton smiled. "That would have gotten you court-martialed for fraternization."

"It would have been worth it." Kate smiled back at him, and he ran his hand down her arm. As much as she didn't want to, she stepped back away from him and dropped her arms to her sides. *Now say good-bye and go.* "G—"

"Ms. Howard?" SAC Dupree's deep voice assailed her from the other side of the curtain.

She should have left when she had the chance. Kate needed a shower, a nap, and a Snickers—not necessarily in that order—and Dupree was standing in her way. The fluttery feeling turning into a tornado.

"Twelve-oh-two voice mail. Twelve-thirty-eight text." The whispered words rushed out of Paxton.

"What?"

Paxton shoved his chin toward the curtain. "Repeat it."

"Twelve-oh-two voice mail. Twelve-thirty-eight text."

Paxton nodded. "In here, sir."

Dupree threw the curtain back. Kate gulped and stood at attention to greet him. "Looking for me, sir?"

"That was the most blatant disregard for rules I've ever seen on display in all my years at the bureau." His tone was more gravely than usual. He crossed his arms high over his chest. "Give me one reason why I shouldn't arrest you for impeding an investigation and endangering a federal agent."

On the list of things Kate needed, spending another night in jail was not included. "He ordered me to shoot him, sir. It was all part of the plan. That's why he was wearing a Kevlar suit."

"The plan." Dupree huffed. "And the storage company? I suppose he told you to break in and get your friend shot?"

A mortar of remorse landed in the pit of her stomach. Paxton's words echoed in her mind. *Twelve-oh-two voice mail, twelve-thirty-eight text.* She glanced over her shoulder at Paxton, but he kept his eyes on Dupree. "Not specifically." She cleared her throat, putting her shoulders back. "I received a voice mail from Pa—uh—Special Agent Banks at twelve-oh-two indicating he was on the way to obtain the warrant. I was on-site at approximately twelve-fifteen—"

"With the Moss kid?"

"Yes, sir. Kyle Moss." Her chest warmed, sending heat in every direction. Kate wiped her sweaty palms on her slacks. "And I received a text at twelve-thirty-eight that he had the warrant. Moments later we—I took down the security system."

SAC Dupree gave her an I-wasn't-born-yesterday look. "Sounds suspiciously similar to the statement Special Agent Banks put in his report."

"I already deleted the messages, but you're welcome to subpoena my phone records if you like." Kate forced her client-smile.

He was quiet for a few moments, drawing out a bead of sweat along her hairline. If he was waiting for her to crack under the pressure, he'd be waiting a long time. Paxton had trained her far too well for that. She put her chin up a fraction higher.

"Why didn't you wait for the team to arrive?" he finally blurted out.

"Women are perceived as less threatening than men. I make a living exploiting that assumption. Especially in John's mental and emotional state, we knew if he was there, coming in hot with a tactical team could spook him. The sirens and lights could have made a dangerous situation worse." She used Paxton's words from a few days earlier.

Dupree let out a gruff laugh. It was clear he was not buying one bit of her bullshit, but he didn't seem like the kind of guy who enjoyed extraneous paperwork. She opened her mouth to speak but closed it when he put his hand up. "The storage company has agreed to drop the breaking and entering and identity theft charges, seeing as a warrant was already issued before their system went down, the keys to their file cabinet had been left behind, and nothing was taken *provided* you pay the property damage to repair the security system."

All the charges dropped, and only paying for repairs? She let out a relieved sigh. "Yes." Kate nodded. "Yes, absolutely sir. Thank you, sir."

"Don't thank me." He slid Paxton a look. "I'm not the reason they dropped the charges."

Kate clenched her fists and released them to ease her tingling fingers. Paxton had saved her ass again.

"Banks." Dupree cleared his throat. "Unorthodox use of a temporary consultant. Do not let it happen again."

"Yes, sir." Paxton's tone was full-on Special Agent.

"But a fine example in teamwork to bring John Scott in safely." He looked from Paxton to Kate and back.

"Yes, sir," they said in unison.

Dupree pointed to Paxton. "Get some rest, and we'll see you in the office on Monday." He turned and left the way he came in.

"You didn't have to do that. I would have figured out a way to fix it." Kate wrapped her arms around her waist.

"You did the wrong thing. But it was for the right reason.

And I did already have the warrant." Paxton stood, holding on to the bed.

She wanted to hug him, but that wouldn't help her situation or his pain level. "Thank you." Kate's phone chirped, and she pulled it out of her pocket to see a text from Maggie. *I'm here.*

Back of the emergency room on rt, she texted back.

When she turned, Paxton had buttoned his shirt. "Maggie's here." Kate shoved her phone back in her pocket. "I texted her for a ride after I asked the nurse to bring Kyle down."

"Katie—"

"Kate? Paxton?" Kyle rolled in on a wheelchair in an *I'm a New Brother* T-shirt and Phoenix Suns basketball shorts. They were the closest things to his size they had in the gift shop. She'd had a hospital aide run them up to his room while she was waiting for Paxton to have his tests done. "Jeez, am I glad to see you. This place is Snoozeville."

"Kyle?" The tightness in her chest released. Kate resisted the urge to mess up his hair. He looked good. Better than the last time she'd seen him at the storage place. "Are you okay?" She pointed to his thigh, bulky from the bandages.

He shrugged. "Did you know they have an endless supply of Jell-O? Endless."

Kate laughed. "I guess that means you're feeling better?"

"My leg hurts, but who else can say they got shot taking down a bad dude?"

Paxton could.

Kyle wheeled closer, looking up at them in confusion like he just realized they were in the emergency room. "What are you guys doing here?"

"Katie shot me." Paxton laughed, then groaned, holding his side.

"Shot?" Maggie strolled in looking camera-ready in her

black jeans and pink-on-pink polka dot sweater. "You shot Paxton?" Her tone was high-pitched and full of panic.

"Whoa. He's like the man of steel." Kyle was enjoying this too much. "Batman and Superman are best friends, so this makes sense." He pointed between them.

"He *asked* me to shoot him. It was part of his plan."

"I'm not a superhero." Paxton looked from Kyle to Maggie. "I think what Katie is trying to say is I'm okay. Thanks to your suit, it's only two fractured ribs."

Maggie propped her hand on her hip. Whatever lecture she was about to give was defused by the compliment. "And who's this?"

The small space was starting to feel crowded, but Kate didn't entirely mind it. "Maggie, this is Kyle. He lives downstairs from me. Kyle this is Maggie, my best friend and sister."

"Well, neighbor, I'm giving Kate a ride home. You wanna bust out of this place?" Maggie looked down at Kyle.

"That'd be great. I've been jonesing for some video game time and Cheetos."

"How about you?" Maggie looked over at Paxton. "Can we drop you off at home?"

"Yes, thank you. The longer I can keep this from my sister the better." Paxton leaned on Kate's good shoulder. His hand was warm even through her jacket. "Why don't you guys head out? It's going to take me a while. I'm moving slow."

"You want me to get you a wheelchair? We could race." Kyle's voice was too excited.

"No, thanks. The doctor said I needed to walk."

"I'll pull the car up." Maggie smiled at them, grabbed the rest of Paxton's stuff from the bed, and tossed it over her arm. "Let's go, new guy." She grabbed the back of the wheelchair and pulled him out of the triage bay. "Those two look like they need to talk."

Kate slid under his arm so he could lean on her. His

weight on her was comforting and disturbing. The heaviness in her limbs had nothing to do with him and everything to do with finishing her reason for being there. Her eyelids were gummy, and she blinked away the threat of tears. She had to do it now. Had to just get the word out. *Good-bye.*

"Before anyone else interrupts us"—he turned to look down at her—"did you mean what you said?"

She'd said a lot of things over the week, but she still hadn't said the one word she promised herself. "When?"

"Before you shot me?"

I'm in. It was only two little words, but their meaning was massive. Kate swallowed back the realization that she meant it. She was in, but if he wasn't…ugh. "There were so many things going on. Dynamite, a suspect having a mental break-down, trying to save your ass—"

"You said, 'I'm in.' "

Her heart rate increased at the vibrancy in his voice. Kate nodded absentmindedly, fiddling with the button on her blazer. "I said that." Her voice was a whisper.

"You did. I heard it." Paxton covered her hand with his, sending tingles up her arm. "Did you mean it?"

"I wanted to give verbal confirmation of my orders."

"And?"

She looked up at him. His steely, blue-gray eyes watching her. Beckoning her. "I thought you said you were out."

"I was angry and worried and I never should have said all those things." Paxton pushed a piece of hair behind her ear. "I've always been in when it comes to you and me."

Always? Kate sucked in a breath of air. She stared up at the fluorescent lights, fighting off the tears that filled the corners of her eyes. "I suck at relationship stuff."

Paxton laughed and groaned. He took a few labored breaths. "Apparently, both of us do. As long as you're in, we can figure it out." He rested his head against hers. "And if I remember right, we already found *something* we were both good at."

Heat rose up from her chest settling on her cheeks. Kate pulled away enough to look into his eyes. "You have two fractured ribs. It will be weeks before we can be good at *that* again."

"I've waited for twelve years." Paxton's gaze dropped to her mouth and back up again. "A few weeks is nothing."

Her temperature and pulse ticked up a notch. Kate's muscles relaxed, and she smiled up at him. "After everything I put you through this week?"

"Let's just say I like a challenge." He held her close, their noses almost touching. "Are you in or out?"

"We do make a pretty good team, you and me." Kate raised up on her tiptoes, closing the space between them. "I'm in." She claimed his lips. The kiss, soft but seductive, warmed her to her core.

"Maybe next time you'll follow orders."

"Orders?" Kate rolled her eyes. "Maybe next time you'll trust my instincts."

The End

A review is the greatest compliment you can give an author. If you enjoyed reading High Heels and Handguns, I'd appreciate your feedback so other readers, like you, can discover the story.

Acknowledgments

Jeff, I appreciate all your help keeping the FBI lingo and procedures straight. I took a few creative liberties, which you'll have to ignore. My deepest gratitude to my good friends and beta readers, Caryn, Lynnae, Nikki, and Sara, as well as my critique partners, Jenn and Justine. It has been a crazy, exciting, and sometimes bumpy road full of late writing nights, tearful edits, and mind-numbing research, but I couldn't have done it without you (and coffee). I'm grateful to my parents for always encouraging me to do what sets my soul on fire. Instead of becoming an FBI agent, I decided to write about them. It's a whole lot safer this way, and I get to wear my pajamas to work. Last but not least to my husband, Jayson, for letting me pick his brains on all things guns and weapons. Thank you for your love and support on the good days and the bad. Falafel, baby!

About the Author

Lisa is a coffee-swilling, sass-spewing romance writer who believes love is messy and magnificent. She writes things she wishes she had said, and some she wishes she hadn't, delighting readers with exhilarating stories and swoon-worthy characters in a world *where danger and desire collide.*[©]

For more information, visit www.LisaHeartman.com or follow Lisa on social media @heartmanlisa.